THE IDEAL BRIDE

NONNIE ST. GEORGE

ZEBRA BOOKS
KENSINGTON PUBLISHING CORP.
http://www.kensingtonbooks.com

ZEBRA BOOKS are published by

Kensington Publishing Corp.
850 Third Avenue
New York, NY 10022

All Kensington titles, imprints and distributed lines are available at special quantity discounts for bulk purchases for sales
promotion, premiums, fund-raising, educational or institutional
use.

Special book excerpts or customized printings can also be
created to fit specific needs. For details, write or phone the
office of the Kensington Special Sales Manager: Kensington
Publishing Corp., 850 Third Avenue, New York, NY 10022.
Attn. Special Sales Department. Phone: 1-800-221-2647.

First Printing: October 2003
10 9 8 7 6 5 4 3 2 1

Printed in the United States of America

**It was a relief the entire misadventure with
Lady Nola was over.**

Now that he was free of her distracting demands
for his warehouse, he could concentrate on interviewing the women recommended to him by his
tenants. By the time Lady Nola returned to London
he would have found and married the ideal bride.

Who most certainly was not Lady Nola.

He opened the door to the breakfast room.

Lady Nola was seated at his place at the table.
Bartlett hovered behind her with the coffee pot.

"Good morning, sir." The butler reached past
Lady Nola's shoulder to pour coffee into her cup.
"We did not expect you back until tomorrow."

Gabriel stood rooted in the doorway, the blood
roaring in his ears. His gaze swivelled from the
sideboard heavy with all the makings of an old-
fashioned English breakfast to the dog under the
table, gobbling a ham slice off a Swann china dinner plate, back to the table where Lady Nola returned his stare, her mouth open and her eyes
wide.

She blushed so fiercely her face turned as red as
her wild curly red hair.

BOOK YOUR PLACE ON OUR WEBSITE AND MAKE THE READING CONNECTION!

We've created a customized website just for our very special readers, where you can get the inside scoop on everything that's going on with Zebra, Pinnacle and Kensington books.

When you come online, you'll have the exciting opportunity to:

- View covers of upcoming books

- Read sample chapters

- Learn about our future publishing schedule (listed by publication month *and author*)

- Find out when your favorite authors will be visiting a city near you

- Search for and order backlist books from our online catalog

- Check out author bios and background information

- Send e-mail to your favorite authors

- Meet the Kensington staff online

- Join us in weekly chats with authors, readers and other guests

- Get writing guidelines

- AND MUCH MORE!

**Visit our website at
http://www.kensingtonbooks.com**

ACKNOWLEDGMENTS

There are many people I need to thank: family, friends, colleagues, all of whom helped so much I couldn't have finished this book without them, including Alice Chiu, Claire Huffaker, Susan Lantz, Lorie Root, and, of course, Kate Duffy. But there actually were innocent people trapped in the house with me during the process: Glen, Annie, and Maggie. Remember all of the times you mentioned I seemed to be a tad grouchy and possibly insane? Well, I'm not admitting you were right, but here, have a book. I love you.

ONE

At exactly twenty-nine minutes past the morning hour of nine o'clock, Mr. Gabriel Carr, immaculately groomed in sober blue superfine with simple cravat and blameless collar points, inspected his reflection in his bedchamber looking glass. The cut of his tailored jacket did nothing to emphasize his broad shoulders. His buff breeches were too slack to reveal his muscular calves. The dignified style of his raven hair lent no special charm to his cheekbones. Nor did it call attention to his eyes, even when he peered carefully at his reflection to ensure no twinkle sparked them to a deeper blue.

He gave his valet a satisfied nod, taking care not to smile. Smiling only encouraged his dimples.

Precisely one minute later, he marched down the wide staircase of his elegant Brook Street town house.

He nodded once to Bartlett, who stood at attention in the foyer, and proceeded down the hall to the breakfast room.

He took his seat at the head of the table. As always, the silver gleamed, the china sparkled, and his morning business correspondence lay neatly stacked beside his plate.

A place had been set for his mother. Excellent. He had been obliged to repeat the order twice to Bartlett last night. The butler had been of the opinion the only time Eleanor Carr would arrive downstairs before noon would be on the sad day her lifeless body was carried down feet first.

Normally, Gabriel would have agreed. But not today. Not after she read the note he had left for her last night. He would wager a pony she would search him out this morning, if he was a gambling man, which, of course, he was not.

The only question was what her attitude would be when she did appear. In normal circumstances, his mother had the disposition of a kindly mule—she always smiled gaily as she did exactly as she pleased.

He selected a slice of ham and a bun from the warming dishes on the oak sideboard. He declined to sample a third dish, the gelatinous contents of which he could not identify. No doubt Chef had been prompted to be creative by Mother's anticipated attendance this morning. Gabriel frowned. He was not fond of innovation at breakfast. There was nothing wrong with ordinary stirred eggs and herring. He would have to speak to Chef again about keeping a firmer rein on his artistic tendencies, though at least this dish was not aflame.

When he had arranged his napkin to his satisfaction, he picked up his fork in one hand and his pencil in the other and began his breakfast.

The first report was from his clerk about the new merchant tenant in the Bridge Street building. Londoners' enthusiasm for bisque-colored porcelain had made Swann's Fine China Emporium a brilliant success. Gabriel smiled at the figures at the bottom of the page. His decision to accept a percentage of the profits in lieu of a fixed sum for rent had already paid off to advantage.

When he saw the subject matter of the second report, he poured himself a cup of coffee to better savor the experience. Garrard House in Pall Mall was his most recent acquisition and his most ambitious venture to date. According to the construction manager's account, the refurbishment of the building was proceeding according to schedule. By the end of the month, five of the most prestigious merchants in London would move into their shared premises.

Gabriel permitted himself a small smile, dimples notwithstanding. A client could visit the dressmaker, the tailor, the milliner, buy gloves and shoes and furs and fans, even furniture and fabrics, all within the same elegant building. There was even a restaurant to serve refined refreshment on the third floor.

Every fancy furbelow ladies and gentlemen of good breeding needed to make their lives complete, under one roof. His roof. His soon-to-be very profitable roof.

He leaned back in his chair and crossed his hands behind his head. At times like these he regretted he no longer drank brandy. Not that the pleasure of a sound business transaction could compete with an idle nasty habit like drinking brandy, of course, but the near completion of Garrard House needed to be marked by some kind of celebration. He poured himself another cup of coffee and added twice his normal amount of cream.

As he raised the brimming cup to his lips, the door slammed open.

"Good Lord, Gabriel, what the devil do you mean you don't need my help in finding yourself a bride?" Eleanor Carr lurched to the table in her billowing purple dress like a round grape rolling down a matron's heaving bosom. She collapsed in her chair, leaned her elbows on the table, clasped her head in her plump hands, and moaned. The plumes in her headdress bobbed in waves of purple sympathy.

"Good morning, Mother." He wrapped his napkin around his scalded fingers. "I apologize for making you rise so early. I would have spoken to you last night, but you had not yet returned home when I was ready to retire."

"Are you saying I stayed out later than your bedtime?" she asked without lifting her head. "Do you have a bedtime now, Gabriel? The thought fills me with despair."

He pursed his lips. Of course he had a bedtime. He could hardly gallop around London all night and make clearheaded business decisions the next day. Unlike his mother, he had other responsibilities besides frivolous self-indulgence. She had only arrived in London yesterday afternoon and nevertheless had managed to find a party to go to last night. She had a genius for finding the party. Despite it being September when none of her *ton* cronies were supposed to be in town.

A glance at the morning's third report increased his irritation. Another complaint from the latest tenant in the Soho Square warehouse. This time, Smith the wine merchant was demanding better lighting on the outside of the building to discourage night thievery. Gabriel drummed his pencil on the table. The warehouse had been the first property he had acquired, yet in five years, not one of its tenants had prospered.

"In any event, you're not waking me up." His mother squinted in the sunshine streaming through the bow window. "I should hope even a man as hell-bent on becoming a monk as yourself would recognize an evening gown when he saw it. I have just returned from the Goodacre's rout. I came down as soon as I read your note."

"As I have always maintained I would set up my nursery at age thirty," he said absently, as he calculated the cost of Smith's new gas lamps, "I should think you would be pleased to know I was ready to acquire a bride."

She slammed her hand down on the tablecloth. "There is no need to remind me of your pigheaded adherence to the schedule you have devised for your life! It is your perverse way of meeting it that oversets me." She extracted a sheet of paper from somewhere on her person and read aloud. " 'Dear Mother. I am ready to commence my search for a bride. I shall notify you as soon as I have found a woman who meets all of my specifications. Sincerely, your loving son Gabriel.' " She wadded the note and hurled it across the table. It landed in his cup.

He gritted his teeth and dabbed at the drops of coffee spattered on his papers. His letter succinctly and accurately explained the situation. He could hope for nothing better from any of his clerks and managers when they wrote their daily reports.

She jutted out her chins. "Your birthday is in less than three months. There isn't time for your usual intransigence if you want to marry by then. I shall make a list of my friends who are firing off females this year."

"I have no intention of marrying a daughter of one of your friends." He fished the soggy paper from his cup with his fork and poured himself a fresh cup of coffee. One could never have enough coffee when faced with his mother in a mulish mood.

"Certainly not." She reached for the silver coffee-pot and filled her own cup to the brim. "The daughters gave up on you long ago. We shall have to resort to nieces and second cousins now. I will begin making calls this afternoon."

"No, you will not." He leaned forward to emphasize his point. "Your assistance is not needed because my first requirement is that my wife come from a family whose background is in trade or commerce."

Her eyes bulged as her round face froze in her best expression of horror. She clutched both hands to her heart for added effect.

He sighed. "Come now, Mother. It is not so unusual for a gentleman to look for a bride amongst the merchant class. I could name any number of dukes and earls who have done the same."

"They married for money! Surely you have all the blasted money you need by now! Besides, you are not a peer. You are only the second cousin of a baronet."

"Nevertheless, I am still a gentleman and I believe this holds considerable attraction for a family wishing to move beyond its connections to trade."

"A gentleman? Ha. Your life is so dull, no one would know it. The only thing you bother with is your buildings. It is bad enough you insist on rising at this ludicrous hour every morning. But to sit there and read about business all through breakfast is the outside of enough."

He smiled triumphantly. "Which is precisely why I need a bride from a family involved in trade. This is the way I live. My wife must understand that. A young woman from a merchant family would be proud of my business interests, but the same thing would inspire nothing but disgust in a well-brought up girl from the *ton*. She would forever be longing for the day when I could be an idle gentleman again." He tried not to gloat too overtly. That always made her more stubborn.

She plucked one of her plumes and fanned herself with it. "Could you not look for a well-bred girl who would not object to your preoccupation with business? You would be surprised what a woman is willing to overlook if her husband does not resemble a toad."

"I have no intention of using my appearance to procure a wife." He felt his cravat contract an inch.

"Why the devil not? There isn't a man in England who wouldn't give his right arm to look like you."

"I do not care for fusses," was the best he could croak out as he ran his finger under the noose around his neck. How on earth had he gotten trapped in this idiotic conversation? It was absurd. He had no intention of discussing with his mother the wearying siege of tearful scenes and swooning dramatics women had plagued him with since he hit puberty. All because of his appearance.

"Fusses? Is that what young men call it nowadays?" She tucked the plume back into her headdress at a combative angle. "There is nothing wrong with making a fuss if one is doing it with the right person. Why, your father and I often enjoyed making a fuss, especially when—"

"Mother!" He slammed his cup back into its saucer. "My list of requirements provides a sounder foundation for marriage than whether or not a woman is overcome by the cut of my jacket."

"I do not believe it is the thought of you wearing your jacket they find so affecting," she muttered.

He glared at her as she heaved herself to her feet and tottered over to the sideboard. Marriage was a very serious matter. He could buy and sell buildings as he pleased, at a loss if he had to, but marriage was forever. He was going to acquire a wifely asset that would profit his life in every respect and he would not relinquish control of the process to anyone. Not to his mother. Not to any woman, especially based on mindless admiration of his—

"Well, are you going to tell me about your precious list?" she demanded. "Or are you too embarrassed to discuss it?"

"I am not the least embarrassed. Each one of my requirements has been carefully selected to ensure a successful marriage. I devoted the summer to studying the matter."

She heaped her plate with Chef's surprise. "That is exactly the kind of mischief one would expect from someone who insisted on spending the summer in London, instead of going off to the country like every other gentleman."

He frowned. "I hardly think careful deliberation about the features one requires in a bride is mischief. Surely it is essential before one considers embarking on the state of matrimony."

"Piffle." She flapped her fingers under his nose on her way back to her chair. "Furthermore, if you are going to use the phrase 'embarking on the state of matrimony' when you propose to the girl, I cannot guarantee your suit will be accepted. Unless henwitted is one of your requirements."

"My requirements are perfectly reasonable," he said in his most long-suffering tone.

She balanced a dab of Chef's substance on her fork, raised it to her nose, and sniffed.

"For example," he continued, "in addition to the expected criteria of superior character and agreeable disposition, I have specified that my wife-to-be must have a calm and deliberate temperament, with a natural dignity and composure."

She rolled the morsel of food between her fingers and held it up to her eye.

He crushed his napkin into a ball. "Not only will this ensure my household is run in a calm and orderly fashion, it reflects my belief that a husband and wife must be in harmony in their essential nature."

She spiked the morsel back onto her fork and placed it gingerly into her mouth and chewed, eyes closed, moving the food from cheek to cheek like a squirrel with a newfound nut. Finally, slowly, with pained concentration, she swallowed.

"Because a restrained and dignified manner of deportment," he continued grimly, "is a fundamental characteristic I like to think my wife and I would share."

She remained motionless, her head tilted to one side, her eyes still squeezed shut.

"Well, what on earth is it?" He could not stop himself from shouting.

She blinked once and smiled before she answered. "Eggs à la Portugese. Or perhaps à la Russe. You know how Chef enjoys paying homage to all of the participants in the war."

He clutched the table and forced himself to draw a slow steady breath through his clenched teeth. Fifteen minutes with his mother or fifteen rounds with Gentleman Jackson. He had done both. It was debatable which was worse.

He snapped open the cover of his pocket watch. Nearly ten o'clock. The carriage would be ready. He bundled his papers into an orderly pile and stood to take his leave.

His mother scrambled to her feet after him. "But you have not told me the rest of the requirements you have for your bride. Surely you want more in a wife than being docile and boring—"

"Calm and dignified"—he gritted his teeth—"do not mean boring." They did mean a soothing and restful home, something his mother couldn't possibly understand. "My wife must also be reasonable in figure and face and be skilled at household management." He swung open the door. "I am, however, willing to be flexible about whether she is blond or brunette."

"How broad-minded." She linked her arm with his as they stepped into the hallway. "But I still do not understand why you refuse my help. I am one of the most well-connected women in town. Perhaps I could locate some young women whose families are in trade and invite them to an afternoon entertainment."

His house full of chattering chits and motivated mamas, with every eye on him to see which of their darling chicks he would cull from the flock? He shuddered.

"I have a better plan," he said. "I have made a list of my most successful tenants. Today I shall ask each if they have any suitable family members for my consideration."

She ground her heels into the marble floor. "Have you gone mad?"

He batted aside a particularly quarrelsome plume. "My tenants are among the most prestigious and successful merchants and tradespeople in London. This is the most efficient way to obtain a bride who meets my specifications."

"Specifications!" Her shout made the Swann urn in the foyer chime on its plaster pedestal. "You speak as if finding a wife is exactly like buying another one of your blasted buildings!"

"But it is." He began to mark off the points on his fingers. "First I identify the area in which I propose to make my investment. In this case, it is the

City, metaphorically speaking. Next, I investigate the available properties in the chosen area, carefully inspecting the soundness of each, the structure, the foundation, the upper stories..." he trailed off, his face burning. His wretched cravat began to throttle him again.

"Do continue, darling." She looked up, her blue eyes wide in an innocent expression.

"Never mind." He lowered his voice in an attempt to dampen Bartlett's fascination. "You know perfectly well what I mean."

"Yes, dear, you were examining the girl's foundations." She patted his arm. "I may have misjudged you when I accused you of having become dull."

Bartlett stood at the front door, holding Gabriel's beaver hat and gloves and avoiding his eyes. Gabriel snatched his beaver and jammed it on his head.

"Of course," his mother added as she trailed him down the front steps, "I am comforted by the knowledge that all gentlemen make lists of requirements they wish to have in a bride. Then they meet a nice young girl, fall in love, and the list goes out the window."

"The selection of my bride is not a matter to be left to whim and windows." He climbed into the carriage and slammed the door. The woman was impossible. A man would have to be dicked in the nob to want the kind of wife his mother's help would get him.

He thumped on the roof and fell back against the leather squabs as the carriage jolted forward into the morning traffic. Every requirement on his list was essential to a perfect marriage and he would never yield a single one. Compromise was the refuge of the weak-minded. It was a pity his mother was too stubborn to see it.

* * *

"I know it is not exactly what she wanted, but I hope your client will accept it nonetheless." Lady Nola Grenvale peeled off her worn gloves and unrolled the corset from its muslin wrapping as the elderly Latour sisters hovered round the Chippendale desk. "It would be a shame to let such fine quality go to waste for lack of a little reasonable compromise."

She smoothed the undergarment out on the mahogany desktop, careful not to let her damp hands mark the delicate white cotton. The late afternoon sunshine made the air in the tiny office over the Latours' exclusive dress shop even more stifling than usual, and Nola felt as if she were melting in her gray bombazine dress and tight straw bonnet.

"The lady who ordered it is very particular," Mademoiselle Aline Latour said dubiously. "The corset was commissioned with a particular evening in mind."

Mademoiselle Eloise chided her sister for such indelicacy of expression. Nola bit her lip to keep from giggling. At five-and-twenty she was no green girl. It was no surprise to her the elegant undergarment had been designed for an intimate encounter. Merely because she could not perceive the attraction of such a thing did not mean she was unaware of its appeal to others.

Mademoiselle Aline put on her spectacles and ran her bony fingers over the embroidery. Ice blue swans with verdigris ivy sprigs in their beaks floated along the undergarment's tiny high waist, exquisitely picked out in minuscule silk thread stitches. Scattered ivy leaves dotted the generous allotment of fabric for the bust.

Whoever the client was, she had the perfect

feminine shape. Nola looked down ruefully at her own figure. She was uncommonly tall, but at least her waist was slender. Unfortunately, so was her bosom.

"It is the work of *pauvre* Madame Chapman—the one whose husband was killed at Ciudad Rodrigo, yes?" Mademoiselle Eloise asked.

Nola nodded. It had taken Mrs. Chapman a week to embroider the design. It was only when Nola went to collect it that they realized the birds were supposed to be green and the ivy blue to match a dress that had already been made. As if anyone had ever heard of green swans.

"You are so good, my lady." Eloise shoved several books of patterns off one of the battered armchairs and insisted that Nola be seated. "What would the widows do without you?"

Nola shook her head. "All I do is collect the work and bring it back when it is done."

"But because you do, they are free to attend to their families." Eloise began to clear a second chair.

Nola seized the bolt of sprigged muslin from the tiny woman's frail hands and dragged it to the corner, where dozens of other rolls of fabric were piled in a dusty heap. "When I think of all of the men who were lost in the fighting, it is a very small thing I do to help the women they left behind," she said honestly.

Mademoiselle Eloise perched on her seat with a grateful smile. "But to devote your days to walking around London to distribute the work and the money, instead of enjoying the frivolous diversions that distract the other ladies in the *ton*. You are an example to everyone, my lady."

"But I must walk," Nola protested, "for surely you know we have been forced to give up the carriage. As for most *ton* social diversions, it has been no great sacrifice to forego them." She bent down and whispered in Mademoiselle Eloise's ear. "In truth, Almack's was quite horribly, interminably, dreadfully, boring."

Eloise snickered. Aline snorted in reproof from the other side of the desk.

Nola tried to look suitably chastened. But it was a familiar conversation and the outcome was always the same. No matter what she said, she could not dissuade Mademoiselle Eloise from her stated opinion that Lady Nola was the most virtuous woman in all of London. Perhaps England. Nor was Eloise Latour the only one who thought so. Nola had no idea why people persisted in believing she was a self-sacrificing saint. She certainly did not feel like one. Every person in London with any sensibility was moved by the pitiful situation of those orphaned and widowed by the war on the Continent. She was just the only one with nothing better to do and no better way of helping than to be a go-between for the widows and the merchants who commissioned their work.

"Madame Chapman's work is magnificent, as always," Eloise said. "We shall take it, shall we not, sister?"

"Bah," Aline said. "If we do not pay for it, you will, my lady. Eloise and I met Mrs. Forbes in the Hungerford Market last week and she thanked us very prettily for the half crown we had paid her for the pelisse." She removed her spectacles and looked Nola in the eye. "I did not tell her we only gave you two shillings."

Nola flushed. "I did not mean to suggest you did not offer a fair price." Unfortunately, sometimes a fair price was not enough to support a family in crowded London.

Eloise wrapped the corset back in the clean

muslin. "We shall tell the client reversing the colors on the undergarment is the latest mode from Paris."

Aline unlocked the desk drawer and counted out the agreed-upon price in coins. "Better we should tell her any man who cares so much about the color of the swans does not deserve to see her in her undergarments." She tossed an extra coin on the pile and looked away when Nola thanked her.

Nola smiled and tucked the money into her reticule.

A tap at the door heralded the arrival of Gaston, the Latours' equally ancient clerk, who staggered through the doorway panting as he balanced a heavy silver tea tray in his palsied hands. Nola held her breath until he dropped it safely on the desk.

"It will be so much easier for him when we move to our new premises next month," Eloise whispered as Gaston shuffled out of the room. "The stairs in Garrard House are not nearly so steep."

Nola accepted the cup that Eloise passed to her. "I am eager to hear about your new shop premises. You barely had time to tell me anything before you left for Brighton. I passed by Garrard House whenever I was on Pall Mall this summer. There were always a great many workmen going to and fro inside."

"You were obliged to stay in London all summer?" Aline pursed her lips in disapproval.

Nola laughed. "I do not understand why everyone rushes off to the countryside when there is so much to do in town when the weather is fine. In any event, soon enough I shall be obliged to leave London."

Eloise clucked in sympathy. "The earl is still determined to find a tenant for Belcraven House?"

"After five years in the army my brother has returned to find he has no choice. As soon as he finds a tenant, I shall join my aunts in Kent."

"Lady Hortensia and Lady Caroline," Aline said. "We remember them well, do we not, sister?" The pinched expression on her narrow face suggested the memory was not a fond one.

"Yes, of course," Eloise answered. "Lady Hortensia wishes for the hoops and Lady Caroline . . ." she trailed off, tilting her head as she considered the choicest word.

"Does not," Nola offered helpfully. Aunt Caroline's passion for the latest crack in fashion rivaled Aunt Hortensia's nostalgia for powder and patch. It was only one of the manifestations of the bitter feud between the two sisters-in-law. Nola did not want to go to Kent. But she knew better than anyone that after years of neglect by her uncles and Papa, the Belcraven finances could not support another establishment.

"I am certain there will be many interesting things to do in Kent," she said.

The Latour sisters said nothing. Nola sighed and took a desultory sip of tea.

"But you have not told me about your new shop," she said brightly after a few moments of silence.

Eloise's face lit up. She perched at the edge of her seat and her tiny hands flew as she described the latest visit she and Aline had made to Garrard House. "The building is magnificent! Each shop has the most tasteful appointments. And you must see the mahogany partitions between each merchant. The artistry! Exquisite! Monsieur Carr is a true visionary. I was moved to tears!"

"Everything moves you to tears," Aline said. "You are a hopeless romantic. However, the quality of workmanship is good, and Mr. Carr's notion is a sound one, otherwise he could not have persuaded us and the others to move from our present profitable locations."

"Sound? It is brilliant." Eloise leaned toward Nola to explain. "We will be between Madame Sophia the milliner and Monsieur Pottenger's haberdashery. Which is exactly *comme il faut,* since so many of our clients patronize them already."

"That is exactly why we are together in one building," Aline said. "We each sell different things, but we have the most important thing in common. We are the best in London. That is why the customer will come. She knows she will find only the best merchants in Garrard House."

Nola looked at her in astonishment as the words echoed in her ears. One building with many merchants. It was an original idea. Nola's heart began to race. A clever idea. Merchants who had something in common. Brilliant, in fact. She caught her breath. Something customers would know and draw them to the location. Her thoughts swirled into one shining notion.

"That is exactly what the widows of London need!" she exclaimed.

The sisters gazed at her blankly.

"They need to sell their work to the public, all together in a single location!" Nola beamed at them. She balanced her cup and saucer on a stack of pattern books, snatched up her gloves, and fanned herself.

"But why?" Eloise asked.

Aline answered. "So the customers may know they are supporting the worthy widows, and only the worthy widows when they shop at the market?"

"Exactly!" Nola clapped her hands together. "A bazaar exclusively for widows."

"The problem is how," Aline said. "A few widows sell in the markets now, but one cannot simply move a stall like a chessboard piece."

"And of course, there are those who cannot take a market stall because they have families to care for," Nola added. "But if there was a location uniquely for widows, perhaps some could share a stall."

"It would have to be built," Aline said.

"The difficulty is where." Nola tapped her gloves against her lips.

"Do you mean a market or a bazaar?" Eloise still frowned in puzzlement.

"What difference can it possibly make, sister?" Aline demanded in an exasperated tone.

"A market is outside," Eloise explained patiently, "and it is difficult to see where in London one could put it." She ignored her sister's snort. "But a bazaar could be indoors, and I think a lovely location would be Mr. Carr's warehouse across the square."

"*Mon dieu*, Eloise!" Aline looked astonished. "You have an excellent idea. The warehouse has been a trial from the moment it was built."

"Monsieur Smith the wine merchant wishes to leave," Eloise told Nola. "He says Soho Square is not the right place for a warehouse."

"I am certain the warehouse has never brought Mr. Carr one sou of profit." Aline said.

Nola went to the front windows and pushed aside a bolt of calico to better look outside. The elegant three-story yellow brick warehouse occupied nearly a third of the north side of the square. Although she had lived in Soho since she had come to London six years ago, she had never much noticed it despite its imposing size. The Latours were right. The location was ideal for a bazaar.

"Do you think Mr. Carr would consider it?" She asked as she picked her way back to her seat.

"Oh, Mr. Carr is the best of men!" Eloise exclaimed. "Most intelligent, and charming, and extremely handsome as well, which is why Aline and I were so amazed when he called on us this morning." She leaned toward Nola and lowered her voice to a confiding whisper. "We could scarce believe it, but he came to ask us if we knew of someone—"

"Someone who could advise him about his warehouse," Aline finished loudly for her. "Is it not the most astonishing coincidence?"

"I do not think—" Eloise began.

"Yes, I can see you do not," Aline said. She picked up the plate of ginger biscuits and offered them to Nola. "Do you not like Mr. Carr, sister?"

"Yes, of course I do, but—"

"Do you not want him to find the best possible person to advise him on his warehouse—the matter which prompted his visit to us this morning?" Aline shoved the biscuit plate at her sister. "Likely that is what put the notion of the warehouse in your bird-witted brain."

"No," Eloise answered, taking a biscuit, "I was watching the pigeons land on the warehouse roof while I was drinking my chocolate this morning. That is why it was in my mind. It could not have been Mr. Carr's visit, for he did not—"

"Eloise!" Aline snatched another biscuit and pressed it into her sister's hand. "Do you not think kind and amiable Lady Nola would be the perfect person to help Mr. Carr with his problem?"

"Ah." Eloise paused, then turned to Nola and smiled. "Yes. Of course."

Aline snorted. "Well, then *tais toi*, and we shall arrange a time for them to meet."

"Should not you and Mademoiselle Eloise be the ones to speak to him?" Nola asked. "I am not certain it would be appropriate to impose my views on a such a matter to someone I have never met."

"Nonsense." Aline pried the cup and saucer from Nola's hands even though it was still half full. "You have been out of society for too long, my dear Lady Nola. Now it is all the thing for ladies to hold forth on the plight of the less fortunate. It becomes most tedious for their friends, so it is only natural to discuss the matter with people upon the merest acquaintance. Is it not so, sister?"

Eloise, wide-eyed with her mouth full of biscuit, nodded.

Aline seized Nola's arm and pulled her toward the door. "If you believe in your little widows, you must be prepared to put yourself forward on their behalf."

Nola took a deep breath. Even though the idea for a widows' bazaar was the product of a moment's inspiration, it was the embodiment of opinions she had been mulling over for quite some time, ever since she realized her days of acting as a go-between would end when she was obliged to remove to Kent. The desperate families living on the edge of subsistence needed a more permanent solution than her modest services, and the idea of a widows' bazaar was sound, she was convinced of it. She threw back her shoulders and drew herself up to her full height.

"When should we approach Mr. Carr?" she asked.

"Tomorrow afternoon," Aline answered. "We will send word to him immediately."

"Tomorrow?" Nola's stomach fluttered. "Should we not spend some time preparing our idea so we may present it in the best light possible?"

Aline shook her head. "Time is of the essence. Mr. Carr is approaching a number of people to see if they had anyone to help him with his warehouse."

"Oh, yes," Eloise said, "he has a list."

"Precisely." Aline handed Nola her pelisse. "You must present yourself before he has the chance to consider any others."

Nola made sure the ribbons of her bonnet were snug beneath her chin before she slipped the pelisse around her shoulders. "But what if he asks questions or requires more information? An indoor bazaar with stalls operated by war widows is hardly a commonplace notion. Surely it will require considerable vision for Mr. Carr to be convinced it is a suitable enterprise?"

Mademoiselle Aline swung open the door to the hallway. "Do not worry yourself unduly, my lady. Sometimes a problem has an obvious solution. After all, what sensible man could fail to be persuaded by the vision you shall present?"

TWO

"I do not wish to meet the daughter of an earl."
Gabriel struggled to keep his tone level.

Eloise Latour looked at him like a sparrow who
had unearthed a particularly bewildering bug, head
tilted, with an inquiring expression on her gentle
face. Mademoiselle Aline, however, was frowning,
and Gabriel felt himself flush beneath her hawkish
regard. Or maybe it was the baking heat of the
Latours' office. The first thing he had done when
he had stepped over the stack of fabric bolts in the
doorway was offer to open the windows. The sisters
had enthusiastically declined, insisting the temper-
ature was ideal. Perfect for roasting pigeons, no
doubt. He did not intend to become one.

The meeting was not proceeding smoothly. To
begin with, he had been delayed when Smith saw
Gabriel's carriage pull up in front of the Latour
dress shop. The wine merchant sprinted across the
square to deliver a new litany of grievances about
the warehouse. Gabriel extracted himself with the
promise to discuss the matter as soon as his business with the Latours was complete, but by the

time Gaston had ushered him into the sisters' office, he was fifteen minutes late.

He did not like being late.

He rubbed his temples. The Latour sisters were among his best tenants. He did not want to antagonize them on the brink of their move to Garrard House, but there was no point in discussing a completely unsuitable candidate. What kind of an earl's daughter required her dressmakers to run her suitors to earth? He had never heard of the lady or the Earl of Belcraven. Not that it mattered in the least. He was not going to waste time on some *beau monde* belle. Or *beau monde* beast.

"I am sorry, but the lady will not do," he said in a more soothing tone. "When I asked if you knew of any suitable young women, I thought I specified I was not interested in meeting any of your clients."

Eloise's face brightened. "But Lady Nola is not a client."

He clenched his jaw. "I do not care where the woman buys her clothes. She is an earl's daughter, and therefore out of the question. I wish to marry someone from a family in trade or commerce."

"Why do you not wish to marry a lady? You are a gentleman." Aline Latour's voice made it clear she thought only the greatest of nodcocks would prefer someone from the bourgeoisie to a daughter of a peer.

"Perhaps Mr. Carr is a member of the sansculottes." Eloise offered hesitantly.

"Bah," said Aline. "Republicans do not own buildings. At least, not so many and so profitable as Mr. Carr's."

He stood up. "This has nothing to do with politics. It is merely a matter of the requirements I have set down for the woman I will marry. The background of the young woman is one of my most important conditions, and I have clearly stipulated she is to be from the merchant class."

"What about your other requirements?" Aline Latour frowned. "Superior character and congenial disposition?"

"Yes." Mademoiselle Eloise clasped her hands together. "Lady Nola is the kindest, most generous woman. She is a saint! Everyone agrees, is it not true, sister?"

"She is of a most superior character," Aline said.

Gabriel mopped his forehead with his handkerchief. Homely and holier-than-thou. Gad, this Lady Nola, whoever she was, sounded the complete prunes-and-prisms miss.

Aline pursed her lips. "As for her personality, Lady Nola is extremely amiable."

"You will find no more amiable woman in all of London," Eloise said.

Amiable. The polite term for vacuous. No wonder she had given up on marrying a title. Lady Nola was a complete antidote. Gabriel collected his hat and gloves from the desk. "No doubt she also dances divinely?" The antidotes always did.

Eloise hesitated. "I am not certain. Lady Nola seldom goes out in society."

Gabriel choked back a laugh. In addition to virtuous and vacuous, the ugly Lady Nola was too freakish to be unleashed in public. Who would have thought the Latour sisters would demonstrate such poor judgment? True, they were spinsters, but they were also successful businesswomen in a competitive profession. A Latour dress was obligatory for any London woman of fashion. But it seemed that even the shrewd Mademoiselle Aline could not resist romantic matchmaking, no matter how ridiculous.

"I thank you both for your interest on my behalf." He bowed over Mademoiselle Aline's hand.

"But you have not even met her!" Eloise said. "And you have so many things in common!"

"I do not need to meet her. We will not suit."

There was a knock at the door. For the first time since his arrival, Aline Latour smiled. "That is a shame, Mr. Carr, for here is Lady Nola now."

He gasped. "You were only supposed to suggest the name of a suitable candidate, not arrange for a meeting."

Aline shrugged. "You said you wanted to be married in a few months. That does not leave very much time to waste going back and forth."

He clutched his head. He had no idea why some people insisted on believing three months was not enough time. It was enough time. More than enough time. Especially if he did not waste it interviewing completely inappropriate, unacceptable, impossible daughters of earls.

"We would have told you earlier, but you were late in arriving," Eloise said. "Most unusual."

Gabriel cursed Smith and the warehouse as he peered around the cluttered office. There was no other door. No balcony beyond the second floor windows. Not even a ledge.

There was another knock on the door.

He ran his finger under his collar. "Are you certain that is her?"

"Lady Nola is very punctual," Eloise said. "That is one of the things you have in common."

"I don't suppose there is a priest's hole in the wall?" he asked.

Aline Latour shook her head. Eloise clucked sadly.

He clapped his hat on his head and faced the door squarely.

"You cannot simply tramp past her like Napoleon," Aline said.

"Would you prefer I bow over her ladyship's hand and then announce I will not offer for her?"

"There is no need for dramatics," Aline answered. "Lady Nola does not realize you are looking for a wife."

Of course. He should have known. Homely, holier-than-thou, vacuous, freakish and stupid. He had forgotten stupid.

Nola frowned at the heavy oak door as Gaston rapped on it again. The elderly clerk insisted that the Latours and Mr. Carr were waiting for her in the office, yet the door remained solidly shut despite their knocks.

She swung her reticule indecisively, her spirits ricocheting between disappointment and giddy relief. Her stomach had somersaulted the entire journey here and by the time Gaston had led her up the dark staircase above the dress shop, her hands were soaking and her throat was parched. She was not normally unnerved by the thought of speaking to a stranger—she had often done so when she approached merchants soliciting needlework for widows. But a bazaar was an enormous undertaking. It would involve considerable investment in alterations to the warehouse. A successful businessman like Mr. Carr would have many questions about its profitability and feasibility. None of which could she answer.

The widows' bazaar required someone with his experience in London commerce and real estate to make it succeed. She gripped the ribbon of her reticule more tightly. It could help so many needy women and children. She must convince Mr. Carr of the merit of the idea.

Gaston motioned for her to listen.

Nola held her ear to the door. The thick wood muffled the sound, but he was right. There were animated voices coming from inside the Latours' office.

Of course. Poor Gaston's feeble knock could not rouse anyone, no more than her timid tap. Certainly not when the occupants of the room were engaged in lively conversation.

She smiled at the old man, peeled off her gloves, clenched her hand, brought her arm back behind her head and swung her fist down as hard as she could.

Just as her fist would have struck the oak panel, the door was yanked inward.

As she flew across the threshold, Nola had a brief impression of a tall dark and handsome man stepping aside. She had a better impression of his powerful hands catching her tight around her waist before she hit the ground.

She was trapped facedown in his muscular arms, her nose bobbing inches away from the oak floor planks. The man's firm grip squeezed the wind from her lungs. She gulped for air and twisted herself around to find herself gazing into the deepest blue eyes she had ever seen.

She stopped trying to breathe.

Then, in the briefest moment that passed as slowly as if she were trapped in treacle, she watched helplessly as her reticule arced gracefully upward on its long silken ribbon and smacked him flush on the nose.

He did not drop her. He could have dropped her, for she did not have far to fall. Nor would she have blamed him in the least if he had dropped her, for the reticule struck him a fair facer. But his hold on her did not falter for an instant. He smoothly withdrew one hand from her waist to reach into his pocket for his handkerchief and held it to his nose.

She stared in fascination as a deep red stain began to seep through the snowy linen.

Mademoiselle Eloise's frantic fluttering wrenched her back to her senses. Nola scrambled to her feet and disentangled herself from the strong arms of Mr. Carr, for obviously that's who the man was, according to Eloise's exclamations and Aline's remonstrances as they dragged him to sit in one of the chairs and pushed his head back.

Aline ordered him to remain still until she returned with cold cloths. His broad shoulders lifted in a sigh and he closed his eyes, his long slender fingers still holding the bloody handkerchief to his nose.

Nola clutched the offending reticule to her pounding heart. Mr. Carr was not what she had expected. True, yesterday Mademoiselle Eloise had called him handsome, but Nola had assumed she meant handsome in the way as to appeal to a seventy-year-old spinster. Not handsome as in the embodiment of every Englishwoman's idea of what a handsome man should look like. Nola forced herself to take a deep breath. Mr. Carr looked like Robin Hood. Like Lancelot. Like every hero every fifteen-year-old girl dreamed would carry her off on his snow white charger.

She had seen plenty of handsome men. Most of Henry's friends were not only handsome men, they were handsome men in uniform. But none of them looked like Mr. Carr. She had never seen eyes so blue, such long curling black lashes, such a noble nose. Well, she couldn't really see his nose now, of course, not with his head tilted back and the handkerchief pressed to it to staunch the streaming blood. But in the seconds she looked into his face before the reticule struck, it seemed to be a perfect nose. To match his exquisitely chiseled cheekbones and his sensitive lips. And that was before one even considered his superb physique.

Mr. Carr was quite simply ridiculously handsome.

Nola giggled. One of Mr. Carr's elegant eyebrows flared upward although his eyes remained shut.

Mademoiselle Eloise immediately scurried over, chirping about how my lady was overset by the strain. She whisked the cloak from Nola's shoulders, pushed her down into the chair next to Mr. Carr's, dropped her bonnet on her lap, and flitted out the door, imploring Nola to keep watch on Mr. Carr until she returned with tea.

Nola hid her smile behind her hand. She would be happy to watch Mr. Carr. What woman would not? Of course, the poor man was probably married with a dozen children and spent his time reviewing ledger sheets rather than rescuing fair maidens or kissing sleeping princesses. Nonetheless, she found it impossible to avert her gaze from the impossibly perfect Mr. Carr.

He opened one brilliant blue eye and stared right back at her. Her cheeks flamed.

"I'm terribly sorry." The squeak in her voice added to her mortification.

Mr. Carr murmured that it was quite all right. Or that was what she thought he said. It was difficult to distinguish his words with the cloth pressed so tightly against his nose.

She had a sudden dreadful thought. What if her reticule had broken his nose? Why, it would be a crime against the human race. Likely women across London would riot. Her name would be reviled through history as the one who had marred the perfect profile. She would have to wander the earth—

"I am relieved the sight of blood amuses you." He lifted his handkerchief an inch. "I suppose gales of laughter are preferable to a swoon."

She flushed guiltily. "I am—I am merely happy you were not seriously injured." Goodness! Perhaps he was more delicate than his height and athletic physique suggested. "Are you seriously injured?"

"Certainly not." He bristled. It made his broad shoulders seem even wider. "Although this is the first time I have had my cork drawn by a reticule. I do not wish to pry, but what exactly was in it?"

"My reticule?" She swallowed even though her mouth was dry.

He nodded, then quickly pressed the handkerchief to his nose as the blood once again began to stream.

"Mrs. Fisher's fee for the waistcoat she just completed." Nola said. "It was very intricate. Mr. Stultz paid two pound six."

Both of his eyebrows went up.

"In shillings." She twisted the reticule's ribbon. "Mrs. Fisher sends money to her sisters. She has six, so she likes to be paid in small coin. In my reticule, I have her forty-six shillings." She knew she was chattering, but it was impossible to think while looking into his magnificent blue eyes. Furthermore, the tiny office was even hotter than it was yesterday. Her dress felt pasted to her back. She fanned herself with her straw bonnet.

Her bonnet!

She leaped to her feet and clutched her head. Her fingers sank into her tangled curls. She gasped. Her head was bare. Her bonnet must have fallen off when she landed in Mr. Carr's arms. Her red hair was bouncing unbound. Her reckless, tempestuous, impulsive hair. The kind of hair that couldn't convince anyone she had a responsible idea in her madcap head, never mind persuade an important businessman to dedicate his building to the benefit of others. She bit back a shriek.

Mr. Carr peered up at her over his bloody handkerchief. "You will forgive me if I do not stand," he said.

She dropped her hands as if her curls had burnt them. "I appear to have lost my—"

"Head?" he offered.

"Bonnet," she whispered.

"I believe it is now under your left heel."

She retrieved what was left of the mangled straw and her reticule from the floor and fell back into her chair. Her face was on fire. No doubt her cheeks were now as red as her hair.

He shifted his handkerchief slightly. She had a clear view of his face. He was smiling.

Goodness! He had dimples. Darling, delightful dimples. One in each cheek. Perfectly positioned, peeping and precious.

"Are you unwell?" he asked. The dimples disappeared.

Nola shook her head. Her hair dangled disastrously against the nape of her neck. She kneaded her bonnet and reticule together on her lap. Where on earth were the Latour sisters? It couldn't possibly take a lifetime to fetch a clean cloth and order tea.

Mr. Carr peeled the sodden handkerchief away from his face. He waited a moment, then got to his feet with a satisfied grunt. The blood began to gush from his nose. He sat down again.

The linen muffled his words, but she was fairly certain he was cursing.

She stifled a moan. This was not an auspicious introduction to the widows' bazaar. Nor was she helping matters by ogling the poor man. It wasn't his fault he looked the way he did. His appearance had nothing to do with his business acumen. She was acting like a pea-goose over a few curls and dimples—allowing the cleft in his chin to distract her from the desperate plight of London's war widows.

She took a steadying breath and leaned toward his chair. "I hope the manner of our meeting will not influence your opinion of our mutual business."

"I assure you, my lady, I have not been moved in the least from my original opinion of our mutual business. In fact—"

Aline Latour shot through the door, Eloise bobbing behind in her wake.

Mr. Carr fixed Mademoiselle Aline with a grim look. "I was about to say the events of our meeting merely confirm my conviction that if one deviates from one's plan, one is always punished."

Aline snatched his bloody handkerchief away and slapped a fresh cloth in his hand. "Perhaps the punishment is for making hasty judgments."

Mr. Carr's reply was forestalled by Mademoiselle Eloise's attempt to inspect his nose.

Nola's heart sank as she watched Mr. Carr and Eloise wrestle over the cloth. If Aline was rebuking him for making hasty judgments, Mr. Carr must have already turned down the suggestion for the widows' bazaar. Without even giving her a chance to explain.

Mr. Carr won the battle. Mademoiselle Eloise was relegated to clucking and hovering behind his chair.

Nola wove her reticule ribbon through the splintered straw of her bonnet crown. Just because Mr. Carr would not lend his warehouse to it did not mean the bazaar could not be built. His was not the only building in London.

But Soho Square was a perfect location. The

more she considered it since Eloise's suggestion, the more she realized it was true. Situated between exclusive Mayfair and the poorer neighborhoods in the East End, it was easily accessible both to the widows and the clients who would purchase their work. The warehouse was an excellent size and the square ideal for retail enterprise. One would have thought the building's lack of profitability as a warehouse in the past would make its owner more amenable to useful suggestions.

Mr. Carr removed the cloth and gingerly raised his head. His hair had become disarranged and a single raven curl fell against his forehead.

Nola sighed. The handsomest man in England. And he didn't even have the decency to give a fair hearing to a good idea.

She stuffed her reticule into her bonnet and gripped the arms of her chair. She cleared her throat. Mr. Carr and the Latour sisters looked at her.

"I must tell you, sir," she said in her firmest tone, "I am very disappointed in your rejection of my proposal."

Mr. Carr's jaw dropped. His eyes darted from her to Mademoiselle Aline.

Nola had to disguise her amusement with a discreet cough. The man was obviously unnerved by plain speaking. How absurd.

"I am sorry if straightforward discussion is not the standard in your business dealings," she continued, "but if you had agreed, you could have improved the lives of hundreds of women in London."

"Indeed?" His smile was crooked. "I foolishly believed any proposal I was involved in would only bring happiness to one woman."

"I do not understand this conversation." Eloise wrung her hands together. "How did Lady Nola discover—"

Aline Latour grabbed her sister's arm. "We shall continue this discussion another time. Everyone is overset by the sight of blood."

Nola forced herself to stop goggling at Mr. Carr's dimples. "I do not see the purpose in wasting any more of Mr. Carr's time. He is obviously not interested in doing something useful with his warehouse."

"My warehouse?"

The forceful tone of his voice made Nola jump in her chair.

"Lady Nola is here to speak to you about your warehouse." Mademoiselle Aline enunciated her words clearly. "She wishes you to convert it into a bazaar where war widows would be able to sell their wares directly to the customers."

"Who on earth asked her for an opinion on my warehouse?"

Nola watched him scowl as if he had no idea what Mademoiselle Aline was saying. The blow from the reticule must have scrambled his wits, if the poor man had forgotten he was seeking advice on his warehouse.

His face was flushed but Nola wasn't certain if this was a symptom of a serious head injury, although it certainly made his splendid cheekbones more prominent. "Should we not fetch a surgeon?" she whispered to Mademoiselle Aline.

"I do not need a surgeon any more than I need opinions about my warehouse from a clutch of addled women!" He leapt to his feet.

Nola gripped her reticule in alarm.

Eloise shook her head sadly.

Aline charged. She shook her bony finger under his aquiline nose. "With that attitude you will remain a bachelor for a very long time. It is no surprise your mother refuses to introduce you to any eligible women herself."

"Aline!" Eloise gasped. "We are not supposed to tell Lady Nola that Mr. Carr is looking for a bride. Do you not remember?"

Aline groaned and clutched her head. Eloise looked at Nola with watery eyes.

Nola stood up on unsteady legs. Her reticule and bonnet tumbled to the floor. She turned to the sisters. "Do you mean he is meeting me merely to determine if I would suit as his wife?"

"Merely is not the term I would use," Mr. Carr said.

She whirled to face him. "I was not speaking to you, sir. Although if marriage to you is such an honor, I do not understand why you are so coy about your intentions." She was satisfied to see him frown. "In any event, it is irrelevant. I do not want marry you."

She didn't want to marry anyone, never mind some stranger she had never met before today. She pressed her hands against her hammering heart. It was preposterous.

"You do not have to convince me." He leaned against the Latours' desk and crossed his long legs at the ankles. "But I warn you the mademoiselles seem to have their hearts set on it."

"But what about the bazaar?" Nola asked. Despite her best efforts, her voice quavered. "I believed the notion of the widows' bazaar was sound."

Both Eloise and Aline loudly assured her it was. Mr. Carr folded his arms across his chest and said nothing.

Nola strode to where he stood. As tall as she was, she was disconcerted to find her eyes were only level with his lips. His fine, sensitive lips. She shook herself and tilted her head back to meet his eyes, annoyed to see amusement in their dark blue depths. "Mr. Carr, are you interested in my proposal—proposition—offer—" He smothered a cough. She took a deep breath and tried again. "Will you consider installing a widows' bazaar on the site of your warehouse?"

"Certainly not," he drawled. "It is a stupid idea."

She gasped. "How can you possibly say so when you have not given it more that a moment's consideration?"

He shrugged. "Some alternatives are obvious upon first impression. A widows' bazaar would involve a lot of women. Therefore it would be too much trouble to manage and hardly likely to be profitable."

"Very well then." She extracted the remains of her bonnet and her reticule from the dressmaking debris on the floor and collected her cloak. She marched out of the office, closing the door smartly behind her.

A moment later, she opened it again and freed the hem of her dress. "I will deliver Mrs. Forrest's spencer on Tuesday," she told the Latours sternly.

THREE

Gabriel stormed down the Latours' dark narrow staircase. It had taken half an hour to convince the mademoiselles he was sufficiently sorry about the distress he had caused their earl's daughter. Half an hour while they rattled on about the many interests he shared with their dear Lady Nola. A love of London. An understanding of commerce. A plainspoken candor, a complete disregard for the vagaries of fashion, and a shared impatience with society's superficial entertainments. Eloise Latour had even crowed about how he and dear Lady Nola both found the upstairs office too warm, although Aline was not impressed that this was a sufficient reason for matrimony.

Half an hour of keeping his tongue between his teeth while the dressmakers pronounced that with her fine family background and her cleverness and her kindness and excessive amiability, there could be no better wife for him than dear Lady Nola.

Dear Lady Nola? He shuddered. Disastrous Lady Nola was more like it. From her dive across the threshold, to her impertinent giggling and unseemly interest in his warehouse, the woman was a complete catastrophe. Even her appearance was vexatious. Tall and skinny with red corkscrew hair—in her black cloak, she looked exactly like a Pall Mall gas lamppost.

As for marrying an earl's daughter, he'd sooner start selling blue ruin in the Garrard House dining room at a penny a glass than take a wife who'd trumpet her superior connections over him for the rest of his days. They would be Mr. Carr and his highborn wife Lady Nola wherever they went, and he knew precisely where an earl's daughter would need to go. Almack's. Holland House. Morning calls all afternoon followed by tedious tours of Hyde Park. Balls, routs, musicales, stifling summers in the country and winters somewhere worse.

Furthermore, this particular earl's daughter seemed to have devoted her life to a Cause. Not that helping war widows wasn't an admirable goal. But a woman with a Cause did not make for a soothing wife. An earl's daughter with a Cause was a positive nightmare. She would likely expect him to present her at Carleton House every second Tuesday so she could buttonhole Prinny himself, as an earl's daughter no doubt felt it was her due to edify the Regent on matters of concern.

He grinned. But by some miraculous stroke of good fortune, Lady Nola had taken a fit at the mention of matrimony. He ought to be on his knees in the family pew this Sunday to give his heartfelt thanks.

Besides, the afternoon had not been a complete waste of time. He had gained two benefits by listening to the Latours ramble on about the earl's daughter. The first was that Lady Nola's brother, the Earl of Belcraven, sought a tenant for his Soho

mansion. If the Latours' description of the place
was accurate, it was exactly what Joseph Swann
wanted.

But the second benefit of the Latours' lecture
was of much greater value. With half an hour's
headstart, dear Lady Nola's carriage would have
borne her far away by now.

He would never set eyes on the woman again.

He bolted through the Latours' elegant ground
floor dress shop. It was faster to walk to the warehouse than to drive, especially this time of day when
the streets were inundated with carriages and carts.

It was not only the streets of the square that
were busy, he noted with satisfaction as he closed
the shop door behind him. Soho Square was an
excellent location for retail commerce. The side-
walks were choked with people, as were the paths
that bisected the square's central park. Most carried a parcel.

He stepped around an elegant couple debating
the merits of a mackerel in a fishmonger's window.
He hadn't yet decided what kind of enterprise he
would solicit for the dress shop premises once the
Latours were in Garrard House. A trade which re-
lied on spontaneous custom would do well. A confectioner, perhaps, or a maker of ices like Gunter.
It might even be possible to arrange for customers
to consume their treats in the central park.
Whatever he decided, it would be easy to find a
successful tenant by Michaelmas.

Unlike the warehouse. He eyed it critically
across the square as he walked toward it. It was a
sound building of commodious size, barely fifteen
years old. He loved the simple arches of the
ground floor windows and the massive central
door. Yet it had been nothing but trouble since he
had taken possession of the deed. Tenants should

have thrived. Not one did. The cabinetmaker failed. The wool merchant had hightailed it back to Gloucester. Now Smith was floundering.

But surely Lady Nola's scheme was completely round the bend? An indoor bazaar for widows? Grief-stricken novices in mourning who wouldn't know the difference between taking inventory on account and taking account of inventory. He was perfectly justified in turning down the cracked-brained notion. It didn't require great deliberation to recognize a disaster in the making. He wasn't merely being stubborn. It would have been cruel to encourage the woman. He stopped behind the cluster of pedestrians waiting for Carlisle Street to clear enough to cross.

Suddenly, the steady din of carriage wheels and clattering hooves was overlaid by a woman's laugh. A soft rolling chuckle. A chill rolled down his spine.

He squeezed his eyes shut and tried to shake off the shudder that seized his body. It could not be. He heard the laugh again. His eyes flew open. It was.

Lady Nola was crouched on the cobblestones less than six feet in front of him, peering at something underneath a carter's wagon that was drawn up to the curb. She had managed to resurrect her bonnet by strapping a scarf around the top and the wide brim limited her range of vision, so thankfully, she hadn't spotted him. Behind her bobbed a pair of identical hatchet-faced young women in grim gray dresses.

Gabriel ducked behind the life-sized wooden Highlander in the tobacconist's doorway. Whatever new disaster the earl's daughter was fomenting, he had no intention of hanging about in the open like a shop signboard flapping in the breeze.

"I can't reach him, my lady," one of the gray girls moaned. "They keep shifting away from my hand."

The second girl put her hands on her hips. "It's all the fault of the costermonger's bitch, my lady. There's no telling what tricks she gets up to."

Gabriel shook his head. The beaked gray girls must be Lady Nola's maids. A matching pair of maids. Obviously the latest idiotic vogue to sweep the *ton*, to compete with the craze for matched pairs of horseflesh for the men.

"Naughty dogs!" Lady Nola stood up and swiped at the dust on her skirts. "I suppose there is nothing for it but to wait until they are finished."

Good Lord! Gabriel snorted in dismay, then yelped as a bolt of pain stabbed his nose.

He looked up in horror. Sure enough, Lady Nola's gaze was fixed squarely upon him.

"Mr. Carr?" She stepped toward him, her maids flocking behind her like vultures trailing a stork. "Are you unwell again, sir? You look exceedingly pale." She reached into her cloak pocket and pulled out a scrap of linen and lace and thrust it under his nose.

Perspiration dripped between his shoulder blades. He was trapped, trapped like a shiny gold band in a jeweler's display case.

"Perhaps one of my maids can assist you to your carriage," she said, enunciating her words slowly, as if she thought he was too addled by injury to understand clearly. "I am afraid I cannot accompany you myself because I must wait for my dog. He is under this wagon."

The blood roared in his ears. He clung to the wooden Highlander. Why was this happening to him? He was just trying to live a useful life, deal responsibly with his business matters, find himself a congenial bride. Now he was in the middle of Soho Square trying not to have a conversation about the sexual activity of her dog with the daughter of an earl who less than an hour ago had denounced the very idea of marrying him. There wasn't an etiquette manual in all of England that could explain this. Even his mother, the mistress of every social occasion, would not have a pattern card for him to follow on this one.

He stifled a moan. If God was merciful, his mother would never discover his perfectly sensible scheme to find a bride had brought him to this hellish pass.

Lady Nola continued to pin him with her level gaze, a small smile hovering on her lips and her sandy eyebrows arched in polite inquiry. The small part of his brain which still functioned noted the useless fact that her eyes seemed to have changed color. In the Latours' office, he could have sworn they were brown. Now they were green.

Without any conscious volition on his part, his hand rose to tip the brim of his hat. As if from far away, he heard his voice ask, proof of the immutable nature of a lifetime of training, "May I offer some assistance?"

He goggled at her, aghast at his own words. What possible assistance would she expect him to offer, pray? He kept his mouth fixed in a smiling grimace and silently cursed his upbringing as a gentleman.

She shook her head. "I am afraid there is nothing to do. Fig is extremely stubborn. He will not come out until he is done." Her casual tone implied this was a common occurrence.

Gabriel stared at her in mute horror.

"But it should be fine as long as there are no donkeys," she continued. "Since we hardly need worry about cows in Soho Square."

Perhaps Lady Nola was mad.

She frowned. "I suppose you think I am making a fuss about nothing?"

"No—no, of course not." Good Lord. He clenched his jaw. Now she had reduced him to stammering.

She sighed. "It is merely that Fig has run to fat ever since—" She dropped her eyes and a pink blush spread over her cheeks. It did nothing to disguise the freckles sprinkling her nose. "Ever since he was gelded."

"Gelded?" He winced in instinctive sympathy. Then he realized the implications of her words. "Gelded?" he repeated. A small bubble of hope rose in his chest. A gelded dog could not possibly—he dropped to his knees on the cobblestones and peered under the wagon. Two dogs were crouched, each gnawing one end of a bone. That was the only thing they were sharing.

He leapt back to his feet, giddy with relief. The earl's daughter's dog was not being lewd! "These dogs are eating!"

"Yes," she said, "the costermonger's dog stole a mutton bone and Fig followed her—"

"How splendid!" He fought the urge to do a jig around the wagon.

She smiled. "You are a lover of dogs, sir?"

"Of course not!" He beamed back at her.

She shot him a worried glance. "Are you certain you are well? Perhaps you should not leap about so after a blow to the head."

He seized her hand and bowed over it with a flourish. "I am excellent, my lady. Excellent. In fact, I assure you at this moment, I feel better than I have all afternoon." Now all he had to do was tip his hat farewell and the whole hideous episode would be over.

Her eyes darted down to her hand clasped in

his and a look of dismay struck her face like a slap. "Mr. Carr, I worry you may be under a grave misapprehension."

Blast. Now what was the matter? Gabriel dropped her hand.

She glanced over to where the maids prowled on the street side of the wagon and lowered her voice to a confidential tone. "I cannot allow you to continue to believe I would make you a suitable wife."

He choked. "Not at all—I assure you, I think no such thing!"

She narrowed her eyes in suspicion. "So you are not following me to see if I will reconsider my opinion about marrying you?"

"Certainly not!"

Her face lit up and she took a step toward him. "Then you are following me to say you have reconsidered your opinion about installing the bazaar in your warehouse!"

"Of course not!" He backed away. The woman was obsessed with his warehouse. As for her delusion he was interested in marrying her, the sooner he disabused her of it, the better. "I am afraid you are the one under a grave misapprehension," he said. "It is outrageous—"

"How can you call the plan for the bazaar outrageous when you refuse to listen to it?"

"I am not talking about the bazaar! I am referring to the subject of marriage."

She frowned. "I thought we settled the matter. I will not marry you, sir. I must ask you not to speak of it again, no matter how much you wish my opinion to be different."

"I do not wish your opinion to be different!"

"Then we are in perfect agreement," she said. "There is no reason for you to be so agitated."

"I am not agitated!" He clutched his head and leaned limply against the side of the wagon. He gazed at the warehouse across the street and contemplated with longing the relative relaxation of listening to Smith's litany of complaints.

Lady Nola followed the direction of his gaze. "It is a very handsome building."

"Yes, it—" He wiped the smile off his face. "No, you will not butter me into handing over my warehouse. I thought you were above idle flattery. The Latours told me you prided yourself on plain-speaking."

"I am being honest! It is a lovely building. Such fine arches." Her smile deepened. "In any event, there are more flattering compliments I could pay you, if I thought it would persuade you about the bazaar."

Blast. He felt as if she had struck him with her reticule again. She was going to mention his appearance, of course. Possibly even make a fuss. He turned around and scanned Carlisle Street. After the next carriage passed, he might be able to dash across before—

"Garrard House," she said.

"I beg your pardon?" Did the woman's conversation ever proceed upon a predictable line? He turned back to face her.

"Garrard House." She smiled brightly at him. "That is the compliment I would pay you. I think your idea is brilliant. Original, yet it makes perfect sense to put different merchants with a common theme into the same building."

He dipped his head in a polite gesture of acknowledgment. Likely she would offer any Spanish coin to try to wheedle the warehouse out of him. She wouldn't understand why Garrard House was an innovation. Still, it was better to be complimented about one of his buildings than on his appearance.

She nodded. "Yes, it is really quite clever because while there are many markets which sell similar products, like the Smithfield cattle market or Hungerford for household provisions, you have diversified the product yet given the vendors a common theme."

Good Lord. His jaw dropped. She really did understand what he was creating in Garrard House.

"I do not think anyone has ever done it before, do you?" She looked up at him, an inquiring expression in her bright green eyes.

He clasped his hands behind his back in what he hoped was a modest gesture, but he couldn't stop himself from beaming with pride. "I do not think so."

"I do not think so either." She smiled back.

"I can tell you something else about Garrard House that is unique," he found himself saying, suddenly interested to see her reaction. "There will be a dining room on the third floor." He paused for effect then added, "In the middle of the display of the furnishing fabrics."

Her brow furrowed in thought. "Full meals?" she asked after a moment.

"No. Wines, tea, coffee, and sweetmeats."

"Ah." She nodded. "Then I think it is another inspired notion. The Latours were right when they said you were clever."

She approved. Excellent. He smiled and realized he had been holding his breath. "Thank you," he said.

"No, I must thank you. It was the Latours' description of Garrard House yesterday which inspired me to think the war widows should do the same."

"Well perhaps the notion could be applied to ventures other than—yesterday?" He stopped abruptly and shook his head in astonishment. "The idea of the bazaar occurred to you yesterday, yet you expected me to commit a very valuable building to it today?"

She sighed. "Yes, I hoped we would have a few days to prepare before we approached you but the Mademoiselles Latour were adamant."

"A few days?" He snorted despite the pain in his nose. "A few days will not make your scheme any less of a spur-of-the-moment impulse."

"I concede I am still missing some of the details." She drew herself up to her considerable full height. "But it is still obvious creating a bazaar exclusively for war widows is a good plan."

"No," he said. "A good plan is one which involves actual planning."

She planted her hands on her hips. "There will be planning! Considerable planning! But in the meantime, why won't you admit the notion of the widows' bazaar is a good one?"

"Because it is not." He pointed across the street to the warehouse. "My building has room enough for two hundred vendors' stalls, possibly more—

"Really?" A look of rapture lit her face.

He threw his hands in the air. This was ridiculous. He had to disabuse her of the idiotic notion or that would be all she ever spoke to him about. "I will not be saddled with hundreds of women—by definition in mourning, all weeping and missing the heads of their households—completely inexperienced in the business of retail. The mere thought gives me chills. I must ask you never to mention it again." He flushed—not that he would ever see her again if he did not agree to her bazaar.

Her cheeks turned pink and she clenched her

fists at her side. He waited for her to begin hurling insults, but she merely panted and glared at him. Panting did little to improve her flat chest, he couldn't help but notice. He was reminded of her performance in the Latours' office when at the height of her temper the best she could do was collect her things and leave. Perhaps the mademoiselles were right—Lady Nola was the most amiable woman in London.

"Oh! You!" she said.

He laughed.

"I am thinking of something quite cutting, I assure you." She pursed her lips but he could see the amusement glinting in her eyes. "I am nearly tempted to call you—"

"Donkey!" One of her maids shouted from the other side of the wagon.

Lady Nola nearly bowled him over in her scramble to reach the back of the wagon and in the few seconds it took for Gabriel to follow her, she was already on her knees in the street.

"Fig! Fig! Come here at once!" she shouted.

Gabriel looked down Carlisle Street. A ragman's donkey cart plodded toward the square. Both maids dashed down the street toward it. He shrugged. The cart didn't look particularly evil, but neither had Lady Nola's reticule.

Lady Nola scrambled back to her feet and dusted her hands. "Honestly! I do not know why I bother to take him for a walk. He never wants to go and it always ends in disaster. He is a Welsh herding dog and he reverts to his childhood whenever he happens upon a donkey—"

"Or a cow," Gabriel said, comprehension dawning. "But surely disaster is an exaggeration?" Neither dog under the wagon seemed particularly large and the maids had intercepted the donkey cart fifty feet away.

Lady Nola snorted. "Trust me. He is the most stubborn creature in London. It will end in disaster."

Gabriel squared his shoulders. "Since I am here to assist you, I am sure I will be able—"

The donkey brayed. A clump of brown fur shot out from underneath the wagon, a leather lead whipping behind it. It dodged Lady Nola and streaked past Gabriel. There was but one way to stop it before it reached the donkey cart. Gabriel lunged and managed to stamp down on the lead and trap it under the heel of his boot. Just as it trailed through a fresh pile of horse droppings. For an instant, he looked down in dismay. Then the dog yanked hard, and Gabriel found himself looking up. From a seated position on the cobblestones of Carlisle Street. In manure.

Lady Nola flew to his side. "Are you all right?" she asked over the din of barking, braying, and shouting maids.

"I am fine," he muttered through clenched teeth. "I suppose you are going to laugh or say you told me so?"

Her green eyes sparkled as she tapped her chin with her finger. "Actually, I was thinking of doing both."

"I told you so!" Cook dabbed the tears in her eyes with the corner of her broad apron. "You can never trust a Frenchy."

"How's that?" Nanny cupped her hand to her ear.

Cook positioned another onion on her wooden

chopping block. "I said it's all the fault of those Latours," she bellowed. "Everyone knows Frenchies are romantical fools."

Nanny snorted. "A handsome man can turn any woman into a fool."

"Especially an old Frenchwoman," Cook muttered.

Nola looked up in exasperation from the papers she was laying out at the other end of the pine kitchen worktable. "I told you the Latours sent a note to apologize. The whole thing was simply a misunderstanding." She lined up the slips of paper with the names of the widows on the left side of the table. On the right, she arranged those with the names of the merchants.

"What kind of misunderstanding makes a man offer for a lady without so much as an introduction to her family?" Cook slid the heap of chopped onions into the kettle.

"Mr. Carr did not offer for me," Nola repeated for what seemed like the hundredth time since Agnes and Mavis had rushed home yesterday to blurt out the whole sorry incident in Soho Square. But the Belcraven House kitchen was cosy, and if Nola collected her papers and tried to hide in the south parlor Nanny and Cook would merely follow and deliver their lecture there.

Nola sighed. Organizing a schedule for the delivery of the widows' work was a useful occupation. Speculation about Mr. Carr was not. Taking a clean sheet of paper, she wrote the name of Mrs. Philip's ten-year-old son Daniel at the top. Daniel Philips could bring his mother's work to the milliner on Grafton Street. But could he also be the go-between for the milliner and Mrs. Conway in Cheapside? Or was that too far for a ten-year-old boy to travel?

Nanny tucked a wisp of her iron gray hair back into its tidy bun. "I still think his lordship ought to be told about Mr. Carr."

"There is nothing to tell," Nola said without looking up.

"Well, I still say those Frenchies were up to no good." Cook executed another onion. "Taking it upon themselves to introduce a lady of quality to a man who's in the marriage market. It's scandalous."

Nanny sniffed. "If you ask me, a handsome man like Mr. Carr likely had something other than marriage on his mind."

Nola bit her lip to keep from laughing. Years of supervising the female servants had made Nanny think every man had ulterior plans.

Agnes emerged from the scullery, drying her hands on her apron. "Oh, no, that can't be true," she said, sitting on the bench at the table opposite Nanny. "Mr. Carr has to marry."

Mavis followed her sister to the table. "The Latours' shop assistants told us all about it. Mr. Carr must marry before he turns thirty—"

"Or he'll lose his fortune—" Agnes explained.

"At the stroke of midnight—"

"He'll die a hideous death—"

"Then be turned into a frog—"

"Locked in a dungeon—"

"And thrown from the highest tower!" Mavis concluded in breathless triumph as Nanny reached across the table to try to knock her and her sister's heads together while Cook waved her knife and sprayed onion on them all.

Nola rolled her eyes. It was past time the twins stopped reading Minerva press novels. They had a disconcerting effect on the minds of sixteen-year-old girls.

"But you shall be the one to save him, my lady!"

Agnes cried over the gasps from Cook and Nanny. "His one true love!"

"His one true love he never set eyes on before yesterday?" Nola asked dryly.

"But you saw how he followed you down Soho Square," Mavis said.

"Shocking!" Nanny's eyes bulged.

Nola gritted her teeth. "In the first place, Mr. Carr was not following me. He was merely on his way to his warehouse."

"Then why was he hiding behind the tobacconist's Highlander?" Mavis asked.

"Appalling!" Cook slammed her knife into the board.

"The way he looked at you," Agnes said. "All pale and overwrought, then so merry when you condescended to speak to him?"

Mavis nodded. "And he was so grateful in the end after he fell in the street. When you did not laugh, but merely offered to fetch his coachman for him."

"Oh for heaven's sake!" Nola flung her pencil down. "I asked him myself if he was trying to persuade me to marry him! He said not!"

Cook's knife clattered to the floor.

Nanny's face turned bright red. "Sometimes you take plain-speaking to an extreme, my lady. In any event, men lie. Especially—"

"I know, especially handsome ones," Nola finished for her. "But there is also the letter from the Latours. They said Mr. Carr would never dream of seeking so advantageous an alliance such as marriage to an earl's daughter."

"Frenchies!" Cook snorted. "You can't believe a word they say."

Nola pressed her fingers to her temples. The incident with Mr. Carr had taken on epic proportions. It was beyond ridiculous. It was all very well for Gabriel Carr to arrange to marry without love, but she would not. Not that she had high hopes of ever being in love, not at her age, with her unromantic nature. But all the Belcraven marriages had been alliances of convenience, and they all had turned out miserably. Besides, had she been interested in marriage merely for the sake of convenience, she would have accepted one of the men who offered for her in the year she made her London come-out.

Of course, neither of them had looked like Gabriel Carr.

She shuffled through the pile of widows' addresses. It was preposterous to find a man appealing solely on his looks. Especially when the man had betrayed a less-than-excellent character by flatly refusing to listen to anything about the widows' bazaar. Only a featherheaded widgeon would continue to think of him, or review their conversations together, or keep rereading the letter from the Latours, looking for clues about his intentions toward her.

Never mind that the man had expressly said he didn't want to marry her. Of course, she had said she didn't want to marry him first. She only hoped he remembered that when he considered the matter. Not that he would consider the matter. Because there was nothing to consider. Only the romantic fancies of sixteen-year-old maids.

It was all so unsettling! She covered her burning cheeks with the palms of her hands. She looked up to find the eyes of the four other women staring at her, Cook and Nanny with concerned scowls, Agnes and Mavis beaming in approval.

Nola snatched up her papers and pressed them to her chest. Brooding about Gabriel Carr was pointless. Working on behalf of the widows was not.

She looked down the length of the table. "The only meaningful result of my meeting with Mr. Carr is that the Mademoiselles Latour were so stricken with remorse over his rude refusal to consider the bazaar they have offered to devote themselves to helping find a better place for it than his warehouse." She tilted her chin defiantly. "And when we find it and when the London Widows' Bazaar is a glorious success, Mr. Gabriel Carr will be very sorry he so summarily rejected me!"

Nanny shrieked. Cook's onions flew across the table. Agnes and Mavis clutched each other and gasped.

"Goodness!" Nola glared at them, feeling her face burn even hotter. "You know perfectly well I meant to say the plan for the bazaar, of course. You are all kicking up a dust about nothing. Frankly, I will not be sorry if we never hear the man's name again."

"What man's name?" Henry asked as he strolled through the doorway.

"Your lordship!" Nanny scrambled to her feet, Cook hovering in alarm behind her. "You should not be down in the kitchen."

Henry laughed. "Just because I am earl now doesn't mean I have forgotten this is the only warm room in this old barn. What man's name does my sister not want to ever hear again?"

Nola leaned her head in her hands. "Gabriel Carr," she muttered.

"Gabriel Carr?" He sounded surprised.

Nola looked up to see a peculiar smile on her brother's face. "Do you know him?" she asked, a sinking feeling in her stomach.

Henry fished a letter from his jacket pocket. "I

received this just this morning—that's why I'm down here now. I had been wondering how to broach it, but now that you have raised the subject . . ." He unfolded the letter and showed her the bold looping signature at the bottom of the vellum sheet.

Nola's stomach plunged. The letter was from Gabriel Carr.

FOUR

"Lady Nola Grenvale is here to see you, sir."

Gabriel looked up from his morning correspondence and scowled. Bartlett hovered in the doorway of the breakfast room, and for a moment Gabriel thought the old man had just announced Lady Nola Grenvale was calling on him. He shook his head and poured himself another cup of coffee. Lord only knew what the butler was actually trying to say.

"Sir." Bartlett cleared his throat. "I said Lady Nola Grenvale is here to see you."

"Impossible." Gabriel's cup fell from his nerveless fingers.

He pushed his chair back to avoid the streaming liquid. He was not shocked Lady Nola wanted to see him. Certainly not. For the past fortnight, whenever he was about his business in Soho Square, he kept expecting her to spring out like a highwayman and demand that he hand over his warehouse. He even found himself waiting for her letter on the subject whenever the mail was delivered, not that it would have been proper for an unmarried woman to write a bachelor. But Lady Nola did not seem like the kind of woman who was overly concerned with propriety. Had she not uttered the word "gelded" to him in the middle of Soho Square? He repressed the chuckle that rose in his throat at the memory.

But to visit a bachelor uninvited at this hour of the morning? Shocking. It was the kind of behavior that invited scandal, and scandal between an eligible bachelor and a marriageable spinster might easily result in his being required to offer for her. A forced marriage to Lady Nola Grenvale? No wonder his heart was pounding and his breath seemed to be coming in short gasps.

"Are you sure it is her?" he asked.

The butler shrugged his bony shoulders. "Everyone knows Lady Nola. She helps the poor widows."

Gabriel ran his hands through his hair. He did not want to marry Lady Nola. She did not meet his requirements for a bride—she wasn't from a family in trade, she was too plainspoken to be dignified, and the way she seemed to be constantly laughing at him was not soothing in the least. As for her figure, it was anything but reasonable.

Any fleeting moments of sympathy that may have passed between them during their encounter in Soho Square could not possibly be a better foundation for marriage than his list of requirements. He had spent a long time determining the requirements of his list. They weren't to be trifled with at the impulse of some earl's daughter who was merely here to pester him about her unworkable scheme for a bazaar.

"You may tell her I am not at home," he said.

"It may be too late, sir." Bartlett made a show of

studying the coffee stain on the tablecloth as he dabbed it with a napkin. "She is waiting for you in your study."

Gabriel bolted to the breakfast room door and slammed it shut. He leaned his weight against it and glared at Bartlett. "Have you taken leave of your senses?"

The butler shrugged. "She insisted she had an urgent business matter to discuss with you."

Gabriel rolled his eyes. As if by calling it an urgent business matter, she thought he would be fooled about why she was here. Very well. He folded his arms across his chest. Perhaps one elderly butler was no match for Lady Nola and her bedlamite bazaar. But she would soon learn he had a far more powerful weapon at his disposal. "Bartlett," he said with a grim smile, "fetch my mother."

The butler shook his head sadly. "Madam has not yet returned from the Danford ball."

Gabriel seized the old man's shoulders and aimed him toward the door. "You may tell Lady Nola no matter how long she camps in my study, I will not see her. Nor will I ever agree to give her my warehouse."

"Warehouse?" Bartlett looked over his shoulder, his expression brightening. "But Lady Nola said to tell you it had nothing to do with your warehouse!"

Gabriel frowned. Not about his warehouse? Good Lord. The blood drained from his face as a sudden thought occurred to him. He sank back down into his chair.

"You don't think she is here to make a fuss, do you?" he croaked.

Bartlett looked horrified. "Lady Nola? Certainly not sir! She is a paragon of virtue. Saint Nola, some people call her—not in a popish way, of course."

Gabriel tugged at his cravat. It did seem unlikely a young woman of Lady Nola's respectability was ready to throw herself at a man in such an abandoned way. However, a few times in the Latours' office, he thought he glimpsed in her eyes the kind of glazed expression which usually indicated appreciation of his appearance. He pursed his lips. But Lady Nola had burst into laughter, not the usual declarations of devotion.

"Furthermore," Bartlett said, "in my opinion Lady Nola is not dressed appropriately for the making of a fuss."

Gabriel smiled. Lady Nola must be wearing something as hideous as the last time he saw her. "Clothing does not always remain an issue throughout the making a fuss," he said. Perhaps Lady Nola would look better without her clothes. He flushed at the thought.

"Sir!" Bartlett's ears turned pink. "Lady Nola has two maids with her as chaperones."

"Maids merely mean they are interested in marriage, not—"

Bartlett gasped. "Lady Nola is not the kind of woman who would make a fuss!"

Gabriel stood up. Except when she was laughing at him, Lady Nola was plainspoken and amiable, not the kind of woman who usually made a fuss. Furthermore, she had mentioned she did not want to marry him. A number of times. Anyway, he didn't want her to make a fuss. He didn't find her attractive, and even if he did, she didn't meet his list of requirements in a bride.

"Of course you are right." He sighed. "I am being ridiculous."

"Quite so, sir." Bartlett opened the door.

"Likely she has simply lied and she is here about my warehouse."

"Saint Nola lie?" Bartlett followed Gabriel to the staircase. "I hardly think so, sir. Is there no other business she could have with you?"

"I did send a letter introducing Swann to her brother and they have arranged for Swann to let Belcraven House. Perhaps she is here to thank me." It didn't seem likely, but it was possible.

When they reached the first floor hallway, Gabriel stared at the closed study door and swallowed. Lady Nola might not be here to harangue him about his warehouse or to make a fuss, but she laughed at him, struck him with her reticule, and her conversation was unpredictable.

"Perhaps you should tell the carriage to collect me round back," he whispered to Bartlett.

The butler clucked. "Running away is hardly heroic, sir."

"I am no hero and you have not spent an hour with Lady Nola."

"Every man is a hero in his own life, sir."

"You have been reading Byron again, Bartlett."

The butler nodded sadly and gave him a push toward the study.

Gabriel squared his shoulders, seized the brass doorknob, and yanked open the door.

"Mr. Carr!" Lady Nola squeaked and bobbled the china figurine she was examining.

He gasped. She was standing in front of the marble hearth, fumbling with the Golden Shepherdess. The one Swann had made to celebrate their first thousand pounds of joint profit. There were three in existence. If Lady Nola continued juggling, there would only be two.

Gabriel charged across the room. Unfortunately,

he hadn't noticed her maids lurking in the shadow of the corner bookcase. Not until they sprang out in front of their mistress and he was forced to veer around them.

His hip slammed into the corner of his desk. He bit back his howl of pain.

Lady Nola raced toward him, stopping abruptly just before she knocked him down. "Mr. Carr! Are you injur—"

"I beg you do not say it!" he snapped at her more harshly than he intended as he clenched his fists to stop himself from rubbing his impending bruise. But it would have been pleasant to spend a moment in her company without being asked about the state of his health. Furthermore, the way her gaze lingered on his hip where he had struck the desk was disconcerting. Distracting. Disturbing.

Damnation.

He glanced over his shoulder at the door. Why the devil had he not chosen running away?

The giggling of the maids as they slunk off to the window seat at the far end of the room brought him back to the moment. He muttered an apology to Lady Nola and tried not to limp as he escorted her to the pair of armchairs in front of the fireplace.

She was not as tall nor as bony as he remembered. It wasn't her clothing that made her seem different—he would swear she was wearing the same ugly pink dress she was wearing the day he met her. He remembered the long tight sleeves and the neckline so high her slim throat looked like she was being strangled by a ruffle. Did the woman not own a looking glass? A decent dress might do wonders for her figure. Not that it mattered in the least. She was still freakishly tall and flat-chested.

Certainly not the kind of woman he found attractive.

Positively not the woman he pictured as his wife.

She smiled at him as he took the seat across from her. She had wedged her head in another bucket-shaped bonnet today. Not a single red curl could be seen. She must not like her hair. He couldn't blame her. It was unruly and not at all dignified. For the sake of further confusion, today her eyes were neither green nor brown but a mix of both and flecked with amber.

Such inconsistent eyes were irritating. As irritating as the tilt of her chin and the small smile that flitted on her lips and the entreating way she clasped her hands together in her lap, still cupping the china figurine.

"That is a Swann," he said, pointing at the figurine in her hands.

She looked at him as if he were an idiot. "It looks like a shepherdess to me."

"No—I mean, yes, it is, but it was manufactured by Joseph Swann of Swann's Fine China Emporium. The new tenant of Belcraven House," he muttered, knowing perfectly well he sounded like a pompous dolt, even to himself.

"It is very nice." She set the figurine down on the table between them. He laced his fingers together to help fight the urge to replace it on the mantel to the right of the miniature of his grandfather where it belonged.

"The Swanns take possession of Belcraven House soon, do they not?" he said, giving her the opportunity to thank him.

She nodded. "I leave for Kent tomorrow."

"You must be looking forward to missing the worst of London's fogs," he said, giving her another opportunity to thank him.

She looked at him sideways. "Have you ever been to Kent, Mr. Carr?"

"Once. Lovely place." Incredibly dull. Many cows. Except for Dover. Many cows and ships.

"I lived there for most of my life. We did not come to London until my father became earl. My aunts live in the Belcraven Dower Cottage three miles from Milton where the best thing about it is that it is only a five-hour journey from London."

"Ah." He leaned back in his chair. A fit of temper. That is what warranted the early morning call to a bachelor. Although her fit of temper looked no stormier than it had in Soho Square. "You have come to ring a peal over my head? I do not blame you. I would not care to leave town either." He smiled encouragingly.

Her eyes widened in surprise. "But it is not your fault! If not Mr. Swann, we were still obliged to find a tenant because after Papa and Uncle Edgar and Uncle Frederick, Henry can barely cover the window tax and Mr. Swann seems very kind, his daughters as well and they can afford to heat all of the rooms, because if there isn't a fire in every room, the only decent place to sit is the kitchen and—Goodness!" Her hand flew up to cover her mouth and she ducked her head down so the bonnet hid her eyes.

Gabriel's heart began to pound. If her business wasn't about Belcraven House, she must be here to try to stick him with her bazaar. No doubt her babbling was prompted by her remorse about lying her way into his study. He folded his arms across his chest. He certainly wasn't going to help her by bringing it up first. If the last time they met was any indication, she'd be hectoring him about it soon enough.

But a minute passed and she didn't say anything.

She kept her head bent, her long slim fingers trembling as they pleated the fabric of her skirt. As he watched, a pink blush spread up her throat and her cheeks. He looked over to her maids. They were on their knees on the window seat looking out at Brook Street. Useless chaperones.

He frowned. In his experience, only one thing made a woman blush and quiver the way Lady Nola did now. Romance. The making of a fuss. Which, of course, could not possibly be the reason for her agitation. Because paragons of virtue were not interested in such matters and she had plainly said she didn't want to marry him. Three times.

She must be here about his warehouse. But still—he bit his lip—her face was now completely red.

She picked up the figurine again without meeting his gaze. "It is very nice," she squeaked.

"So you have already mentioned." He eyed the way she rolled it back and forth in between her palms. Perspiration began to bead his brow. Her kid gloves looked soft and supple and he couldn't help but wonder what it would be like to take them off her slender hands, finger by finger.

Damnation!

He took a deep, calming breath. He must be imagining things. She must be here about her blasted bazaar. She would tell him so in the next instant and they would argue and tomorrow she would go to Kent and he wouldn't see her again until after he was married to a woman who met his requirements and didn't insist on stroking his china.

"The shepherdess's crook is delicate," he snapped at her.

Lady Nola put the figurine down on the table again. "I am terribly sorry, but I am nervous and when I am nervous I like to do something with my hands. Normally I fiddle with my reticule strap but I did not bring a reticule today because I did not want to frighten you and now I am babbling."

Her eyes were glassy and she seemed to be looking at his cheeks. His damned dimples! He stopped smiling. Her gaze dropped down to her lap but only for a second and when she looked up again, she impossibly blushed an even deeper shade of crimson. She was looking at his dimples!

"I wish you would not stare at me, sir, not that you do not have very fine eyes, you do, of course . . ."

He flushed. She had noticed his fine eyes as well.

". . . but I am already feeling quite ashamed of myself this morning for coming here and guilty for telling your butler I had urgent business . . ."

Shame. Guilt. Fuss. His breath grew ragged.

". . . and I know we agreed never again to discuss the subject . . ."

She had told him in Soho Square never to mention marriage again. He ran his finger under his constricting cravat.

". . . but I feel so strongly about the matter I have no choice but to ask you—"

"I cannot!" He leaped to his feet. "Please do not speak of it!"

"But I am desperate!" She followed him to the fireplace. "If I cannot get you to agree before I leave, I will not have another opportunity until my aunts return to town for the Season. That is months away!"

He turned to face her and sighed at the plea in her big green eyes. He couldn't blame her for wanting to marry him. Not only was there the appeal of his looks and fortune, but her praise of

Garrard House showed she appreciated his skill in business as well. Likely a woman of her impertinent attitude and scrawny looks did not meet a lot of eligible men, even if she was the daughter of an earl. But she didn't meet the requirements of his list. He couldn't marry her. He shouldn't marry her.

What he should do was bring the matter to an immediate conclusion by explaining in clear terms he had no intention of marrying her. Ever. A simple and brutal yet effective solution. Then her maids could carry her out and he could get on with his business of the day.

"You should go home before we begin a conversation we shall both regret," he said gently. On the other hand, there was no reason to be cruel. After all, it wasn't her fault she found him attractive.

Her cheeks turned an even brighter shade of red. "You know why I have come this morning?"

He nodded kindly. "I am afraid it is rather obvious."

"Yes." She sighed. "Still, is very kind of you not to be overset."

"I am more flattered than overset."

She frowned. "But I have not said anything flattering yet."

"Your mere presence is flattery enough."

"I suppose you are right," she said. "It is not a simple matter for an unmarried woman to visit a bachelor. It shows how important this is to me, which is why you must give me the opportunity to plead my case before—"

"Wait!" He knew by now there was no way to stop a woman hell-bent on making a fuss, but somehow she had managed to pick up the figurine again. No reason to sacrifice a valuable object to the fit of female temper which would follow his rejection. He held out his hand and she dropped it in his palm. It was shockingly hot from her touch.

She took another deep breath and looked into his eyes. "We must have your warehouse for the widows' bazaar."

"My warehouse!" The shepherdess's crook snapped off in his fist.

"I knew you were going to be overset!"

"This whole charade has been about my warehouse?"

"Of course it is about your warehouse." She blinked at him in confusion. "What other reason could I possibly have to be here?"

"You lied!"

She had the grace to turn pink again. "Of course I lied. I told you I felt ashamed about it. It is very upsetting. I am not the kind of person who lies, but you would not have seen me otherwise."

"I most certainly would not!"

She tilted her head and eyed him with a considering look. "If you thought my visit was not about the warehouse, why did you think I was here?"

Damnation. Why the devil did she have to be so clever? "I knew perfectly well it was about my warehouse and your bazaar," he muttered.

She frowned. "But you just said you would not have seen me if you knew I was calling about the bazaar."

"You are quite right! I have been most unfair." He seized her arm and led her to his desk. "I have never given you the opportunity to explain your notion of the widows' bazaar. You must tell me all about it right now."

"Truly?" Her voice quavered.

"Absolutely. I insist." He pulled out the chair opposite his desk for her.

She beamed at him over her shoulder as she sat down. "I knew you were not so buffle-headed as you seemed."

He gritted his teeth and took his chair behind his desk. She'd have a good laugh at his expense if she ever did find out how buffle-headed he was. He yanked open the bottom drawer and tossed in the Swann figurine, trying not to wince at the merry jingle made by the pieces of formerly valuable china. All he had to do was humor her for a few minutes and send her on her way. He pasted an interested expression on his face and looked up at her to say something encouraging—the blaze in her eyes killed the words in his throat.

"I know why you thought I came to see you this morning!" She jutted out her chin in challenge.

His heart sank. "I thought you were here about the bazaar, of course. Which I look forward to hearing—"

"Do not bother to deny it! It is writ plain as day on your face."

"There is nothing wrong with my face!" Not that she noticed anything right about his face.

She snorted. "You are red as a beet. You think I came here to throw myself at you!"

She sounded as if she would soon be throwing something at him. At least she had not armed herself with a reticule today. He surreptitiously eyed the wax jack on the corner of his desk and wished he had thought to move it out of her range. To do so now would only alert her to its presence.

Without taking her narrowed eyes off him, she leaned forward in her chair, gripped the edge of his desk with both her hands, and burst into laughter.

Of course. "It is not so funny as all that," he

snapped. "It is outrageously early for calls and my mother is not home."

She shuddered for breath between gales of laughter. "How was I supposed to know your mother was out? I do not have a carriage to chase you through London and everyone insisted this was the best time to find you home. Your schedule is notorious." She leaned back in her chair and wiped the tears from her eyes. "Besides, I have two chaperones."

They both looked over to the bow window, where her maids were still on their knees looking outside. They appeared to have caught the attention of someone on the street below because they were both giggling and one seemed to be pantomiming the equivalent of meet you out back in fifteen minutes.

"They are not very good chaperones," Lady Nola conceded, "but I am sure they would have noticed if we had . . ." She pursed her lips together and turned an excellent shade of pink.

For an instant, he was gripped by an insane devilish urge to try to make her describe what she thought they might have done, but he quickly shook himself back to his senses. "Actually, I may have believed you were here about marriage," he admitted in the interest of being fair, hoping she did not think his voice was as sulky as it sounded to his own ears.

"Yes of course. You are looking for a bride." She brought her knuckle to her lips to stifle another chuckle that bubbled in her flat chest. "I had no idea you expected one to be delivered."

This had gone on quite enough. He stood up. "Now that we have shared this happy moment, I am sure you will excuse me. I have work to do."

She stayed in her chair. "That is completely unfair!" The laughter was still in her voice, making him smile despite himself. "You were willing to let me tell you about the bazaar to try to distract me. Now I am being punished for realizing the truth."

She was right. It didn't make him any happier.

Her tone became serious. "All I need is for you to listen to me for fifteen minutes."

Gabriel looked at the pleading expression on her face. Tomorrow she would be in Kent and he would never see her again. "I will give you five minutes," he said.

"Ten."

"Fine." He sat down again, then realized ten minutes was closer than halfway to fifteen minutes. He could see why the widows appreciated having her negotiate their commissions.

She leaned toward him, her eyes sparkling with enthusiasm. "If your warehouse is large enough to house two hundred stalls—"

"Two hundred weeping women—" He snapped his mouth shut, mindful of her pursed lips and glare. He folded his hands meekly on the desktop. "Please continue."

"I realize extensive renovations will be required—"

"Two new floors, a new staircase, which, by the way, is extremely expensive, then there is the construction of the actual stalls themselves."

She bristled. "I understand perfectly well setting up a bazaar is not a matter of repainting the signboard and flinging open the doors!"

"Good, because I cannot help but wonder how your poor widows will pay a rent to justify such expenses?"

"Since the expense will be shared by so many tenants, the cost to each could be quite reasonable."

"Reasonable!" he sputtered. "That is hardly the

adjective I would use to describe hundreds of women crowded into my building all weeping—"

"Oh, for goodness' sake! You are not the slightest bit interested in listening!" She flung herself back in her chair and glared at him.

"What I would like to listen to is why you have it fixed in your head you must have my building and nothing else will do. I should warn you such inflexibility does not lead to success in business."

"I shall not bother to comment on your having the nerve to lecture on inflexibility, sir, but I assure you, we have looked at other buildings."

He snorted. "I find it hard to believe nothing else in the entire city of London was suitable."

"Some had potential," she said. "I had high hopes for the Pantheon Theater on Oxford Street."

"Ha! The Pantheon Theater on Oxford Street! That is . . ." He frowned. The Pantheon Theater. Just sitting there since it was stripped of its fittings after the Lord Chamberlain ordered it closed. It was an excellent building. On Oxford Street, a superior retail street. Good Lord. She was right.

"I suppose it might not be too bad a location for a bazaar," he said casually, the derisive expression on her face making it clear she knew perfectly well he was impressed. He sighed. "It is a very good location." The brilliant smile that lit up her face made him glad he had said it. She was rather pretty when she smiled, once one got over the sprinkling of freckles. Fortunately, she had one of those faces that always looked on the verge of smiling. He supposed that meant she was pretty.

"Why do you not put your bazaar in the Pantheon then?" he asked.

She sighed. "You and I might recognize it is an excellent idea, but Mr. Cundy does not. He said it was a crackbrained notion."

"Cundy has never been known as a man of vision," he said, regretting it immediately when she gave him a pointed look. Surely she didn't think he was as big a cabbage-head as that cawker Cundy? "I cannot believe that is the only other possibility," he said quickly.

"It is no longer a matter of finding the right premises. The bazaar needs someone with experience to set it up."

"I thought that was what you were doing."

"I was." She smiled. "Until Mr. Swann took our London house. I must leave for Kent tomorrow, thanks to you."

"What about the Latours?"

"They are in their seventies and in the middle of moving their premises, thanks to you."

He sighed. "You are not actually thanking me, are you?"

She leaned forward across the desk, the pleading expression back in her wide eyes. "The Latours say Mr. Smith is desperate to vacate the premises and you do not have another tenant at hand. All you would have to do is start organizing it. I will be back in the spring and—"

"Start organizing two hundred women? You must be joking!"

"If you cared for the poor unfortunate widows of our gallant officers who died so tragically—"

"Just because I do not want to midwife a mare's nest of competing, duplicating merchandise, offered by weeping women with children to mind, no business sense, and less common sense does not mean I do not care for worthy widows! I shall prove it to you!" He snatched up a sheet of vellum. "I will write you a bank draft for their benefit."

"The widows would prefer to offer a useful ser-

vice rather than sit back and receive your charity."
She folded her hands in her lap primly. "A bank
draft for how much?"

"Five hundred pounds." He dipped his pen in
ink.

Her eyebrows shot up in admiration. "That is
exceedingly generous."

He smiled to himself as he wrote the instructions to his bank. Lady Nola was no different from
any woman. It was merely a matter of finding the
best way to handle her. He blotted the letter to his
bank and handed it to her.

"Thank you." She inspected the letter, then passed
it right back to him. "You may put it toward our
rent."

He flung his pen down, spattering ink across
the mahogany desktop. "I have been telling you I
do not want your bazaar since I first heard of the
scheme in the Latours' office, yet you ignore what
I say. I have made up my mind. I will not change
it."

"But you made up your mind in the Latours' office without giving it more than a second's deliberation. Surely a hastily given opinion is worthy of
reconsideration?"

"Really?" He crossed his arms and tilted his
head back to look down his nose at her. "If I recall
our introduction in the Latour office, you did not
spend an instant deliberating before you announced
you did not want to be married to me. And yet, I
do not hear you volunteering to reconsider your
hastily given opinion."

"There lies the difference between you and me,
Mr. Carr. Unlike you, I am not irrationally stubborn. Nor am I afraid to endure personal sacrifice
for the benefit of a greater good." She lifted her

chin, the gold flecks in her eyes glinting. "If marrying you is the only way to get your warehouse for the widows' bazaar, then I will marry you."

She gasped and covered her scarlet cheeks with both hands.

Gabriel swallowed. His heart pounded. His temples ached. What the devil was he supposed to do now?

From the hallway, an ominous titter cleaved the silence.

FIVE

Gabriel lunged to the door. His mother, in full bedraggled evening regalia, stood in the hall, whispering into Bartlett's ear. She waggled her fingers at Gabriel in greeting.

He glanced back at his desk. Lady Nola still sat goggle-eyed and beet red, her hands glued to her cheeks.

For a hellish minute, Gabriel hovered in the doorway, debating his choices. To continue to be insulted by a woman whose only interest in him was his warehouse. Who considered marriage to him a sacrifice to be endured. Who acknowledged his expertise in business one minute, only to berate him for his stupidity in not following her orders in the next. Who did not even notice he was tolerably good-looking—no, staggeringly good-looking. She didn't even seem to understand he had a sizable fortune. She should be grateful he was interested in speaking to her at all, not bristling with indignation every time they met.

Damnation.

He darted into the hall.

"Gabriel, darling!" His mother tried to peer past him into the study. "When I complained you had become dull, I never dreamed you would feel compelled to begin entertaining young women in your study. Alone."

He grabbed her arm and marched her down the hall as quickly and quietly as he could. "If you were eavesdropping with the slightest efficiency, you would know the whole thing was hardly entertaining."

"Eavesdropping? Certainly not! I will be forced to rely on Bartlett's account of what happened, and you know how poor his hearing is at his age. Anyway, your study is far too large, one cannot hear a thing from the door. I've always said you should have made the smaller room the study and the larger room the drawing room. You can see for yourself it is at least ten feet shorter—" She frowned as he pulled her into the drawing room. "Why on earth are we in here?"

He shut the door. "We are going to give Lady Nola a chance to—"

"Lady Nola Grenvale?" Her eyes bulged.

His heart sunk. "You know her?"

"Good heavens, Gabriel! Everybody knows Lady Nola. She helps the helpless widows."

He groaned.

His mother ignored him. "Her father died last year. Her poor mother, of course, died when her children were young, but at least she produced a Belcraven heir. He is the same age as St. Fell's third brother, Toby. Or is it Frederick? They're both officers in the Guards, not both of St. Fell's brothers of course, but one of them and Belcraven, although Belcraven is a captain, and Toby or Frederick—"

"Mother!" Gabriel flung himself down on the sofa and pressed his fingers to his throbbing temples. "It is a pity you cannot find a more useful purpose for your endless store of pointless information, but now is not the time!"

"Of course not, dear. We must return to your study so you may introduce us properly."

"Certainly not! Lady Nola might slip out of the house if we give her a few moments alone." If there was a merciful God in heaven.

"Oh no, dear, she will not leave." His mother settled herself next to him. "In the first place, that would be unspeakably rude."

"I suspect that might not be a problem for Lady Nola," he muttered.

She glanced at him sideways. "Secondly, I told Bartlett to send her maids down to the kitchen. She cannot leave without her maids."

He leaned his head against the back of the sofa and took a deep breath. He had to get a hold of himself. What did it matter if the only thing about him that Lady Nola noticed was his well-endowed warehouse? She didn't meet his requirements either.

"How do you come to know Lady Nola?" his mother asked.

Wonderful. Now he'd be treated to a lecture on the stupidity of asking his tenants to recommend prospective brides. "The Latours introduced us. I will leave the house through the back," he added quickly, hoping to divert her, "and you will go inform her I have been called away on business and will not return to town for a week. It would not be a lie, because I was planning to go to Uxbridge anyway, and I shall merely leave a day early—"

"The Mademoiselles Latours who own the dress

shop in your Soho building?" his mother continued. "Your tenants?"

"Yes. I will go to my club and wait until my bags
are packed—"

"Never say they introduced you to Lady Nola in
the belief she would be a suitable candidate for
your wife?" She peered at him through narrowed
eyes.

He nodded, miserable, and braced himself for
her to crow about the spectacular failure of his plan.

She clapped her hands together. "How marve-
lous! Here I thought your scheme was stupid and
rigid and heartless and doomed to failure—" She
tucked her fan under her arm and extracted a handkerchief from her sleeve and dabbed at her eyes.
"Oh, never mind what I thought. I was completely
mistaken. Lady Nola is the perfect wife for you!"

He stared at her, dumbfounded. "Does no one
listen to my list of requirements?"

"A brilliant match!"

"The list of requirements I spent months refin-
ing?"

"You are perfect for each other!"

"Perfect? The day my brains are dashed out the
side of my head. The woman is lecturing, managing, unappreciative—" He snapped his mouth shut
at the speculative look that flashed across his
mother's face. "Do you not recall my first requirement?" he demanded. "Lady Nola is the daughter
of an earl!"

"Piffle!" She flicked her fan at him. "You said
you needed a wife from the merchant class so she
would not object to your preoccupation with business. Lady Nola knows all about London commerce. She would love your business interests."

He folded his arms across his chest. "I want a

wife who admires my own interest in business—not one who thinks she can run my business better herself."

His mother frowned. "Perhaps you should let Lady Nola run your business, dear. I hear she is quite clever about matters of commerce."

"There is nothing so blasted clever about her!" If Lady Nola was so clever, she would not think he was an idiot. "Anyway, I do not want a clever wife. It is not one of my requirements."

"Gabriel, your language! You said 'blasted'!"

"You say 'blasted' all the time."

She shook her head sadly. "Yes, dear, but I am a matron. You never use bad language. I do not know what is come over you."

"Damnation, Mother! Nothing is come over me!"

She gasped and fell back against the sofa cushions.

He rolled his eyes. "Do not bother clutching your heart. Will you help me get her out of my study or not?"

She struggled to push herself upright against the cushions. "But you wanted someone of morally superior character. You cannot get much more morally superior than a girl who devotes herself tirelessly to the cause of unfortunate widows."

"All I want is Lady Nola out of my study."

"What about your requirement of an amiable nature? Lady Nola is known to be very pleasant, not the least sign of temper. Which given your excitability of late, I can see why this would be very important."

"Are you going to help me get her out of here or not?" He glared at her.

"Furthermore, I distinctly recall your saying you wanted a girl with a reasonable figure. Lady Nola has a lovely figure, I remember watching her dance at Almack's."

"Listen to me, Mother!" He leaned over to put his face before hers. "I want her amiable and morally superior person out of my study without a scandal or a scene. Are you going to help me or not?"

"Do you not find her figure reasonable? She is so tall and slender. As graceful as a willow tree."

"Yes, you are right," he ground out between clenched teeth. "Her figure clearly resembles that of a tree. Now will you please go speak to her while I sneak out the back? Just make sure you see her to the door. If anyone is watching, they will assume she called to visit you."

"You compare her figure to a tree? I expect you to be more generous than that."

Just as his ideal bride's figure would be more generous than Lady Nola's. He tugged his cravat.

"For goodness' sake, Gabriel! You are going to reject the girl because of the size of her bosom? That is most unfair!"

"Have you listened to a word I have said? Lady Nola does not meet the criteria of my list. Her bosom is the least of the reasons why I do not want to marry the girl!"

His mother gasped.

He tried again. "I mean, her bosom does not signify."

She smacked him with her fan.

"Damnation, Mother!" He leaped to his feet and out of her reach. "I do not know how we have managed to fixate on this idiotic topic."

"I do not know either," she said with a sniff. "This kind of superficial judgment is the last thing a mother wants to hear from a son."

"The only important point is I do not want to

marry Lady Nola. She does not meet the requirements of my list."

"Which goes to show what I have said all along—your list is stupid. You and Lady Nola are perfect for each other. Any idiot could see it—even you."

He folded his arms across his chest. "Well, that would make Lady Nola and me idiots both, for she does not want to marry me either. She is only interested in my warehouse."

"Your warehouse?" His mother frowned. "That isn't a cant term for something improper, is it?"

"My warehouse in Soho Square," he groaned. "She wants it for a bazaar for her widows."

"Well, why don't you give it to her?"

"I don't want to give it to her! I want her to leave me alone!" He put his hands on his hips and glowered at his mother.

"Then why did you invite her into your study?"

"I did not invite her! She just showed up."

"Why did you agree to see her? You could have snuck out the back way ages ago if you did not want to give her your warehouse."

"Because Bartlett made—Because I thought she was here about marr—Damnation! I am going to Uxbridge."

She pursed her lips and eyed him thoughtfully. "Yes, dear, I can see why you would."

Nola rubbed her temples with the tips of her fingers. The clock on the mantel struck the hour of eleven. The Carr butler kept insisting that Agnes and Mavis were on their way. Nola supposed she could march through the house and roust them out herself, but she did not want to take the chance she would see Mr. Carr again. Nor could she possibly leave without her maids. The last thing she wanted after this morning was any hint of a scandal between herself and Mr. Carr.

Not that there was any rush to leave Mr. Carr's study. He certainly was not coming back, not after his choking reaction to her insane offer to marry him for his warehouse. She had never seen such an expression of horror on a man's face. She buried her head in her hands.

To think an hour ago she had been ashamed about lying to the Carr butler so she could try to persuade Gabriel Carr one last time to change his mind about the bazaar. She felt terrible about lying, guilty she had tricked her way into his home.

Any embarrassment about that lie dissolved into nothing after the humiliation of her subsequent behavior.

Of course, she had enjoyed a brief moment of moral superiority in between her two humiliations. She lifted her head and snickered. To think Mr. Carr believed she had come to his house to try to marry him. How ridiculous.

But much less ridiculous than her blurted offer to marry the man for his warehouse. She sunk her head back in her hands. How had it happened? She closed her eyes and tried to review the conversation, but the only thing that came to her mind was the tilt of his chin.

Would she really have been willing to marry the man just to get his warehouse for the widows? She stared at the wall of bookshelves behind his desk, the volumes blurring as the tears welled in her eyes. Personal happiness was not the only legitimate motivation for wedlock—surely service to others was a valid reason to acquire a husband? There were worse reasons to marry.

Another rush of mortification made her fumble for her handkerchief.

Of course there were worse reasons to marry, and she knew perfectly well what they were. Dimples. Mr. Carr's dimples. She had been sitting opposite him, scowling at him while he argued, when he had smiled. Not a friendly, warm smile, either, but an annoyed, sarcastic smile. A smirk, even. Nonetheless it had made the little dimples appear in his cheeks. Each one a tiny half-moon crease in his smooth-shaven face, no farther than an inch and a half from his lips on either side of his smile.

She buried her burning face in her hands. She hadn't only suggested she would marry Mr. Carr for his warehouse. She had designs on his dimples. There he was, a businessman trying to have a discussion about his warehouse, and she wanted to take advantage of him so she might be able to stroke his dimples. His dimples, and worse!

The worst thing of all was her attraction to him was merely for the way he looked. It certainly wasn't for his character. He was stubborn, smug, and completely unsympathetic about the cause she cared about deeply. She was ready to sacrifice her independence, her personality, her integrity, for a pretty face. She dabbed her flaming cheeks with her handkerchief. And an excellent set of shoulders too. Not to mention his muscular legs.

The strange pang that gripped her whenever she contemplated Mr. Carr's legs returned, and Nola was obliged to unfurl her handkerchief and fan herself.

The whole morning had been a nightmare. It was wretched enough the dream of a widows' bazaar in Soho Square was as dead and dry as the dust behind her post chaise to Kent tomorrow. But

in addition her moral and intelligent approach to
life had nearly vanished in the wink of a dimple.

And she had been willing to pretend it was only
about helping widows! Nola sniffed and blew her
nose. She was a hypocrite. A liar!

"If you ask me, there is nothing wrong with a
well-placed lie." A short, plump woman in a rumpled peach silk ball gown padded across the plush
carpet to the desk. "Especially when one is dealing
with men."

Nola stared at her, aghast. Surely she had not
been speaking aloud?

"Such trying circumstances in which to make
proper acquaintance." The woman installed herself in the chair next to Nola's. "No third party to
make sure we keep precedence, my son skulking
off and you obviously still overset."

So the woman was Gabriel Carr's mother. She
had the same deep blue eyes and raven hair as her
son. Nola was so relieved she had not blurted out
the extent of her humiliation she could barely make
the appropriate responses while Mrs. Carr per-
formed the introductions and proceeded to describe a complex chain of mutual acquaintances. It
seemed Gabriel Carr's mother knew every member of the *ton*, and had pertinent information
about each. Fortunately she did not require more
than the occasional nod, so Nola had the chance
to regain her composure.

"And of course, I am well acquainted with the
Countesses of Belcraven," Mrs. Carr said, finally
stopping to draw a breath. "Your aunts. In Kent . . ."

Nola took advantage of the awkward lull which
inevitably followed any mention of Aunt Caroline
and Aunt Hortensia to rise to her feet, thank her
hostess, and ask for her maids to be sent so she
might leave.

"So soon?" Mrs. Carr looked bereft. "But I have ordered coffee so we may spill it on Gabriel's blotter."

To her shame, Nola found the thought tempting, spurred by the memory of Mr. Carr's jaw dropping before he scrambled out of his study. She decided against it, however. "I'm afraid I must go. I leave for Kent tomorrow, I must see to the packing."

"Piffle. You only wish to leave because you are overset. You will feel much better once we have had a nice chat."

Nola shook her head. "No, really, I must go."

"If you insist." Mrs. Carr's casual shrug was belied by the alarming intensity with which her eyes bore into Nola's. "I suppose rushing off is the only sensible alternative if one has suffered a devastating emotional upset."

Nola sat down.

Mrs. Carr smiled.

A knock on the door heralded the Carrs' butler bearing a tray with coffee and pastries. Nola could have sworn he winked at her as he set it down on the desktop.

"We do not actually have to spill coffee." Mrs. Carr poured them each a cup. "Merely eating at the desk is sufficient to vex Gabriel."

Nola smiled. Unlike her son, Mrs. Carr seemed very easygoing.

Mrs. Carr drained her coffee in one go and poured herself another cup. "Gabriel has a host of unreasonable matters that drive him to distraction. Oh! Look!" She pointed at the plate of pastries. "Chef has made Congreve rockets!"

She passed the silver dish to Nola. The Carr chef's rockets were tiny pancakes rolled into cylinders with a cream filling, which one apparently ate with the fingers, as if it were a biscuit. Nola took one. When she bit into it, cream spattered the front of her dress.

Mrs. Carr handed her another napkin from the high stack on the tray. "They explode so authentically, do they not? It drives Gabriel mad."

Nola wiped the blobs of cream off her dress. Perhaps, just in this one instance, Gabriel Carr's irritation was justified.

"Just the thing to divert us from my son's morning intransigence." Mrs. Carr let her rocket explode into her coffee, then stirred the cream until it dissolved in the hot liquid.

"Mr. Carr does appear to be somewhat fixed in his opinions," Nola said, succeeding with effort at achieving an even tone of voice. It wouldn't be good manners to attack the man's character in front of his mother, no matter how justified. It must already be difficult for the poor woman to share a home with someone as obstinate as Gabriel Carr.

Mrs. Carr licked her spoon. "I suppose you are right, if by fixed in his opinion you mean he is a pigheaded mule."

Nola laughed. Mrs. Carr was definitely more pleasant than her son.

"I blame it on his father." Mrs. Carr plucked another rocket from the dish.

"Your husband was stubborn as well?" Nola asked.

"Heavens no. Mr. Carr was very easygoing. But he passed away five years ago, poor dear, so it is quite convenient to blame him for everything."

Nola took another sip of coffee. Of course, it might be possible Mr. Carr and his mother annoyed each other with mutual equality.

"Not that being stubborn is all bad. On his twenty-fifth birthday, Gabriel decided it was time to make his fortune." Mrs. Carr waved her plump hand and Nola's gaze followed it from the plush Aubusson rug to the elegant furniture that graced the enormous study in the Mayfair town house. "I am sure I do not need to tell you how well he has succeeded, although I could provide exact figures, if anyone asked."

Nola leaned back in her chair and took another bite of the sweet rocket and then a sip of her coffee. It was pleasant to sit in the study and listen to Mrs. Carr chat.

"Oh yes," Mrs. Carr continued. "Gabriel works very hard at his business interests even though all his friends continue to idle away their days. His best friend is the Duke of St. Fell. Have you met him? Tall, fair, and handsome. He comes here often."

Nola nodded. He was the brother of Henry's friend Toby. Handsome, but not nearly as handsome as Gabriel Carr.

"He is very charming. Much better manners than Gabriel. But he is not worth a bean, so Gabriel's stubbornness does have its rewards."

"Material ones, at least," Nola said.

"Exactly my dear! I can see we shall get along quite nicely." Mrs. Carr took another rocket. "I am glad you are not still overset by being forced to lie in order to speak to my son."

Nola flushed. "Mr. Carr told you I lied about the reason for my visit?"

"No, Bartlett did," Mrs. Carr said. "He also said had you told the truth, Gabriel would have refused to see you. So you should not be the slightest bit overset about telling your lie."

"But it made no difference. Mr. Carr still refused to consider the widows' bazaar."

"It was very unreasonable of Gabriel to refuse to

listen to your excellent arguments on behalf of your widows."

A glow of pride warmed Nola. "Mr. Carr told you my arguments were excellent?"

"No, Bartlett did," Mrs. Carr said. "He overheard you. It is the nature of arguments that they are audible. He said you were most convincing."

Nola sighed. "Not to your son."

"Yes, my dear. I can see you have had a very trying morning. I do not know how a man can reject such a perfectly sensible offer."

Nola's face burned. She lowered her eyes. "I suppose Bartlett told you I offered to marry Mr. Carr if he would give the widows his warehouse?" she whispered.

Mrs. Carr blinked. "No, dear, Bartlett quite missed that part of the conversation. You must not have been shouting loud enough. I was referring to your offer to install the bazaar in his warehouse."

"Oh." Nola's hand trembled so much her cup rattled in its saucer.

Mrs. Carr studied her own cup for a moment, then looked up with a peculiar smile on her face. "You offered to marry Gabriel if he would give you his warehouse?" she asked.

Nola nodded miserably.

"He did not accept?"

Nola's face burned so hotly her ears stung. "He bolted from the room as if his hair were on fire," she said.

"But you must not be embarrassed about that, my dear, for it had absolutely nothing to do with you. Gabriel has made a list of requirements he wants in a bride, and the first one is she must come from the merchant class."

Nola's breath caught in her throat. Gabriel Carr had made a list of requirements for a bride? As if

getting a wife were like going to Tattersall's to choose
a horse. Or ordering a tilbury carriage to one's
specifications. "That is so"—she took a deep rasping breath—"That is so . . ."

"Yes, words fail, do they not?" Mrs. Carr sipped
her coffee. "But I wager you are feeling less undone."

Nola leaned back in her chair and let the memory wash over her of Gabriel Carr's goggling eyes
and slack jaw just before he sprinted out of his
study. Her heart hammered and her stomach knot-
ted. She still wanted to bury her head in her hands.
Now, however, she also wanted to say something
really quite cutting to Gabriel Carr and a small part
of her wanted to sulk in disappointment that someone as clever at business as Gabriel Carr would be
so stupid.

Mrs. Carr held the silver coffeepot out and offered the handle. "I believe if you aim for the
right-hand corner it will soak all the way through
to the second drawer."

Nola eyed the coffeepot and the polished mahogany desktop and sighed.

The older woman dropped the pot back down
in the tray with a clatter. "Oh for heaven's sake!
You cannot possibly be that amiable!"

Nola wrung her hands together. "I am afraid I
simply do not have a passionate nature. I cannot
begin spilling coffee or hurling insults just because
your son is a self-absorbed egotistical cabbage-
head! Goodness!" She covered her mouth with her
hand.

Mrs. Carr laughed.

Nola smiled and lowered her hand. The declaration was strangely satisfying, but it didn't change
what had happened. "I still made an idiot of myself, even if your son is an idiot himself."

Mrs. Carr took another rocket. "That is easily answered. Do you not find my son handsome?"

"Handsome?" Nola tried not to squeak. "I had not particularly noticed."

"Do you require spectacles, my dear?"

Nola shrugged. "I suppose one might say he is handsome."

Mrs. Carr's steady gaze pinned her to her seat.

"Very well!" Nola dropped her cup onto the tray and shot to her feet. She pressed her hands to her flaming cheeks. "You know perfectly well he is ridiculously handsome! But it does not signify."

"It always signifies, my dear." The older woman stirred the cream into her coffee. "Tell me, do you recall how you came to make this offer?"

Nola paced the width of the room. "No, I do not! One moment I was trying to convince him to take money as rent, the next I was saying I would marry him for his warehouse. I never intended to say it. It is ridiculous, because I most certainly would not!"

"Now my dear, there is nothing to be embarrassed about. I know exactly how you feel. The next moment you noticed the set of his shoulders, or the way his hair curled around his ears, or his dimples—"

Nola nodded. She would admit to dimples. Not more. Not to his mother.

"Dimples." Mrs. Carr made a knowing sound. "Gabriel has excellent dimples. And when you are looking at his dimples, do you find yourself in the miserable predicament of knowing every word you say is of crucial importance, yet you cannot stop yourself from babbling the most idiotic twaddle?"

"Yes! It is mortifying! I am not the kind of person who judges someone based on their appearance."

"Piffle! All women feel the same when they see a particularly handsome man. Particularly if one is alone with him."

"Truly?" Nola stopped pacing and turned to look at the older woman. Did all women feel the same way when they looked at Gabriel Carr? Somehow the thought was more disconcerting than comforting.

"Certainly." Mrs. Carr nodded her head sagely. "If your mama were alive, she would tell you so herself. All you need is a distraction. When I was a girl, one particular gentleman had the same effect on me. Until I got a lovely little kitten. Then whenever I got a glimpse of the gentleman's calves in his blue silk knee breeches, I would simply pick up my little kitten and dangle a ribbon in front of it until the urge to babble passed. My little kitten grew into a cat, of course, but not before Gabriel's father had proposed."

"Mrs. Carr!" Nola marched back to the desk. "I do not want to marry your son! I merely want to persuade him to put the bazaar in his warehouse." She couldn't marry him anyway. She was the daughter of an earl and he was a very stupid man with a very stupid list.

"I do not blame you in the least for not wanting to marry him, my dear," Mrs. Carr said, "but you cannot convince him to support your bazaar unless you find a way to speak to him without babbling."

The woman was right. The widows deserved better. Nola sank back down into her chair. "I do not have a cat," she said. Fig would likely eat a cat.

Mrs. Carr shrugged. "My sister used to knit. The year of her come-out she made a muffler seventeen feet long."

"I cannot knit, either." Nola sighed. "But I do have a dog."

"There you are! A dog will do the trick nicely."

Nola laced her fingers together in her lap. "I certainly hope so, because I cannot bear to keep acting like a brainless idiot. This has been the most embarrassing morning of my life."

Mrs. Carr reached over and patted her hand. "Don't be absurd, my dear. You are young. I promise there will be many more embarrassing moments to come."

"Damned right, it is embarrassing. Wretched business when a man has to be rescued from the clutches of a woman by his mother." St. Fell leaned forward in his armchair and lowered his voice. "I say, Gabriel, what the devil is a man's warehouse? I thought I knew all the cant terms for the parts of—"

Gabriel ground his fingers into the leather arms of his chair. "My warehouse! My building in Soho Square!" He looked over in alarm at the half-dozen dandies sitting at the table in front of the bow window. Thankfully they were completely absorbed in watching people pass on St. James's Street. It was bad enough his mother knew the low ebb his list had brought him to—if the wags of White's discovered his list had resulted in the encounter with Lady Nola, between their gossip and his mother's, all of London would be laughing at him.

"Ah. An actual building." St. Fell flagged the waiter and signaled for another glass of port. "Goes to show you how shatter-brained women truly are. That's why your list of requirements for a bride is so damned clever. Shows 'em a man who isn't afraid to stand his ground in the war between the sexes."

Gabriel stared into his empty cup. If it was a war, he wasn't sure he was winning. He took a deep breath and straightened his shoulders. Yet.

"So how does your search go? Some fellows were considering putting a wager in the betting book on whether you would marry before your birthday, but I told them not to bother. There's no point betting against Gabriel Carr when he has his mind set. Any prospective candidates?"

"It is still early."

"You haven't turned up a single possibility?"

Gabriel shrugged. "I did make the acquaintance of my Bond Street bookseller's daughter and niece." Three days after his first disastrous encounter with Lady Nola. Nola. What a stupid name.

"And?"

"The daughter was a very nice girl." Gabriel reluctantly met his friend's eye, then sighed. "She was unbelievably boring."

"And the niece?"

Gabriel sighed again. "She made the daughter seem interesting."

"You have met only two girls in nearly three weeks?" St. Fell gawked at him. "Your system sounds like a complete failure."

What business of St. Fell's was it anyway? Gabriel flushed. "I have twenty more recommended to me whom I have been too busy to meet. As soon as I return from Uxbridge, I will make their acquaintance. Any one of them is bound to be better than Lady Nola!" Damnation! He clutched his head in frustration. He hadn't given her name when he told St. Fell out of courtesy for the woman. He might not be a saint—Saint Nola, how ridiculous—but he wasn't a cad either. He lifted his hands and furtively eyed the bow window table. He groaned.

The glitter of quizzing glasses were now aimed in their direction.

St. Fell swiped at the port he had sputtered over his waistcoat. "Lady Nola? Lady Nola Grenvale? She was the woman in your study?"

"Lower your voice," Gabriel muttered. "Why? Do you know her?"

St. Fell grinned. "Everyone knows Saint Nola— Good God, Gabriel! She is the ideal wife for you! She is intelligent, loves London, knows all about retail trade, is perfectly amiable. I have seen her dance at Almack's—"

"I loathe Almack's!"

"Exactly! So does she! She only went when her dragon aunts forced her to go. You see? Perfect!"

Perfect? St. Fell's taste in women had gone downhill. "She does not meet the requirements of my list."

"Forget your list!"

"I thought this was a war?"

"You'll not find a better match no matter how many women you interview."

But one of those women might actually see more to him than his warehouse. And not consider marriage to him a sacrifice to be endured. Gabriel leaned back in the armchair. "I will not abandon my list of requirements."

St. Fell eyed him over the rim of his glass. "Very well, how does she not meet your requirements?"

"In the first place, she is managing."

St. Fell's forehead furrowed in a puzzled frown. "I thought you wanted a managing wife?"

"I said I wanted a wife skilled at household management. Lady Nola wants to manage my business."

"Managing is managing." St. Fell waved his glass.

"You get to decide she must be managing. Doesn't seem quite fair for you to pick what she gets to manage as well."

Gabriel clenched his jaw. "What happened to the war?"

"Doesn't mean you can be unfair. Even war has rules. What's next?"

Obviously St. Fell did not understand the first thing about acquiring a conformable wife. Gabriel folded his arms across his chest. "Every time we meet, Lady Nola laughs at me."

"Everyone laughs at you, Gabriel. Intransigence is amusing."

"Being laughed at is not soothing!" Gabriel flinched at the titter that rolled up from the dandies' table. He leaned forward and lowered his voice. "I want a calm and dignified wife."

"I should think a laughing wife is less likely to bash you over the head with the fireplace poker."

Gabriel threw himself backward in his chair. To think they had been best friends since childhood. "There is no point trying to explain the obvious when you are in one of your moods."

St. Fell shrugged. "It's your moods that lead me to suggest Lady Nola. She is extremely amiable."

"Lady Nola!" Gabriel remembered another reason why she was totally unsuitable. "My first requirement is that my wife come from the business class. I do not want to marry an earl's daughter! Nothing personal, of course."

"I wouldn't want to marry an earl's daughter either," St. Fell said, "and I'm a duke. But Lady Nola isn't the slightest bit high in the instep and you must admit, she's a decent eyeful as well."

Decent eyeful? There was no doubt about it. St. Fell had lost his mind. "Lady Nola does not have a reasonable figure. She is"—Gabriel lowered his voice to a whisper and leaned forward—"lacking in her front."

"Good Lord! You mean you think she is flat-chested?"

"Damnation! Keep your voice down!"

"Did you just say damnation?" St. Fell burst out laughing.

Gabriel gritted his teeth and hunched his shoulders to try to shield himself from the dandies' interest.

"Very well," St. Fell tapped his finger against his lips. "I had never considered the matter of Lady Nola's bosom. I appreciate a slender ankle myself. I say, how are her ankles?"

Gabriel shot him a dampening scowl. "How the devil should I know?" Her ankles, according to the glimpse he had gotten when she had flung herself at the wagon, were shapely. But they were none of St. Fell's business.

"Calm down. I was just wondering. You want a second opinion on the merits of Lady Nola's bosom. Give me a moment." St. Fell leaned his head against the back of his chair and closed his eyes. After a few seconds he smiled. A few more seconds later he moaned.

Melodramatic jackass. Gabriel had a sudden urge to smash his fist into his friend's face. He should have realized St. Fell would take a serious discussion and turn it into something lascivious.

"Never mind Lady Nola's bosom!" Gabriel snarled.

"I do not mind her bosom in the least," St. Fell said, a slight glaze in his eyes when he opened them.

Gabriel clenched his fists. It was a miracle no

one had yet wiped the smirk off the idiot's face with the point of a sword.

"There's no need to get yourself in a pet." St. Fell drained his glass. "I am merely saying since your scheme to solicit brides from your tenants is not working out so well, perhaps you should call on Lady Nola. She lives right around the corner from Soho Square."

"What the devil is it about my saying I will not abandon my list of requirements you do not understand! I won't be paying court to Lady Nola! In any event, I arranged for one of my tenants to take the Belcraven House off her brother. Lady Nola will be in Kent with her aunts tomorrow."

St. Fell leaned forward. "So thanks to you, Lady Nola will be leaving for Kent tomorrow and you have left her and your mother alone in your house and you're going out of town for a week?"

"So?"

"Oh, nothing." St. Fell stood up. "Say, Gabriel, when is your birthday again?"

"December seventh. Why?"

St. Fell gave a little wave in the direction of the dandies' table. Every man at the table waved back. "I think I might place a little wager in the betting book about your bride search after all. You know, something about how you will marry the ideal bride before your birthday."

"It will not be Nola Grenvale!" Gabriel shouted.

St. Fell patted his shoulder soothingly. "How could it possibly be when she doesn't meet your requirements?" He pointed out the window. "Say, isn't that your carriage?"

Gabriel looked out the bow window. His valet must have arrived with his bags. He shifted his gaze slightly and realized that every very pink of

the *ton* at the dandies' table was staring at him.
Gabriel glared back. Let them gossip all they want.
His mother would beat them to it anyway. Between
the dandies and his mother, all of London would
know he had no desire to marry Lady Nola Grenvale.
Good.

SIX

Only a complete idiot was incapable of tying a cravat without the services of a valet. Gabriel flung the neckcloth down on the floor and snatched another from his wardrobe. How difficult could it be to fold a simple style? He glared into the looking glass as he wound the starched white linen around his neck. Again.

It was irritating to have to tie one's own cravat. But when one's valet claimed a country doctor in Uxbridge offered more sartorial satisfaction than working for a London gentleman who wasted the canvas nature had given him, what choice did one have? He hadn't even bothered to make the man work out his notice. Being obliged to remain behind in Uxbridge was punishment enough.

Half an hour later he patted his neck in satisfaction. He had folded a perfectly passable Orientale, particularly if he kept his chin tilted to the right. Excellent. Just as satisfying as the fact that neither his middle-of-the-night return from the wilderness of Uxbridge nor the defection of his valet had altered his schedule in the least. It was precisely thirty minutes past nine as he descended the staircase.

There was no sign of Bartlett in the foyer. Gabriel sighed as he marched down the hall to the breakfast room. Household management had deteriorated in his absence, but fortunately, such disorder would be remedied when he acquired a bride. A wife who met his criteria would ensure that everything ran smoothly in his home at all times. Which was why the requirement that she be skilled in household management was absolutely essential. As was every one of the requirements on his list.

It was a relief the entire misadventure with Lady Nola was over, behind him like his valet in Uxbridge. Now that he was free of her distracting demands for his warehouse, he could concentrate on interviewing the women recommended to him by his tenants. By the time Lady Nola returned to London he would have found and married the ideal bride.

Who most certainly was not Lady Nola.

He opened the door to the breakfast room.

Lady Nola was seated at his place at the table. Bartlett hovered behind her with the coffeepot.

"Good morning, sir." The butler reached past Lady Nola's shoulder to pour coffee into her cup. "We did not expect you back until tomorrow."

Gabriel stood rooted in the doorway, the blood roaring in his ears. His gaze swiveled from the sideboard heavy with all the makings of an old-fashioned English breakfast to the dog under the table, gobbling a ham slice off a Swann china dinner plate, back to the table where Lady Nola returned his stare, her mouth open and her eyes wide.

She blushed so fiercely her face turned as red as her wild curly red hair. Her plainly visible wild curly red hair, for it seemed Lady Nola did not wear her bucket bonnet to breakfast.

To breakfast in his house.

He staggered back into the hall and leaned against the wall out of sight of the doorway.

"Sir?" Bartlett followed him out.

Gabriel grabbed the butler by the lapels of his frock coat. "What the devil is she doing here?"

"Your language, sir!"

"Never mind my language! What is Lady Nola doing in my breakfast room at this hour of the morning, and if you answer eating breakfast, I shall strangle you where you stand."

Bartlett merely shrugged, sly amusement in his rheumy eyes.

"Mr. Carr!" Lady Nola strode into the hall, her dog waddling behind her. Her gaze lit on them and she stopped dead, a stunned expression on her face. Gabriel released the butler. Wonderful. Now she thought he beat his servants. Which was completely false and unfair. Not that her opinion mattered in the least.

Bartlett's smirk deepened. He pointed to Gabriel's neck. "You have lost another valet, sir?"

Gabriel looked down. His cravat was untied. The stiff linen now dangled limply down his front.

Damnation. He felt a blush burn his ears. A gentleman with an untied cravat was most improper. Not only was it embarrassing, but he would have to deal with Lady Nola's maidenly reaction when she caught sight of his bared throat between his collar points. She might very well swoon.

She folded gracefully to her knees, but she wasn't even looking at him. Instead she stooped over her idiotic dog to pat its homely head.

"What a lovely handsome boy," she cooed, scratching the fat cur behind its outsized ears. The dog slouched lopsidedly on its haunches, its tongue hanging out of its patchy brown snout.

The woman obviously had an impaired sense of aesthetics.

She looked up at him from behind her dog's ears. "I think Fig remembers you from Soho Square." The dog's vigorous panting made its head bob as if in agreement and its look of adoration as it gazed up at him was in contrast to the amused glint in the eyes of its mistress.

Her hazel eyes were more green than brown today. He now knew the term for her eyes was hazel because he had happened to overhear a conversation about the matter of eye color in females during luncheon with a few members of the Uxbridge Drapers Society and one knowledgeable gentleman was quite certain green eyes which changed to brown eyes were called hazel, even if on occasions there were clear flecks of gold.

Likely her eyes were green today because her dress was not the pink monstrosity she had been wearing on the previous occasions. Today she wore a gray monstrosity. Obviously, the color of her eyes somehow related to her clothes and whether or not she was indoors or out. It was not any more complicated than that.

Gabriel looked around for Bartlett, but he had snuck off—apparently the heroism of not running away didn't apply to butlers. So Gabriel stayed in the hallway feeling awkward, hands clasped behind his back, rocking back and forth on his heels, trying to calm his racing pulse. There was something not quite right about Lady Nola on her knees on the hall floor and him standing around with a drooping cravat.

A minute later she sprung to her feet, her face red from the exertion of fawning over her ugly pet. "I suppose you are wondering why I am here?"

He folded his arms across his chest and nodded.

She sighed. "To tell the truth, I am not quite certain myself. One minute I was explaining to your mother about the widows' bazaar, the next she was having my trunks sent here."

"My mother invited you to live in my house?" Of course. He should have recognized his mother's heavy hand. Someone as amiable as Lady Nola would have no chance against his mother when she fixed on a plan.

"I told her all about the difficulties we have had between us but she kept insisting it would be petty and selfish to put our personal disputes ahead of the plight of the widows. No matter what I said, she would only have it but that I stay and work on behalf of the widows." She paused for breath, her cheeks pink again. "Goodness! Where is Fig?"

The blasted dog was exactly where she had left it, right at her feet with its fool tongue hanging out, but Lady Nola dropped to the ground and started fondling it again. What the devil was it with women and their pets? Give a woman a kitten or a monkey and she turned into a babbling bubble-head. He would have thought a woman as intelligent as Lady Nola would be above such flummery. He watched her stroke the dog's mangy head. Obviously not.

Lady Nola looked up. "Mrs. Carr was so moved by the plight of the widows she wishes to devote herself to their benefit."

Gabriel snorted. The only thing his mother wanted to devote herself to was leg-shackling him to Lady Nola. Mother's next subtle move would no doubt be to sneak back to Bath in the middle of the night so he and Lady Nola would spend a night in the house alone together. The only question was whether Lady Nola was also seeking marriage, or whether she was still just after his warehouse.

Lady Nola jumped back to her feet. "I am sure you are worried this is merely some sort of trap," she said.

"It had occurred to me," he said, keeping his tone smooth. Was she admitting to trying to catch him in marriage? He should be furious. He would be as soon as she stopped making him dizzy with all her popping up and down like a bilboquet ball.

"You are not obliged, I swear it!" She shook her head so vigorously she had to tuck back a curl that bobbed in front of her nose. "Mrs. Carr assures me that she has so many friends and acquaintances in London we will soon find another building just as suitable as your warehouse."

"My warehouse!" He flung his hands in the air. That was all Lady Nola ever thought about when she considered him. He had no idea what stupidity possessed him to keep imagining there would ever be anything else about him the woman would notice.

"Well of course it is about your warehouse! Surely you do not flatter yourself into imagining I have come here to catch you in marriage?" She looked into his face and burst into laughter. "You do! Again! I would be insulted were it not so amusing."

"Gabriel, darling!" His mother rounded the Swann urn at the foot of the staircase. "I came down as soon as Bartlett fetched me. How clever of you to return a day early."

Gabriel stared at her dressing gown and nightcap in consternation. "Mother, are you ill?"

She laughed. "Of course not! Has Lady Nola not told you? I am completely reformed. Last evening I returned home at the early hour of three o'clock in the morning. I missed all the good gossip just to dedicate myself to the worthy bazaar—" She stopped abruptly, the expression on her face darkening as her gaze traveled from his undone cravat to Lady Nola's pink cheeks and ruffled hair. "For heaven's sake, Gabriel! Can you not be left unchaperoned for one minute without—"

"Nothing happened!"

"Oh. You lost another valet?" She turned to Lady Nola. "As I was saying about the bazaar, Gabriel always said it was a shame I could not find a purpose for all the intelligence I know about matters of society. Now I can use my information for the benefit of the poor unfortunate widows."

"Yes, I would like to speak to you about that." He looked at her meaningfully.

"Excellent! We shall all have a lovely cos while we eat." She squeezed between him and Lady Nola. "Breakfast is so refreshing at this ungodly hour of the morning."

He hooked his arm through hers to stop her before she crossed the threshold into the breakfast room. "You and I will have our discussion in my study."

"Gabriel! What will Lady Nola think?"

"Lady Nola has spent time with you now, Mother. I am certain she knows exactly what to think." He aimed her toward the staircase.

Lady Nola appeared to be trying to smother her laughter. "I understand," she said. "I shall wait in the breakfast room. Although I should warn you about Fig."

"Your dog is the least of my concerns," he said over his shoulder, softening the words with a smile as he steered his mother down the hall. There was no need to berate Lady Nola over the many faults of his mother.

When they reached the first landing, his mother dug in her heels. "I will not go any farther. You are being very discourteous to Lady Nola. We should go down and discuss business or London in the summer or—"

"I know perfectly well why you have installed the woman in the house," he said grimly. "You are trying to make me marry her."

"I am sure I do not know what you are talking about," his mother said in her most practiced innocent tone. "Lady Nola is merely here to work on her bazaar."

He rolled his eyes. "How stupid do you think I am?"

"That is hardly a fair question this early in the morning, Gabriel. I have not even had any coffee yet."

He threw his hands in the air. "How do you suppose we can have an unmarried woman who is no relation to us living here without a scandal? You want to put us in a compromising position so I will be forced to offer for her."

"Piffle! No one could ever force you to do anything. Certainly not marry a woman you do not want. The world does not revolve around you and your offers of marriage, Gabriel. Such arrogance is not attractive. Perhaps that is why you are having so much trouble finding a wife yourself."

"I am not having any trouble finding a wife!" He pressed the heels of his hands against his forehead and forced himself to breathe deeply.

"In any event, I can prove you are completely wrong about worrying you will be trapped into a compromising position and have to make an offer," she said triumphantly. "I have invited Lady Nola's aunts to stay with us as additional chaperones."

The blood drained from his face.

She smiled smugly. "So you see, everything is in perfect order."

He goggled at her at her in stunned silence.

"Mr. Carr," Lady Nola called from the foot of the stairs. "I wonder if I might just mention that Fig—"

"One moment, if you please!" he said, barely able to choke out the words. Countesses of Belcraven? Living in his house?

He clung to the bannister for support.

A strange thumping sounded on the staircase above. One thump followed closely by a second. A short pause. Then another two thumps in close succession.

"What the devil is that?" he asked, not sure if his heart could withstand another one of his mother's answers.

"Gabriel! Your language!" His mother jabbed him in the ribs with her elbow. "It is the Countesses of Belcraven, dear. Stand up straight, Lady Hortensia is a little high in the instep."

"I do not care what they are like, I do not want them here."

"Keep your voice down!" she hissed. "Do you wish them to return to Kent and leave Lady Nola here insufficiently chaperoned? I thought you said you did not want to marry her."

"Mr. Carr," Lady Nola called again from the foot of the stairs. "I'm afraid Fig is following—"

"We shall discuss your dog in just a moment!" he shouted, his heart in his throat as he looked up the stairs. The thumping sounded closer.

Two old women came into view as they descended the staircase toward him. The tall one wore a towering wig and a dress with hoops. She had a half-moon patch on her wrinkled cheek in the latest style of fifty years ago. She descended on

the right side of the staircase, holding the bannister with her right hand and her gold-topped walking stick with her left. The second old woman
clutched the left side of the bannister and had an
identical walking stick in her right hand. She was
tiny and seemed to be wearing a see-through muslin
shift. They thumped slowly down the staircase in
tandem.

His mother made the introductions when they
arrived at the landing. Lady Hortensia was the tall
one in hoops and Lady Caroline the one dressed
as if her come-out had been last week, not fifty
years ago.

Each Countess of Belcraven clung to her stick
with both hands and fixed her beady eyes on his
flaccid cravat.

"In my day," Lady Hortensia said grimly, "gentlemen did not come down to breakfast unless they
were dressed."

"Maybe that is why those days were so ditchwa-
ter dull." Lady Caroline winked suggestively at
him.

Gabriel took a step backward.

His heel landed on something furry. It yelped
and squirmed. Gabriel lost his footing.

The last thing he heard as he flew backward
down the staircase was the euphonious sound of
the Swann urn shattering into a thousand pieces.

He must have lost consciousness when he fell—
no, when he was tripped by Lady Nola's pestilential
dog. The effort of lifting his eyelids made his entire
skull throb, but Gabriel persevered, despite feeling
dizzy and sick. He was lying on his back in his own
four-poster bed. Someone had dressed him in his
nightshirt and tucked the coverlet around him.

He moved to swing his legs over the edge of the bed and collapsed howling when a knife of pain sliced through his right knee. He lay back in his bed, panting, his head throbbing in sympathy with the agony in his knee.

When the pain ebbed enough that his hands stopped shaking, he gingerly lifted the coverlet. A heavy bandage was wrapped around the length of his right leg.

"Don't worry, you're still as handsome as you ever were."

He dropped the coverlet.

An old woman loomed from the shadows to stand by the side of the bed and glower down at him. She was older than the aunts and her gray hair was scraped back into a bun.

She put her hands on her hips. "Doctor says you've got a concussion and shattered your knee. You'll have to stay off your feet for six weeks. Otherwise you'll end up with a limp." She sounded as if she looked forward to it.

"Who are you?" His voice came out in a croak.

"What?" She cupped her hand to her ear.

He repeated the question, the pounding in his head worse when he raised his voice.

She pursed her lips. "You can call me Nanny."

Perhaps he had died and gone to hell.

Gabriel closed his eyes and let the throbbing ache in his head return him to oblivion.

The next time he awoke, the pounding in his skull was echoed by a thudding in his bedchamber. Thump, thump, from the doorway, across the carpet, to the foot of his bed.

He kept his eyes closed.

"I do not see what the fuss is about," a woman

said. Lady Hortensia. "Although I suppose he would be tolerable enough with a patch on his cheek and sufficient hair powder."

"Tolerable? For God's sake, Hortensia. Pour him into a Weston coat and a pair of Hoby Hessians and the man would be a pink of the *ton*."

The Countesses of Belcraven. His temples pounded anew.

"You can't judge a book by its cover." That was from Nanny.

There was no doubt about it. He was in hell.

"We must send for Dr. Smith again." His mother's voice sounded from the left side of the bed near his nightstand. "Gabriel ought to have regained his senses hours ago."

She sounded worried. He struggled to open his eyes and reached out his hand to reassure her.

"Not that he'll ever come to his senses," his mother said.

He dropped his hand back on the bed. Perhaps if he lay perfectly still, they would all go away and leave him in peace. Or give him a decent burial.

His mother flew over to the bed. "Gabriel, darling! You are awake! I never thought I would be so grateful for your thick skull."

He forced his eyes open, then froze in terror at the two mismatched gargoyles at the foot of his bed.

"In my day, gentlemen did not tumble down the stairs like acrobats in Anstey's Amphitheater." Lady Hortensia said.

Lady Caroline snorted. "In your day gentlemen fell off their own three-inch red high heels." The Countesses of Belcraven immediately launched into a debate about the merits of men's footwear, punctuating their points with thumps on the carpet with their walking sticks.

"What the devil are they doing here?" Gabriel whispered, unable to tear his eyes away from the horrifying spectacle.

"They are fighting, dear," his mother said. "That is what they do."

Lady Hortensia began to swing her walking stick ominously in her sister-in-law's direction but Lady Caroline looked quick on her feet.

"I cannot blame them for wanting to kill each other," he said, "but why are they doing it in my room?"

There was a knock at the door before his mother could answer.

"I hate to disturb you." The door opened a crack and Lady Nola stuck her head in. "But I cannot find Fig."

"I believe he is under Gabriel's bed," his mother shouted over the voices of the countesses. "You may as well come in and get him."

Gabriel gaped in astonishment, his gaze bouncing from Lady Nola to his mother, but any thought that Lady Nola would think it improper to march through his bedchamber was quickly dispelled when she strolled past her dueling aunts and came to stand at the side of the bed next to his mother.

Of course. He should have realized Lady Nola wouldn't be affected by seeing him in his nightshirt. It wasn't as if he was in his nightshirt in his warehouse.

"Are you feeling any better, Mr. Carr?" she asked.

He yanked the coverlet up to his chin which moved his head and made the pain in his skull explode so fiercely he jumped and jostled his leg, causing the knife of agony to slice through his knee. "I am fine, thank you," he said through clenched teeth.

"I am terribly sorry," she said. "I feel it is all my fault you tripped over Fig."

His mother answered before he could open his mouth. "It most certainly is not your fault, my dear. I distinctly heard you try to warn Gabriel, but he was too intent on argument to listen." She sniffed. "In any event, given the overly large size of his head, it was only a matter of time before he fell on it."

"Damnation, Mother!"

His mother clucked in admonition. "Gabriel, your language is indecent."

"No more indecent than an audience in my bedchamber," he muttered.

His mother rolled her eyes. "This is a sickroom, not a boudoir for one of your romantic trysts. We are all mature adults."

He clutched the coverlet more tightly to his chest. "But—" He jerked his aching head in the direction of Lady Nola.

"Piffle! Lady Nola is far too morally superior to waste time ogling you. Isn't that right my dear?"

"Yes—yes of course." Lady Nola ducked down beneath the bed and started shouting her dog's name.

"Besides, she knows perfectly well you and she do not suit." His mother settled herself down on the bed beside him. "I told her all about your list of requirements in a bride."

"What?" His face flamed. He pulled the coverlet higher, suddenly feeling even more exposed than before.

His mother waved her hand airily. "I told everyone about your list." She leaned forward and lowered her voice to a whisper. "Of course, in Lady Nola's case, I did gloss over one—or rather a pair—of your requirements."

He stared at her in horrified silence.

"Well for heaven's sake, Gabriel! You cannot really expect me to tell her the truth. Women take that sort of thing very seriously."

"I expect you to mind your own business!" he croaked.

She peered down at him with an annoying smirk on her face. "I believe you are embarrassed. Are you ready to admit you have been completely wrongheaded about your list?"

"Most certainly not." Why the devil was she hounding him about the list? While Lady Nola was in the room? He was injured. He deserved sympathy, not torment.

His mother looked down her nose at him. "Very well, I suppose I must help you find someone who meets your list of requirements. After all, you cannot find yourself a bride while you are confined to your bedchamber." She frowned. "Or at least you ought not to."

He passed his hands over his aching eyes. "You have done quite enough as it is."

"Oh, no, I insist. I am happy to contact your tenants on your behalf." She leaned her face down to his and hissed in his ear. "Although perhaps you should first give me your instructions about the minimum bust measurement you define as reasonable." She darted off to the other side of the room, leaving him clutching the coverlet the way he could have wrapped his hands around her neck.

He sank back against the pillows. Why had he not been fortunate enough to die?

The bed bounced slightly. Lady Nola trying to drag her damned dog out. He looked frantically around the room. Was he the only person of sensitivity in the house? His mother and the Nanny woman were standing in front of the fireplace laughing. The Countesses of Belcraven were at the foot of the bed arguing. The bed bounced again. The only way Lady Nola could have fit under it was by spreading herself completely flat-out on the floor beneath him. It was not right! It was improper! It was indecent . . . in a particularly pleasing way. He leaned over the edge of the bed. Her foot stuck out, her slender ankle—

"Gabriel!" His mother shouted from across the room.

Damnation. He dropped back against the pillows.

"You must be careful you do not fall out of bed!" his mother shouted. "Even a head as hard as yours cannot take another blow."

He swallowed. Young women should not scramble under the beds of gentlemen.

Particularly when they were chaperoned.

The bouncing ceased and Lady Nola jumped to her feet next to the nightstand.

"He has a bone!" she shouted indignantly.

"I beg your pardon!" Gabriel yanked the coverlet higher.

"Fig has got hold of a beef bone," she said. "I will never get him out from under the bed now."

"Just leave him alone!" Gabriel snapped, desperately trying not to look at her bosom. God only knows what his mother had actually told her.

"I thought you did not like dogs," she said. He chanced a glance at her. She was wringing her hands together at her waist. Which was just below her bosom.

He groaned.

"You are in excruciating pain!" She flew to the

bed and landed on his knee. He doubled over in excruciating pain.

Nanny marched over and pulled Lady Nola off the bed. "He's too excitable to be a good patient."

"Who the devil are you?" he asked through clenched teeth.

"Gabriel, your language!" His mother came to stand next to Nanny.

"Exactly the kind of excitable patient who'll end up with a limp." Nanny scowled triumphantly.

"A limp is all the crack," Lady Caroline said. "Lord Byron has a limp and the ladies find him very attractive."

"Nanny is the Belcraven family nurse," his mother said. "We needed someone to look after you, since you have gone and lost another valet. Nanny was sitting in her room in the attic without a thing to do. So when you fell, it all worked out marvelously!"

Lady Nola's smile was kind. "I am sure your mother does not mean it in quite that way."

"Poetry nowadays is self-indulgent rubbish!" Lady Hortensia thumped her walking stick.

Gabriel gazed up at Lady Nola helplessly. "Is there anyone else I should know about?" he whispered.

Her answer was forestalled by the sounds of a scuffle at the door to his bedchamber. A buxom woman in a white apron marched in, brandishing a tureen. "Will someone please tell this Frenchy that recuperating English gentlemen require English beef tea?" she bellowed. "Not some mess of onion slurry."

"Did anyone mention Cook?" Lady Nola murmured.

Chef managed to squeeze his skinny frame past Cook's without spilling the pot he held. "It is consommé! And I am not French. I am a Swiss!"

"Let him pick!" Cook pointed at Gabriel.

Everyone turned to look at him. His head throbbed. His knee ached. Beef tea. He sighed nostalgically. He had not had beef tea since Chef had come to work for him.

Chef's drooping mustaches quivered.

"I will take both," Gabriel said, and passed out.

SEVEN

"It is the siege of Badajoz, my lady." Bartlett pointed to the slivered almonds that climbed up the side of the savory pudding. "I believe these are the ladders scaling the ramparts."

Nola wished she were less exhausted so that she could better appreciate Chef's latest breakfast offering. "And the olives?" she asked.

"The Rifles of the 95th, my lady."

Of course. She rubbed her eyes. The famous green uniforms. "It seems a shame to eat it."

Bartlett sliced off the reinforcements and placed it in her plate. "Chef will be most disappointed if you do not. He has not had a very good morning. He discovered that Mr. Carr drank all of Cook's beef tea but fed the consommé to your dog."

The mention of Gabriel Carr chased away the yawn that had been threatening to overtake her. She sat down at the breakfast table. "How is Mr. Carr this morning?" she asked, trying to keep her voice casual as the butler put her plate down before her.

"He had a restful night, which, if you will permit

me to say, does not appear to be the same for you, my lady."

Nola flushed. "I suppose I am still adjusting to my new accommodations."

Bartlett nodded sympathetically. "It is often difficult get to sleep in a new bedchamber."

She stared at her breakfast blearily. It certainly was difficult to sleep in a new bedchamber. Particularly when it was one floor above the bedchamber of Gabriel Carr. Gabriel Carr in a nightshirt. Gabriel Carr in a nightshirt, the candlelight illuminating the long, strong column of his throat.

"Do you desire anything else this morning, my lady?"

"I beg your pardon?" She blinked up at the butler.

He bowed. "If you do not need anything else, I will leave you to your breakfast."

She smiled wanly and shook her head. The old man backed out of the room.

It was completely ridiculous. She poured herself another cup of coffee. If she had to spend the night tossing in her bed and pounding her pillow, it ought to have been over concern over the widows' bazaar. She should have lit the candle and rewritten the list of suitable districts and available properties. Or sorted the widows into categories of retail interests. In reverse alphabetical order. Anything would have been more useful than brooding about the way she could almost see the muscles of his chest beneath his nightshirt.

As for the giddy feeling of restlessness that seized her whenever she remembered sliding under his bed yesterday evening—that was completely beyond contemplation.

No, if she had to think of Gabriel Carr, it ought to have been about how she could make him relinquish his warehouse to the benefit of the widows. After all, the man was stubborn and self-absorbed and egotistical and too selfish to lend his building to a good cause and had a list of requirements so he could shop for a wife the way he picked a tenant for one of his precious buildings. What did it matter if his appearance was appealing? His character was not.

The only thing that mattered was convincing him to support the bazaar. After the meetings between the widows and the vendors in the trades and as soon as she had enough information about the likely profit a stall could return and the reasonable rent that could be charged, she would write it all down and present it to him. Until then, there was no reason to see him. Arguing the matter wouldn't change his mind.

In any event, he was confined to his bedchamber. It wasn't as if a spinster could just waltz into a bachelor's bedchamber whenever she wished it. Not even to look for her dog. At least, not very often to look for her dog. Certainly not to fling herself under his bed looking for her dog. There was no way on earth Nanny would let her get away with that one again.

Her fork clattered in her empty plate. She had eaten her breakfast without even noticing how it tasted.

She groaned. Aunt Hortensia and Aunt Caroline's coaches and coachmen were making the widows' deliveries today. She was going back to bed. To sleep.

Bartlett was in the foyer arranging a silver epergne on the pedestal that had previously held the Swann urn.

"I suppose you are looking for your dog," he said as she passed him.

She shook her head. Fig had scratched at her door last night and after she had let him out in the back garden he had slept in her room. This morning he waddled straight upstairs after the trip to the garden. "I think he may have gone to Mr. Carr's room."

"Yes. Perhaps you should fetch him for a walk, my lady?"

"I think I will wait until he scratches to come out. Nanny will tell me." She smiled at the old man and started up the stairs.

"Your maids!" he called out.

"Agnes and Mavis?" She halted midstep and looked back at him over her shoulder.

"Yes. Are you looking for them, my lady?"

She walked back down the stairs to where he stood at the pedestal. "They are likely helping Cook and Chef in the kitchen."

He shook his head. "Cook and Chef have gone to visit the butcher to determine if this morning's delivery consisted of properly hung English beef, or rancid tripe foisted upon an unsuspecting Frenchman. Your maids did not go with them."

She stifled a yawn. Why on earth was he being so mysterious? "If you know where Agnes and Mavis are, why do you not just tell me?"

He smiled briefly, then ducked his head down to examine a smudge on the epergne. "They are in Mr. Carr's room."

"With Nanny?" Nanny could always be trusted to keep the twins occupied with a harmless activity.

Bartlett polished the epergne with his sleeve. "I heard Nanny say this morning she needed fresh supplies from the apothecary."

Nola's heart began to race. Surely he wasn't suggesting anything improper about the maids being in his master's room when Nanny was not? "Why are they in Mr. Carr's room?" she asked.

"They brought him his breakfast this morning. They have not come back since."

"What are they doing?"

"I really could not say, my lady."

Goodness! "I think I ought to go up to Mr. Carr's room right now."

He nodded gravely. "I hoped you would."

"Are you not coming with me?" she asked.

He shook his head, a mournful expression on his face. "I am but a poor servant, my lady. Nothing I do has the slightest influence on Mr. Carr."

She sprang up the staircase, raising her skirt to her knees so she could take the steps two at a time. She should have known Gabriel Carr was a rake. What else could he be with his looks? Just because he had a list of exacting requirements for a bride didn't mean he needed them filled to take advantage of a maid. Or two.

She panted as she charged down the hallway. Bartlett had not followed, the coward. Shocking a man of his age thought so little of his master's debauchery.

She flung open Gabriel Carr's bedchamber door.

Agnes flew across the room into her arms. "Oh, my lady, thank goodness you've come!"

"We knew you would find out and save us!" Mavis crowded behind her sister.

Nola blinked at them in horror. Somehow, she had not really believed it, even as she had rushed to the room. Yet the twins were in his bedroom, and they were grateful that she had come to their rescue. Her knees buckled. She clung to the door frame behind her for support.

"Too much goings-on for the room of an invalid. That's what happens when I'm lenient and let a handsome rogue have his own way." Nanny's querulous voice pierced the fog in Nola's head.

Nola opened her eyes. Nanny was standing with her arms folded, glaring at Gabriel Carr. But Mr. Carr wasn't in his bed. He lay on the chaise longue in front of the fireplace, arms folded across his chest glaring right back at Nanny.

"I am the one in need of rescuing," he muttered.

Nola looked from his petulant expression to Nanny's furious face. But Nanny wasn't bristling with the kind of rage Nola would have expected if there had been debauchery involving maids in her care. In the first place, she wasn't armed with one of Cook's cleavers. Secondly, Agnes and Mavis were fully dressed, not a hair out of place. Each girl clutched a sheaf of papers.

Nor did Gabriel Carr look in the least like a man caught in an indiscretion. His white linen shirt was neatly tucked into his fawn pantaloons and he had a wet cloth folded on his forehead.

"He's made us read the most unspeakable things," Agnes whispered in Nola's ear.

"Reports from building managers, account ledgers," moaned Mavis. "Hours and hours of it."

"Fifteen minutes," he muttered. "It only seemed like hours with all the carrying on you both were doing."

"But it was so boring," Mavis wailed. "All those numbers."

"And you scolded," added Agnes.

"Requesting you temper your incessant giggling is not scolding." He leaned back and rearranged the cloth over his forehead. His long, lean legs stretched the entire length of the chaise longue. The bulge formed by the thick bandage around his right knee strained the buckskin, but—

"I suppose you have come for Fig?" Nanny demanded.

"No, Bartlett . . . he mentioned . . . Agnes and Mavis . . ." Nola tore her eyes away from Gabriel Carr's thighs. Fig. Yes. She swallowed. She ought to get the dog.

"What's that? Bartlett?" Nanny snorted. "I suppose the dog wasn't good enough for him. Men!"

"Could I just have my correspondence please?" Mr. Carr said in a long-suffering tone.

Nanny rounded on him. "You still have the headache?"

He shrugged, but Nola saw how the action made him wince. "I have important business," he said. "I have been out of town and I need to catch up."

"Lady Nola could read to Mr. Carr," Mavis said.

Agnes shoved her papers into Nola's hands. "You love this sort of thing, my lady."

Nola shook her head. She wasn't ready to speak to him yet about the warehouse. There was no other reason to be in his bedchamber ogling the man. "I do not think—"

"I am certain I will be well enough to read them myself later this afternoon," Mr. Carr said.

Nanny snatched the rest of the papers from Mavis and thrust them at Nola. "Very well. You may read to the rogue, my lady. But only for one hour."

One hour! That seemed like an excessively long time to read to an invalid. Nola followed the old woman as she shooed the maids out the door with a list of things she wanted from the apothecary's and tugged on her sleeve. "But I do not want to read to—"

"Nay, don't thank me," Nanny boomed. "I know how much you enjoy helping others."

Mr. Carr raised his voice loud enough for Nanny to hear. "I do not want her to—"

"Of course you don't deserve it, you handsome cheeky devil." Nanny settled herself down in the armchair on the other side of the fireplace and picked up her knitting. "You should be thankful Lady Nola is so kind and generous."

Nola looked over at the chaise longue warily. It really was not a good idea for her to linger in Mr. Carr's bedchamber. True, he wasn't in his nightshirt, but he still looked very handsome, his long, lean length stretched out on the chaise longue, his head propped on his elbow. His blue eyes sparkled with amusement. He smiled and the dimples appeared.

Goodness. It was just reading business correspondence in broad daylight. There was no harm in looking at him in broad daylight. Besides, Nanny would be here the whole time. Nola dragged the straight-backed chair from his desk over to the chaise longue.

"Are you going to harangue me about your bazaar before or after you read my correspondence?" he asked as she sat down.

"I am not going to mention the bazaar today," she said primly as she looked through the papers. Most were letters, still with their wax seals.

"I do not believe you," he said. "You have lied before."

"Well at least every time I see you, I do not assume you want to marry me," she said, checking the dates on the letters. She supposed he would have definite opinions on which he wanted read first.

"At least if I did want to marry you, it would not be for a building," he said.

"Oh for goodness' sake!" She put the papers down and glared at him. "You are so much more pleasant when you are unconscious." Not one of her thoughts about him last night included his speaking. Now she realized why. "In any event, you are perfectly safe this morning. I realize I have gone about the matter in completely the wrong manner. You are clearly one of those people who needs to have everything written down and planned ahead of time, so I will wait until I have prepared a report on our plan for the bazaar then present it for your consideration."

"You make it sound as if there was something wrong with wanting to see something in writing," he said.

"Oh no! The only thing wrong is I did not work within your limitations," she said airily.

"Limitations?" He pulled the cloth off his forehead and shot her an indignant look. "You do think there is something wrong with me!"

She smiled. "Limitations is not the right word. Let us say parameters instead." There was no sense in antagonizing him when she needed his building. "You will have to forgive me, I did not have much sleep last night."

"No doubt you spent the night brooding about my warehouse."

"No," she said, then couldn't stop the blush that stung her cheeks. Then she blushed even harder when she realized she should have said yes.

"Oh?" He rolled on his side and leaned his head on his elbow. "See how much more interesting our conversations are when we do not talk about my warehouse? Whatever were you thinking about all night that turns you such a delicious shade of red?" The slow smile he gave her matched the throaty tone of his voice.

She looked down at the papers on her lap and tried to breathe evenly. She could swear he was flirting with her—no, he was flirting with her. Which

would be very flattering if she didn't know he had
a list of requirements he wanted in a bride and
had told all of London what they were and she
would never meet them. She sighed. Therefore his
flirting was not flattering in the least. He probably
flirted because he was a handsome man and used
to it. Likely the only thing he found attractive about
her was that she did not openly swoon at his feet.
Once she did, he would probably want nothing to
do with her. She ought to have these things engraved
on a vinaigrette bottle that she wore around her
neck so she could take a whiff and snap herself out
of it whenever he was charming.

"All right," he said, "I can see you are giving
yourself a good talking-to about whatever it is that
is making you frown so enthusiastically. I will take
pity on you and change the subject myself. Tell
me, is your nanny actually deaf, or is she one of
those women who is only deaf when it suits her?"

Nola smiled in relief. "I am afraid it always suits
Nanny to be deaf." When he laughed at her answer, she refused to look at his dimples.

"Why does she hate me?" he asked.

"She doesn't hate you." At least, not more than
any other handsome man in particular, but there
was no need to tell him that.

"She scowls at me."

"That is her natural expression." Nola glanced
at the old woman out of the corner of her eye.
Nanny's grimace as she glanced up from her knitting looked more benign than any other time Nola
had seen her contemplate the subject of handsome, cheeky men. In fact, Nanny looked besot-
ted. Likely the only reason Gabriel Carr didn't
recognize it was because he was habituated to a
more effusive rate of female adoration.

"Now you are scowling at me." He smiled at her. "And I know that is not your natural expression."

Goodness. More flirting. Her pulse raced. What was it his mother had said he did not want? Fusses? If this was his natural state when not discussing his warehouse, she could see how tempting it would be to make a fuss.

"Between your nanny, your cook, your aunts, and now your maids," he continued in the same bantering tone, "I am becoming quite accustomed to the perpetual scowls. Indeed, amongst your entire entourage, there is only one who looks at me with any admiration."

Her heart sank. Was she so obvious? She clutched the letters and suppressed the urge to lift them up to hide her flaming face.

He grinned. "Your dog likes me."

"Fig?" she squeaked.

Fig stuck his nose out from under the bed. She realized she ought to drag him out, but the time spent in conversation with Gabriel Carr seemed to be racing past so quickly.

"You sound surprised your dog likes me," he said. "I thought dogs were supposed to be a good judge of character."

"Fig is a better judge of a snack," she said in a dampening tone. "Now you have fed him consommé, you may expect him to be constantly underfoot."

"Or under my bed," he said softly, looking at her sideways from under his lashes, a teasing glint flashing in the deep blue of his eyes.

"You are being ridiculous!" The blush flooded her face so fiercely her ears burned. She snatched up a letter at random, ripped open the seal, and stared at it until the words began to sink into her overheated brain. "You have a letter from a Mr. Chalmers," she said, her tone challenging. If Gabriel Carr did not stop using that silky tone of voice, she ought to put down his papers and stalk out of the room.

He laughed. "I am testing the limits of your amiability, and your answer is to resort to serious business." He eyed Nanny. "Probably the best plan."

She took a deep breath to steady herself. Serious business was the only possible plan. He wasn't interested in marrying her and she certainly wasn't going to have an illicit relationship with him. She returned to reading the letter. "He is an apothecary who wishes to take the Soho Square premises being vacated by the Latours."

He rolled over onto his back again and reapplied the cloth to his eyes. "Do not bother reading the whole thing. I do not have an apothecary in mind."

Nola skimmed the rest of the letter. "He says he has been waiting for years for a suitable space in the Square and he prays you will consider his petition. He provides a list of references, one of whom is the Bishop of Durham."

He raised a corner of the cloth and eyed her warily. "You are about to lecture me about deciding too quickly, aren't you? Is it not interesting we seem to have a favorite argument, the way others share a favorite place or a favorite tune?"

She flushed. Favorite places or tunes were for couples. She and Mr. Carr would never be a couple. "You could at least let me read you the entire letter. It is three pages long and his language is most compelling. The poor man's livelihood depends on taking the premises."

"Then he is lucky I will not let him have the place.

There is already an apothecary in the square. Across the green. A very successful one too, if I recall, although the building doesn't belong to me. Since Mr. Chalmers either did not know or did not appreciate that simple fact, I have done him a favor by refusing his petition, do you not agree?"

"No, because Mr. Cole, the apothecary across the square, is seventy years old and declares he will retire this Christmas."

He lifted the cloth off his forehead and struggled to sit up. "Does he not have his own apprentice?"

"He left to start his own shop years ago."

"No family to carry on?"

"None." She stopped pretending she wasn't smug.

"Oh." He looked at her for a minute, then a slow smile lit his face. "You are absolutely right."

She caught her breath. Devastatingly handsome.

"But I still will not take Chalmers as a tenant." He leaned back again and draped the cloth over his face. Even his dimples.

She clenched the letter in her fists. "You are being most unfair."

"What is it about the noble Mr. Chalmers that fixes you so firmly in his camp?"

"How can I not have sympathy for a man whose application to become your tenant is rejected for no valid reason?"

He gave an exaggerated sigh. "Must every conversation we have lead inevitably to my warehouse?"

"I do not know," she said. "Are you always so inevitably stubborn?"

"I am not being stubborn. I have another tenant in mind. My chef."

"Your chef?" she echoed, surprised.

He leaned forward on his elbow. "What did you have for breakfast this morning?" He laughed when she told him. "I had the same," he said, "except mine was the siege of the castle. You can tell because he makes the angle of ascent steeper."

"Oh," was the only thing she could think of saying.

"My sentiments exactly. I fed it to your dog and Nanny smuggled me up some of your cook's excellent breakfast."

"Do you mean Chef would be a confectioner?" she asked.

"Precisely! Do you know he can recreate the battle of Trafalgar using only a bowl of rum punch and a dozen gherkins? It's very moving. The first time. I'm sure there are plenty of people who would love to part with their money for that sort of thing and it would give him the opportunity to cash in on the victory celebrations."

"He could cater at parties, like Gunter," she said.

"And have a few tables in his shop."

She snapped her fingers. "People could bring their food to the green in the center of the square and eat it there!"

He grinned. "We think exactly the same way."

Nola leaned back in her chair, breathless. The admiring light in his eyes made her heart race the same way that thinking about being under his bed while he was in his nightshirt did. Perhaps he wasn't merely flirting with her out of habit. The compliments he paid her seemed particular to her. Could he be reconsidering his list of requirements?

Or perhaps half an hour of looking at dimples had scrambled her brains. She looked over at Nanny, but the old woman's head nodded drowsily over her knitting needles.

"As for your poor Mr. Chalmers," he said, "why don't we just tell him to contact Cole?"

She pursed her lips. That was a kind thing to suggest. She really couldn't deny it. Gabriel Carr was kind. Kind to his chef, whose food he did not like, kind to his butler, who seemed to always be laughing at him. No wonder he needed a wife with good household management skills—he was too softhearted to do it himself. The thought depressed her. She snatched open another letter and ripped through the seal.

In the next half hour, she read him a letter from a tenant about Michealmas rent, another about repairs, and a report on the worthiness of a new fire protection service. They were in agreement on the merits of each. The fourth letter contained the menu for the Garrard House dining room and Nola found herself agreeing to go sample the food before the grand opening next week. In the fifth letter they discovered they both shared the same opinion about the restrictive covenants for the new street Mr. Nash proposed to build for the Regent.

"I think we are the only two people in London who know the covenants will make businesses fail," he said. "Everyone else seems to think banning everything from hawkers to greengrocers will make the street more elegant."

She nodded and stifled a sigh. She and Gabriel Carr seemed to be in perfect harmony about everything except the warehouse. She looked over at him where he lay on his back on the chaise longue with the cloth once again over his eyes. He was still the handsomest man she had ever seen, but she hadn't babbled or thought of the dog once. She had a sinking feeling tonight that she'd be awake thinking of more than his appearance.

He opened his eyes. "Is there some problem with your bazaar?" he asked.

"No," she said, surprised at his question.

He pulled himself upright and looked into her face with an expression of concern. "Whatever is worrying you so this morning? I can hear the wheels turning in your head."

"Nothing," she said quickly. "I am thinking—I am thinking about Chef."

He smiled crookedly. "I do not see how thinking about Chef requires you to scowl at me."

"How could you possibly know I was scowling at you?" she said. "Your eyes were closed and there was a cloth over your head!"

"I am beginning to sense your scowls even when I do not see them." He held up his hand to stem her immediate protest. "I assure you, the idea frightens me even more than it does you. But I thought we agreed I was the one who deliberated excessively. You are the one who is impulsive. Yet here you are brooding. It will not do."

"I am not brooding about anything!" she said as a matter of form, because in fact his words were quite pleasing. She never realized how satisying it was to have a gentleman recognize one's true nature.

"Promise me you will think about what I have said." He smiled. "But not too much."

"Very well." She returned his warm look.

"You must also promise me you will never tell my mother and your aunts I have regained consciousness."

She laughed. "You are afraid of my aunts!"

"Can you suggest a better reaction?"

"They are not so bad as all that once you get used to them."

"Really?"

She sighed. "No. But after a while they become a noise in the distance, like birdsong or bees. Or gnats."

He laughed. "It is hardly fair for me to reproach your aunts when you have been afflicted with my mother."

"There is nothing wrong with your mother!"

"You really are the most amiable woman in London," he said.

"No really! In any event, I cannot say I am sorry your mother insisted I stay in London, although I understand it was a shock to find me installed in your house."

"It was a surprise," he said, "but now I have had the time to think about it, not much of a shock. After all, I did run off and leave you alone with my mother. Someone as amiable as you didn't have a chance against any notion that sprung into her head."

"Still, I was impressed you did not shout." As she said it, she realized it was true. No matter how outrageous Eleanor Carr was, he was never cruel to his mother. Exasperated, annoyed, and frustrated. But never cruel.

"There is never any point yelling at my mother. That just alerts her to what you want her to do, which invariably means she will not do it."

Did he realize the same rule was bound to apply to him? She could use the same strategy to make him reconsider about the bazaar. And any other matter about which he was being stubborn. "How do you get your mother to change her mind?" she asked casually.

"Difficult." He rubbed his chin as if he were pondering the matter, then smiled. "It is much easier to convince yourself you want her to do whatever she is doing. Speaking of which, I wonder if I can persuade you to return tomorrow to finish helping me with my correspondence?"

Footsteps sounded in the hall. Mrs. Carr poked her head through the door.

"Ah, here you are, Lady Nola." She beamed. "No doubt you have come to fetch your dog."

EIGHT

Gabriel held the bedpost with one hand and tugged at the hips of his buckskin pantaloons with the other while he inspected his reflection in the looking glass. The benefit to flouting fashion and refusing to indulge in pantaloons so tight they looked painted on was that he could still fit into them even with the heavy bandage wrapped around his knee. The drawback was that loose-fitting pantaloons did not show to advantage the muscles in one's thighs. Of course, his valets had always claimed this was the case. But this was the first time Gabriel actually understood what they meant. Perhaps tomorrow he would send for a tailor.

He flexed his left leg, making sure his right one did not touch the ground by keeping his hold on the bedpost. Sure enough, the loose buckskin did not reveal the muscles of his thigh. He reached down to feel his leg. Could he be losing the tone in his muscle? He had not boxed in five years. Or ridden a horse since he acquired a carriage and spent his days doing business. He should take up sport again, once his knee recovered. He bent his arm to make sure the bulge of his biceps was visible through his shirtsleeve.

He brushed his hair forward with his fingers. He looked positively shaggy. He'd arrange for a haircut tomorrow. In the meantime, he would try to remember not to rake his hands through his hair.

Nanny stepped between him and the looking glass. "All your primping is destroying my illusions about handsome men."

"You have no illusions," he said, looking at the clock on the mantel for the hundredth time this morning.

"Lady Nola will be here after breakfast," Nanny said.

He shrugged. "It does not matter what time she comes."

The old woman rolled her eyes.

"I am merely looking forward to an intellectual discussion of the business of London retail trades," he said primly as she took his arm and helped him hobble to the chaise longue.

"Right profile or left?" Nanny asked.

For a minute he debated pretending he didn't know what she meant, then he sighed. "Left." He allowed her to help him lie on the chaise longue so he faced away from the doorway. So the dimple on his left side was slightly more attractive than the one on his right. Was it such a crime to be aware of the fact?

Nanny stared down at him for a moment with her arms folded. He gave her the left dimple.

She sighed. "I suppose I could go get her. She's with her aunts. It'd be a kindness, really. To her, not to you." She turned on her heel and darted out the door.

"Gabriel!" His mother charged past Nanny into

his bedchamber. She stopped abruptly when she saw him and smiled. "For a man who claims not to be seeking the making of fusses, I see you are resorting to the left profile."

He straightened his shoulders. "I do not know what you mean."

"Do not bother protesting! Your father was the handsomest man in England long before you. In any event, I am not objecting. I think it is quite hopeful of you, dear. I know perfectly well Lady Nola is on her way."

"Lady Nola is coming to assist me in matters of business," he said. Of course, if she happened to make a fuss over his appearance, he wouldn't necessarily object and embarrass the girl.

His mother's smug expression didn't slip. "Well, if you do not expect her to make a fuss, perhaps you are the one who wishes to make a fuss over her."

He bristled. "I do not make fusses!" The thought was ridiculous.

"I see." She put her hands on her hips. "So you are not ready to admit your method of acquiring a bride was completely wrongheaded."

"Certainly not! There was nothing wrong with my list of requirements. It is merely that I have become injured and confined to my room so I cannot carry out my original plan."

"But I have said I would gladly help you, dear," she said in an irritatingly jovial tone. "I shall write to your tenants to see if they have any young women for you to consider and interview them myself. You could be carried down to the drawing room to meet the ones that fulfill all your requirements."

He lay back on the chaise longue and draped his hand over his eyes and groaned. "I do not feel well enough to go downstairs." He kept his eyes closed until he heard her footsteps recede out of the room. He knew perfectly well she wouldn't write to his tenants. The last thing she wanted was a roomful of other women competing with Nola for his attention.

He settled himself more comfortably. Hopefully Nola would come up soon so they would have a decent visit. Spending time with her was the least he could do since everyone had gone to so much trouble to throw her at him. In any event, time spent with her was pleasant. Very pleasant. As long as they did not discuss her pestilential plans for his warehouse. Fortunately, she wouldn't bother him about it again until she had written up her plan. Not that putting it in writing would make the slightest bit of difference, but at least it would delay the inevitable conflagration that would result when she was forced to finally accept the fact that he had no intention of ever saddling himself with her bazaar.

In any event, surely after their conversation yesterday, she recognized that there was more to him than his warehouse.

"Mr. Carr?" Nola strode into his bedchamber, Nanny right behind her. "We must discuss your warehouse."

He pushed himself upright. "I thought you were going to write a report!"

Nola dragged the desk chair over to the chaise longue across from him and sat down, an earnest light burning in her eyes. "Yes, but I took your advice to heart. I am not the kind of person who broods and waits for a plan. We got along so well yesterday, I shall tell you all about our progress right now. I think you shall be very impressed."

"But the reason we got along yesterday was because we did not discuss my warehouse!"

She smiled warmly. "Which is exactly why we must deal with the matter of your warehouse now. We must get it out of the way."

He reached up to clutch his head, but remembered the arrangement of his hair. He grabbed the back of the chaise longue instead. He looked over at Nanny in her armchair. She was laughing, damn her.

He forced himself to speak in a calm tone of voice. "But whenever we discuss your bazaar and my warehouse it ends in calamity."

She frowned for a moment as she contemplated his statement, then her expression brightened. "Very well," she said, "we shall save our discussion of the warehouse for the very end of our meeting today. That way if there is calamity, it will not spoil the rest of our conversation."

He returned her smile. There would be plenty of chances to turn the discussion away from the warehouse and in any event, how would she know when it was the end of their conversation until it was over? "An excellent notion," he said. "Any other topic would be more congenial."

"Well, last night it did occur to me the reason you—"

"You were thinking of me last night?" he asked, just to see if he could provoke a blush.

She turned a rewarding shade of pink. "No! Well—yes. Last night I was wondering why you have kept a chef whose cooking you do not care to eat—"

"You ask me that? At least I do not have two incompetent maids!"

"They are not incompetent! They are young."

He snorted.

"Will you stop interrupting me!" She looked at him crossly, the amber sparks in her eyes in full flame. "I am trying to explain how I now understand your requirement of good household management skills."

"I beg your pardon?" What the devil was she talking about? Did she know so little about how a household was run she thought Chef was hired for his management skills?

She frowned. "I said now I understand why skill in household management is one of the requirements on your list for a wife and I was thinking perhaps all of your requirements have such a logical foundation."

Damnation! His blasted list! She was talking about his blasted list. Why the devil did she have to mention it? It was bad enough having his mother pop into his room to pester him about it. But for Nola to discuss it—it wasn't seemly.

"I do not want to talk about my list of requirements," he said.

"Oh. Very well." She smiled with her customary amiability. "We can discuss your dining room in Garrard House. I went yesterday."

"Already?" He frowned. She was much more efficient than he expected. On the other hand, he had ten buildings. He could keep her coming to his bedchamber for weeks if he wanted.

"I had another reason to visit Garrard House." She looked at him sideways. "Mrs. Armitage, the Garrard House glove maker, has agreed to take three widows—"

"I know perfectly well who Mrs. Armitage is," he said. "You are trying to bring the conversation around to my warehouse."

She turned a nice shade of guilty pink. Not as deep a pink as when he teased her about thinking of him, but quite diverting nonetheless. This blush only touched her cheeks. Some blushes reached all the way to her ears and her neck and sometimes even down to—

"The view is excellent," she said.

"Excuse me?" He flushed.

"You didn't mention one could see all the way from St. James's Park to Westminster from the dining room windows. It is spectacular. I think I even glimpsed the Surrey hills."

Of course. She was referring to Garrard House. It would be pleasant to take her there for coffee. Perhaps she would attend the opening next week with him. "How was the food?" he asked.

"I sampled everything and it all was delicious. Except for the ratafia. It was so repulsive, I could barely drink a mouthful."

He nodded. "So everything is as it should be?"

She smiled. "Precisely."

He leaned back in his chair in satisfaction. He had never met anyone with whom he shared such perfect sympathy. As long as they did not discuss his warehouse.

"Yes," she said, "I was thinking it would be nice to have a dining room in the bazaar. But not for the clients, but for the widows, since there will be so many of them. If the bazaar were in your warehouse, there would be plenty of room for it."

He groaned. "For a woman with such a fine understanding of the complexities of business, you cannot grasp the simple concept of not discussing a subject."

She smiled. "You think so highly of my opinion in matters of business?"

"I have thought so since the first day we met." He gave her his most melting expression from under his lashes.

"If you esteem my opinion so much," she said, her eyes sparkling with laughter, "why will you not listen to my advice on your warehouse?"

"Can you not think of anything else about me besides my warehouse?" he asked softly.

She blushed again. "You are only trying to divert me from the subject of the warehouse. That is another thing I realized about you after our conversation yesterday—you run like a rabbit from conversations you cannot control."

What the devil? "If this is the kind of thing you are going to come up with, perhaps you should stop devoting so much time to thinking about me."

"Oh do not get in a pet about it." She waved her hand airily. "I think most men behave exactly the same. I only mention it to you because yesterday we seem to have made such an excellent intellectual connection."

He glanced over at Nanny in triumph, but the old woman had already started to doze over her knitting. A shame. It would have been pleasant to show her how even her precious Nola acknowledged their mutual intellectual appreciation. On the other hand, one could not ask for a better chaperone than an old deaf woman who slept.

"Yes," Nola continued, "before yesterday, I thought you were stupid."

"Stupid!" He bolted upright on the chaise longue. "Just because I would not devote my warehouse to your bazaar?"

"Oh, no," she said. "I thought you were stupid because of your list of requirements for a bride." She frowned. "Of course, I may have been willing to overlook your stupidity about your list had you agreed to hand over your warehouse."

"My list is not stupid!" Who the devil made a plain-speaking spinster earl's daughter the judge of him? "In any event, we agreed to not discuss my list."

She shook her head. "I did not say I thought your list was stupid. I said I thought you were stupid."

That was enough. To think he had wasted hours looking forward to her visit. He stood up on his left leg.

"There you go." She crossed her arms. "Off like a rabbit."

"I do not see why you have come to visit someone about whom you obviously think so little." He looked down his nose at her. Interesting. She was wearing the gray monstrosity today. The only good thing about the gray dress was the neckline was lower than the ruffled blockade on the pink one. From this vantage, with her arms folded across her chest like so, he could almost see down the front of her bodice. Of course, there was the possibility her bosom would not benefit from exposure.

"Oh for goodness' sake!" she said. "I said my opinion of you changed after our conversation yesterday. Please sit down before you topple over and Nanny wakes and blames me for your limp."

He sat down. Really, when he took the time to consider it, her bosom was not that bad. Not ample, of course, but she was tall and slender, and a large bosom would look out of place on her. Given her height, her bosom was actually quite proportional.

"You are very clever about business," she said.

He reached for the silver tray on which his business correspondence rested. His hand brushed against the pile of letters he had saved for her to read to him and the top one slid to the floor.

He made as if to reach for it, then flung himself back and clutched his forehead and moaned.

It worked. Nola bent down to pick up the letter. Oh, yes. He leaned forward and got a perfectly acceptable eyeful and confirmed she had a perfectly acceptable handful. He shifted uncomfortably on the chaise longue.

Nola tossed the letter back onto the tray. "I do not believe you have listened to a word I have said."

"You were praising me," he said. "I am old enough to know that is usually followed by criticism."

She pouted. "I am not going to criticize you."

"You are pouting," he said.

"I do not pout!"

"Your lower lip is jutting out." He leaned toward her. "I would say that was pouting." He lifted his gaze from her plump little lip to her glinting green eyes and his breath became ragged.

"You are in a very strange mood today, Mr. Carr," she whispered.

"Perhaps I have been left alone in my room too long." He lowered his head toward hers.

"You are not alone. You have Nanny and Fig. Fig!" She scrambled to her feet, a wild look in her eyes. "I think I had better look for Fig."

Damnation! He hid his face in his hands. What the devil was he doing? He had taken leave of his senses. She was a lady. An earl's daughter, for pity's sake, staying in his home. He was leering down the front of the poor woman's bodice like a filthy old lecher in a penny melodrama.

"No, please!" He blinked up at her from between his fingers. "I am very sorry. It is merely I also had very little sleep last night."

"Really?" She hovered behind her chair.

"Yes," he lied. "And you would scarcely credit how exhaustion makes one vulnerable to flights of emotion."

"But I would! I know exactly how you feel! I have not slept well in days, and I think it is severely affecting my feelings."

"Could I not persuade you to take pity on me and help me with my correspondence?" He pointed to the stack of letters on the tray.

Her eyes narrowed in suspicion. "Nanny told me you had recovered enough to read all of your letters by yesterday afternoon."

Cursed old busybody. "But that was before my sleepless night. My head is aching. If I try to read I may suffer a relapse."

She gave him a long look, but perched on her seat and took the first letter in her slender fingers. She opened the seal and skimmed the pages. "It is from your solicitors." She read the second page, then looked up at him with an expression of dismay. "It is about your warehouse."

He snatched the letter from her and read it for himself. Smith had left London, rent owing, twenty creditors unpaid, more creditors showing up daily. As landlord, his solicitors were pleased to report Gabriel had priority. They begged authorization to begin an action on his behalf. Unfortunately, it was also the opinion of the solicitors that Mr. Smith had no property left to distrain, having sold all his effects in the last month.

If anyone found Mr. Smith, he would go directly to debtors' prison.

Gabriel folded the letter, slumped back against the chaise longue, and waited for Nola to begin hectoring him about her bazaar.

"It is not your fault," she said softly.

"My fault!" He opened his eyes and glared at her.

She smiled. "I read the letter. He has not paid his rent since last Christmas quarter day."

He rubbed his temples. "I should have evicted him last spring. If I had, he would not have had the opportunity to get so far in debt."

"You do not know that," she said.

"I knew he was in over his head. I listened to him complain and blame his troubles on everyone else. I could have told him to settle his debts and close the business before he was forced to flee in the middle of the night."

"You were only his landlord."

He sighed. She was so sweet.

"Now I understand why you do not want to be responsible for the widows' bazaar," she said.

He sighed again. Sweetness deserved honesty. "I have told why I do not want your bazaar. Because two hundred women tenants would drive any man mad."

"You keep saying two hundred, but by my calculations we may be able to fit in two hundred and twenty."

"Were you not listening? I do not want your widows in my building."

"I know you do not want them. But will you take them anyway?"

"No!"

"Well, at least now you are talking about it. That is a good start."

"No, it is the end of the matter. Just because I am feeling bad about Smith and you are clever enough to know why and kind enough to console me does not change the decision I made based on calm consideration of the facts."

It was finally clear he was slamming the door of

his warehouse in her face once and for all. Lord only knew what she would do. Cry, perhaps. She was too amiable to shout or hurl insults or strike him. He watched her stare down at her interlaced fingers, her forehead creased in a worried frown.

After a minute, she looked up at him. "Why do you have such a negative view of women?" she asked.

"What?" When would he remember that her conversation never proceeded upon a predictable path.

"Were you jilted?" she asked, her eyes clouded with concern.

"Certainly not!" Jilted? Him?

"That would explain your list of requirements in a bride."

"What the dev—we are discussing my warehouse, not my requirements in a wife."

"I think they are related."

"I think you are addled!"

"I have given the matter considerable thought," she said. "I believe your refusal to allow the bazaar in your warehouse and your shopping list for a bride are both reflections of your poor opinion of women."

He clutched his head. To hell with his hair. "I believe we have already decided you should stop staying up all night thinking of me!"

"Perhaps you are afraid of women," she said.

"Will you stop saying that?" He'd try bolting, but he wouldn't get very far without triggering the agony in his knee. Anyway, she would just follow and gloat about how he was running away.

"Listen to me," he said through his clenched jaw. "My list of requirements merely ensures I will find a bride without being judged by my appearance or my fortune."

"But that is what I do not understand," she said

with a puzzled frown. "Why do you not wish to be judged by your appearance or fortune? Particularly given the state of each." She ducked her head down and he watched the blush blaze up her cheeks.

Excellent. This was a much more interesting line of conversation. He leaned back and spread his arms across the back of the chaise longue. "Are you saying you have noticed I am handsome?"

"That has nothing to do with it," she said, turning a brighter shade of pink. "We are discussing your view of women."

"I would rather discuss your view of me."

She met his eyes. "After you tell me why you have made a list of requirements for a bride."

He sighed. "I told you. I came up with my list in order to avoid being judged on my appearance."

"Oh." She spent a few moments contemplating this statement, then her face lit up. "I believe I understand what you mean. I have been misjudged because of my appearance my whole life." She reached up and touched her hair with the tips of her fingers. "People"—she flushed again—"gentlemen assume a woman with red hair is temperamental."

"You are not the slightest bit temperamental," Gabriel said, transfixed by the curl at her temple that her fingers had disarranged.

"Yes, it is most unfair!"

"Absolutely," he said. The curl looked soft and it was exactly the width of his finger. If he pulled it, gently of course, it would likely spring back into shape.

"I did not realize a handsome man could suffer the same injustice."

"Absolutely." He leaned forward. She smelled like soap and lavender, the same sweet scent as when he had caught her in the Latours' office.

"To think you have also suffered because of the

misconceptions people—I suppose women, in your case—hold based solely on your appearance."

"Absolutely." He was close enough to count the freckles on her nose. Six. Six adorable freckles.

"How?" she asked.

"How what?" He moved back an inch and blinked at her.

"How have you been misjudged by women based on your appearance?" She tilted her head in inquiry.

"Ah. Well." Somehow this didn't seem like the right time to explain that women had been throwing themselves at him ever since he was old enough to catch. "I see." He took a deep breath. "Everything starts out well enough when one makes the acquaintance of a woman, but soon, her expectations make her want to change my behavior." He swallowed. "I am expected to wear a particular waistcoat. Attend some boring social gathering. Give up my business interests." He looked into her eyes.

He had no idea what he was saying, but it seemed to be having an excellent effect.

She leaned forward and patted his arm. "You poor man. You truly have suffered because you are handsome."

"Absolutely." He caught her hand between his. Her hand was so soft, her fingers long and slender. He turned her palm upward and traced a line down the center with the tip of his finger. She shivered.

"Absolutely," she whispered, her eyes glazing over in a way that made him hold his breath.

He lifted her hand to his lips and gently ran his tongue—

"What do you think you're doing!" Nanny's ball of yarn smacked him between the eyes.

Nola gasped, clapped her hand over her mouth, leaped to her feet, and bolted out of the room.

"I do not know why you woke up." Gabriel scowled at the old woman. "You could not possibly have heard anything."

"Nothing wakes a chaperone faster than silence." Nanny sniffed. "I can't believe a handsome man like you doesn't know that."

NINE

Nola's hot tongue trailed delicately along the inside of his wrist, a mirror image of the caress he had given her this morning. Gabriel shuddered with desire. He reached for her, but she darted tantalizingly out of range, the sound of her passionate panting wrenching a moan from his throat.

He shifted on the chaise longue and opened his eyes. Fig stared up at him, tongue hanging out lopsidedly.

"I knew damned well it was you." Gabriel wiped the drool on his arm off on his pantaloons. "That is the oldest trick in the book."

Wasn't the dog supposed to go for a walk after he had had a nap?

The door opened and Nanny put her head in. "You have company."

Nola! Gabriel scrambled to rearrange his disheveled hair. Hours had passed since she ran out of the room this morning. He had started to think he wouldn't see her again until tomorrow.

"Devil of a clever way to get yourself cooped up in a houseful of women." St. Fell strolled through the door, followed by Bartlett carrying a tray with a decanter and glasses.

Gabriel stood up and balanced on his good leg. "You would not be congratulating me so heartily if you had actually met the Beasts of Belcraven."

St. Fell coughed and rolled his eyes behind him to where a gangly redheaded young man was coming through the doorway.

"The Earl of Belcraven," St. Fell said, announcing the newcomer.

Bartlett winked on his way out the door, naturally.

Belcraven laughed and gripped Gabriel's hand enthusiastically. "If you're referring to my aunts, I must commend you on the restraint of your language."

Gabriel fell back against the chaise longue. It was a good thing Belcraven was not offended by the insult to his aunts. After all, they might end up as brothers-in-law. If Mother had her way. He struggled to think of something more diplomatic to say about the countesses. "I have not made the acquaintance of your aunts much." Thank God.

"Yes, we know." St. Fell poured a generous measure of brandy and offered the glass to Belcraven. "Bartlett says you have been hiding up here like a pudding-hearted poltroon."

"I am not hiding." Gabriel waved away the glass when Belcraven tried to pass it on to him.

Belcraven sat in Nola's desk chair and took a sip from the glass himself. "You ain't had much contact with my aunts if you don't want brandy."

St. Fell poured himself a glass. "Gabriel does not drink hard spirits since his twenty-fifth birthday. It is not part of his plan. Corinthian until twenty-five, make his fortune from twenty-five to thirty, and now marry and set up his nursery."

"Do you think I ought to get myself a plan?" Belcraven looked at them wide-eyed.

"Lord no!" St. Fell sat down in the armchair. "Gabriel has made his life into a special kind of hell, haven't you, old man?" He eyed Gabriel over the rim of his glass. "It's a good thing we have come to rescue you. Where shall we take you? The Clarendon? My place? That's where Belcraven's holed up, but there's always room for more."

"I had better not leave my mother alone. She is hip deep in a scheme, I'm afraid." Trying to make him marry Nola. Which required his attendance.

"Your mother's always hip deep in a scheme, Gabriel. Are you sure there isn't a more compelling reason you want to stay?"

The mocking gleam in St. Fell's eyes was unnerving. "Why the devil are you here?" Gabriel asked.

St. Fell laughed. "Did you just swear?"

"He did," Belcraven said. "It's living with my aunts. Bad influence."

"You'll be drinking next," St. Fell said.

Gabriel clenched his teeth. "Do not be ridiculous."

St. Fell grinned. "It's those kinds of sweeping statements that invite trouble for you, Gabriel. That, and the fact women find you appealing."

"Present sisters excepted, of course," Belcraven said.

Gabriel flushed.

"Come here you hideous fat pest!" Belcraven put his hand down and Fig waddled out from under the bed toward him.

"You had better not let your sister hear you call him that," Gabriel said. "She thinks he is the handsomest dog in England."

Belcraven gave a shout of laughter. "What a

bouncer Nola has told you! Papa made her change the name she had originally given him. Said it was upsetting enough to have a dog that looked like a pig without calling it one too." He scratched the dog behind its ears. "I'm surprised he's not in your kitchen. He usually sticks to where the food is."

"He has taken a liking to me," Gabriel said defensively. "Except for Bartlett and Chef, we are the only males in the house."

Belcraven gave Fig another pat. "Even if one of you is gelded."

"Really?" St. Fell sat up in his chair. "Which one?"

Gabriel rolled his eyes.

Belcraven took a sip of his drink. "I'm sure you will be pleased to learn I mean to persuade my aunts to return to Kent with Nola."

Gabriel started in surprise. "I don't think your sister will abandon the widows' cause so lightly," he said.

Belcraven shook his head. "Perhaps not. But if they insist on remaining in London, they should at least find other lodging."

"I didn't mean to suggest your family was not welcome in my home." Belcraven obviously shared his sister's impulsive streak. There was no reason to throw everyone into upheaval. Nola was installed in his home now. The sensible thing would be to have her stay.

"We appreciate your hospitality, but my aunts are well able to afford a London residence of their own. Especially now that you are incapacitated and confined to your home."

St. Fell gave an exaggerated yawn. "One would think you would be eager to clear your house of superfluous females, Gabriel, so you may forge ahead with the arduous task of finding yourself your ideal bride." He propped his chin on his arm.

"How do you go on, by the way? Any luck finding someone who meets all the requirements on your list?"

Gabriel glared at him. Just because the clunch was desperate to win his stupid bet was no reason to pester him about the list in front of Belcraven. "I have just fallen on my head and shattered my knee."

"What does that have to do with your list?"

"Why the devil do you care?" And why wasn't Nola here with him now instead of these slowtops?

St. Fell stretched languorously. "You don't have to worry about upsetting Belcraven with the news you're looking for a wife. All of London knows about your list."

"That's why I didn't object to my sister staying here in the first place," Belcraven said. "I knew she didn't meet the requirements of your list. Safe as houses for her to stay here. No one in London would ever think otherwise, not knowing Gabriel Carr's capacity for fixing himself on a particular idea."

Gabriel rubbed his temples. "Why does everyone think I am stubborn? I merely adhere to a principle. There is nothing wrong with adhering to a principle."

St. Fell reached for the decanter. "You have your principles. Belcraven has his aunts."

The door opened and Bartlett announced Mr. Joseph Swann was calling for his master.

"My tenant," Belcraven said brightly. "Send him in. Wonderful fellow."

"Wonderful wealthy, isn't he?" drawled St. Fell.

"With two beautiful daughters," Belcraven said. "I've seen 'em myself."

Gabriel swore under his breath. He had forgotten the Misses Swann. Swann had told him about them weeks ago. They were at the top of his list of potential brides. Of course they were in town by now. Living in Belcraven's Soho house. What the devil were their names? He struggled to remember.

Joseph Swann stopped uncertainly in the doorway when he saw that Gabriel was not alone. Belcraven dragged him over to introduce him to St. Fell.

"Your Grace," the merchant murmured, bowing to St. Fell.

"Have a brandy." St. Fell shoved a full glass into the merchant's chubby hand. He refilled his own and Belcraven's.

Swann perched on the edge of the chaise longue next to Gabriel.

Belcraven prowled in front of the fireplace. "I'm not afraid of them. I'll just explain matters in a straightforward way. They must go back to Kent."

St. Fell leaned toward Swann. "We were just discussing Gabriel's wedding plans."

"I cannot believe you do not have anything more useful to do than sit around here drinking my brandy and discussing me."

"Not a thing," St. Fell said cheerfully.

Belcraven did a sharp about turn to the left of the hearth. "I'm waiting to speak to my aunts."

St. Fell stood up to refill Belcraven's glass. "Your marriage plans fascinate me, Gabriel."

Swann eyed Gabriel sideways. "Have you made up your mind, then?"

"Shut up," Gabriel said. Swann swallowed nervously. "I don't mean you," he reassured the merchant. Belcraven pivoted on his heel. "I don't mean you either," Gabriel added.

Belcraven drained his brandy. "Good. I am an earl, you know. Earls carry some influence. Not just in the world, I mean with their aunts as well."

Gabriel sighed.

St. Fell smiled evilly. "Sadly, Gabriel has not found the lady of the list." He sat on the other side of Swann on the chaise longue and patted Swann's knee. "We are hoping you may be able to provide some assistance in this matter."

Swann's chest puffed up to nearly the size of his stomach. "As it happens, I do have two eligible daughters."

"You do? Excellent! We shall celebrate." St. Fell refilled his glass and the merchant's and topped Belcraven's again as well when the young man ambled back from his inspection of the fireplace.

"A toast to the lovely Swann sisters!" Belcraven raised his glass.

"To the future Mrs. Carr," added St. Fell.

Swann shook his head. "Now, I can't say for certain. I don't hold with forcing the girl. Don't much hold with having a list, either, if truth be told. It's up to the girl and Mr. Carr. But both my girls are sensible gels, no reason why either one of them shouldn't get along with a man like Mr. Carr." He took another sip and surveyed Gabriel. "He's got deep pockets and cuts the kind of figure that appeals to the ladies."

"Exactly," St. Fell said.

"Go away," Gabriel said.

"I cannot until I have spoken to my aunts." Belcraven attempted unsuccessfully to straighten his jacket in the looking glass.

Gabriel sighed.

Bartlett tapped on the door and declared that the ladies were available to receive the Earl of Belcraven. Belcraven handed the butler his glass and turned back to salute them.

"My aunts await me." He swayed gently in the doorway. "I am not afraid."

Gabriel struggled to his feet. "I should come with you."

"No need. I fought in the war."

St. Fell raised his glass in the air. "Farewell, brave comrade. We toast your quick success."

Gabriel eyed St. Fell and Swann warily.

"You need a drink." St. Fell grabbed an empty glass.

"Certainly not."

"That's right." St. Fell peered round for the decanter. "No drinking. Just the thing in a son-in-law, right, Swann?"

Swann blinked owlishly at his empty glass.

"But fortunately not required in the father-in-law. Aha!" St. Fell triumphantly produced the missing decanter from underneath his chair.

Gabriel leaned his head back against the chaise longue. Likely the afternoon would end with St. Fell and Swann rolling up the carpet to play dice. He wondered what the women were doing. Would they send Belcraven and his suggestion they leave packing, or would they be packing up themselves? He shifted miserably on the chaise longue. His damned knee ached. He'd give Belcraven ten minutes. Then he'd demand to be taken to where they were.

"I have heard lemon juice, applied twice a day, shows an improvement in only a few months," Aunt Caroline said.

Aunt Hortensia snorted disparagingly. "Asses' milk. Nothing increases the bust as efficaciously as the time-honored method of bathing in asses' milk."

"Well, both take too long." Mrs. Carr opened a box of bonbons and popped one in her mouth.

Nola stood on the hassock in the center of the

small sitting room off Mrs. Carr's bedchamber and let the women's gossip about fashion wash over her. She had thought the fittings for the new dresses her aunts insisted she needed would have been canceled since the Latours were in the middle of their move to Garrard House. Instead, Mademoiselles Aline and Eloise arrived at the Carr town house with everything necessary, and now Nola modeled the pale green Merino walking dress while Mademoiselle Aline adjusted the sleeves and the bodice and Mademoiselle Eloise crouched at her feet pinning the hem.

Ordinarily, Nola would have screamed in impatience with the dull process of acquiring new dresses. But today, she barely noticed the time she had to spend turning this way then that. The women were so preoccupied in their conversation that Nola was free to think about the subject that had consumed her since this morning: Gabriel Carr. Gabriel. The name of an angel. Not that Mr. Carr—Gabriel— was an angel. Certainly not. A hot blush burned through her and Nola was grateful that Mademoiselle Aline's attention was focused on the cuff of the bishop's sleeve of her dress.

An angel would not have done what he had done to her hand and wrist this morning. For the hundredth time, Nola wished she had kept her eyes open when he'd taken her hand in his long, strong fingers. It had all happened so quickly! She was not even sure what exactly had happened. Could he have possibly—she looked around but everyone was still preoccupied with improving their busts—could he have possibly traced his tongue on the inside of her wrist?

"Are you tired of standing, my lady?" Mademoiselle Eloise asked with concern in her voice. "Your knees seem wobbly."

Nola cleared her throat. "No, no. I am quite fine." She smiled and the Latours continued with their pinning. It might have been his tongue. She had run to her room right after and locked the door and drawn the drapes and then tried licking the same spot with her own tongue. It was pleasant. But not the same. Not nearly as intense as when Gabriel—

"There is no reason to moan, my lady, I could not possibly have poked with you a pin." Mademoiselle Aline frowned. "I am only holding the measuring tape."

Nola apologized again. She let the Latours help her out of the walking dress and into the silver gray crepe evening gown.

"Being in a family way is one certain method of increasing the bust." Mrs. Carr chewed another bonbon thoughtfully. "Although frankly, the effect is merely temporary and often in the aftermath matters are worse than before."

"I do not think being in the family way is a good solution." Mademoiselle Eloise looked up with a worried frown. "They are not even betrothed—"

"You must stop your incessant thinking," her sister said. "Be quiet and pin."

"Yes, have a bonbon." Mrs. Carr pushed the box at Eloise.

"Who is not even betrothed?" Nola asked. She didn't want them to think she was completely ignoring their conversation.

"What a lovely dress!" Aunt Hortensia shouted.

"All the crack!" Aunt Caroline thumped her walking stick.

Goodness! Nola looked down at the delicate folds of crepe that swirled around her legs. It must be a fine dress if Aunt Hortensia and Aunt Caroline were in agreement about it. Perhaps she could find a reason to wear it when Gabriel could see it. She sighed. Where was she? Oh, yes—trying to make an interesting contribution to the conversation.

"Mr. Carr asked me to visit the Garrard House dining room on his behalf," she said.

"I am pleased to see you are becoming better acquainted with my son."

It was a shame Mrs. Carr did not say "Gabriel," as she was the only one who could say his first name aloud. "He is very clever about business," Nola said.

"Decent fortune!" Aunt Hortensia thumped her stick once.

"Dashed handsome!" Aunt Caroline thumped twice.

Nola sighed. "Yes, I had never realized before what a burden it was to be so handsome."

Mrs. Carr choked in mid-bonbon. "What kind of Banbury tale has the nodcock been telling you?"

"Oh, yes," Nola said, "the poor man has suffered terribly because of his looks."

"Really?" Mademoiselle Eloise asked. Mademoiselle Aline snorted.

Mrs. Carr swallowed the rest of her bonbon with difficulty. "He truly does not deserve you—I mean your assistance with his affairs—with his affairs of business—where have the blasted bonbons got to?" She snatched the box Mademoiselle Eloise passed her.

"In my day"—Aunt Hortensia tugged on her stomacher—"you could lace up your corset tightly enough to give you a generous bosom even if you did not have one."

Aunt Caroline rolled her eyes. "Gentlemen merely

became skilled in judging the amount of overflow. No, today's high waistlines are much more flattering to a woman's figure."

"Really?" Mrs. Carr asked. "I thought they made everyone's bosom look small."

"It depends on whether or not you have a large bosom to begin with." Mademoiselle Aline puffed the sleeve cap on Nola's gown.

"I do not see why there is so much emphasis on making a bosom look larger than it really is," Mademoiselle Eloise said. "A gentleman is bound to discover the truth sooner or later."

"Sooner, if the illusion is any good," Aunt Caroline said, swiftly parrying the swipe of the stick Aunt Hortensia aimed at her ankles.

"In any event," Mrs. Carr said, "I think the bosom is the least of our obstacles."

Nola bit her lip to keep from laughing. She hadn't realized Mrs. Carr and her aunts were so concerned about their bustlines. But then again, she didn't care much for the fripperies of fashion. Perhaps if she did, she would also waste time worrying about the size of her small bosom.

But it was much more enjoyable to brood about Gabriel. Gabriel in his nightshirt. Gabriel taking her hand in his—

"Do you require a visit to the necessary, my lady?" Mademoiselle Aline stepped back and put her hands on her hips. "I am afraid we will tear the lace inset in your sleeve if you cannot stand still."

Nola apologized profusely and the Frenchwoman bent her head to her task again. If she had to think of Gabriel, she ought to remember his idiotic list of requirements, as she did not meet them all. Of course, he had made the list before he had met her. But he did not seem like the kind of man who would abandon his list. What had his mother called him? The most stubborn man in all of London?

Mademoiselle Aline finished with the sleeve and turned her attention to the neckline of the gown.

"I wonder if perhaps"—Nola struggled to recall Gabriel's words to describe getting around his mother—"perhaps the only way to get Mr. Carr to do what one wants him to do is to go along with what he wants in the first place."

Mademoiselle Aline looked up. "But agreeing with him will not get the widows their bazaar. He has said countless times hundreds of women tenants will be chaos."

The bazaar! Of course, she had forgotten the same could apply to the bazaar. Nola wracked her brains to think of some way of appeasing his requirements for his warehouse. "But what if we set out the rules ahead of time and made the operation of a stall contingent upon the strictest compliance."

"You are so clever, my lady!" Mademoiselle Eloise said around her mouthful of pins.

"I suppose that might work," Aline agreed.

"It is an extremely clever idea." Mrs Carr rifled through the bonbon box. "But perhaps I should be the one to tell him. He might be more receptive to the notion coming from his dear mother."

"The same might apply to other areas as well," Nola said. "Say, for example, his list of requirements in a bride."

"Oh that cursed list!" Mrs. Carr exclaimed. "The mere mention of it gives me the headache."

Nola forged on. "Perhaps the problem is not with his requirements, but with his interpretation of his requirements." She flushed. "Not that I recall precisely what they are, of course."

Mrs. Carr sighed. "He wants a young woman from a family in trade or commerce."

"Of superior character and agreeable disposition," Mademoiselle Eloise said.

"Who is calm and deliberate with a natural dignity and composure," continued Aunt Hortensia.

"Skilled in household management," Mademoiselle Aline said.

"With a reasonable face and figure," Aunt Caroline concluded.

"Do not forget the whole managing complication," Mrs. Carr said.

"Managing?" Nola asked.

"It is a footnote to his text, if you will." Mrs. Carr scowled. "He does not want his wife to be too clever or to manage his business for him."

Nola's shoulders sagged. But he seemed to like her understanding of business. She sighed. Yet another criteria she did not meet. But at least she was amiable and of superior character and had a reasonable figure.

Mademoiselle Aline adjusted the fichu at the neckline of Nola's dress. "What do you mean, Lady Nola, about the interpretation of his requirements?"

"Well, for example," Nola said casually, hoping she wouldn't blush so fiercely that Mademoiselle Aline would ask if she found the room too hot, "about Mr. Carr's stipulation the girl come from a family in trade? Perhaps it could be pointed out to him his requirement may be satisfied if the girl herself has an interest in trade or commerce."

"Ha! That would only work if his list actually determined his behavior," Mrs. Carr said.

"It does not?" Hope soared in Nola's heart. If his list didn't matter, then perhaps she could marry Gabriel.

"Certainly not." Mrs. Carr inspected the remaining bonbons in the box sourly before she selected one. "Gabriel is stubborn and a man. The real problem is he has taken a public position about his requirements."

Nola frowned. "What do you mean?"

Mrs. Carr shrugged uneasily. "He has declared aloud how someone might or might not meet his requirements."

"So?"

Mrs. Carr sighed. "When a man takes a public position on a subject, my dear, getting him to change his mind requires extraordinary measures. When a stubborn man takes a public position, only the greatest strength and cunning can defeat him." She swallowed her bonbon. "I am afraid the only thing left to do now about Gabriel is to trick him." She leaned toward Mademoiselle Aline. "How is that fichu coming?"

Mademoiselle Aline stepped back to inspect the effect. "Better," she said.

Nola looked down. The fichu was pushed all the way inside the front of her neckline.

From her position at the foot of the hassock, Mademoiselle Eloise breathed a heavy sigh. "Well I do not care what Mr. Carr says. I think Lady Nola has a perfectly delightful bosom."

She gasped. The pin dropped from her mouth. The sound rang out throughout the room.

The door crashed open. Belcraven launched himself into the room and slammed the door behind him.

"You're going to have to get married." He leaned against the door, panting.

Gabriel stared at him.

"You made me dribble brandy on Carr's carpet," St. Fell complained.

"You must get yourself married." Belcraven stared wildly at Gabriel. "The sooner the better. Immediately."

The blood roared in Gabriel's ears. What the devil was the young hothead saying? Was Belcraven demanding he marry Nola? He stood up awkwardly on his good leg. "Explain yourself, my lord," he said.

Belcraven threw himself down in the armchair and ran his hands raggedly through his hair. "I can't. Something has happened to them. They've run wild. They're crazed to get someone married. They turned on me and threatened to drag me to the altar."

Gabriel took a gulping breath of air and eased himself back down onto the chaise longue. Belcraven wasn't referring to Nola. "You mean your aunts want you to get married?" he asked.

Belcraven shuddered. "Your mother. My aunts. A couple of French ladies, one of them dashed mean. Marriage, marriage, marriage, that's all they wanted to talk about. Well, that and the inherent evilness of men, but I never pay much mind to that. When one paused for air, the other ones chimed in."

"Nothing wrong with getting married," Swann said.

"Not if you want to," Belcraven said. "I don't know if I do. I'm only twenty-seven. I am just selling my army commission. Don't even have a place of my own, never mind any blunt to spare. I ain't at all sure I want a wife yet." He looked up at Gabriel glumly. "You're the one who wanted a wife. You get yourself leg-shackled and leave the rest of us out of it."

St. Fell laughed. "It can't be that bad."

Belcraven shuddered. "You weren't there. They promised to dedicate themselves to finding me a bride. Continue the Belcraven line, and prove that not all men were idiots, and all that rot."

"They do have a point," St. Fell said. "You are the last in your branch."

"It's not just me. It's everyone. They talked about you too. They know you're in here hiding with Carr."

"I am not hiding," Gabriel said.

"I don't need an heir. I've got six brothers," St. Fell complained. "Five too many, if you ask me."

"That's what I'm saying." Belcraven grabbed the decanter and scouted round the room for a fresh glass. "They don't care whether the person needs or even wants to get married. They're all fired up to get everyone married now. Nola, you, me. Probably marry off poor Swann here, if he lingers long enough. The only one they weren't talking about was Carr. Probably because he's got that stupid list."

"My list isn't stupid!"

"I enjoyed being married," Swann said. "Loved my Elizabeth. Sorry she's gone." He pulled a huge handkerchief from his waistcoat pocket and dabbed at his eyes.

"Wait a moment!" Gabriel's pulse began to race. "They admitted they want to marry off your sister?"

"Admit it? That's all they could talk about. In between threatening me." Belcraven found a glass and filled it. "They must find dear Nola a nice man. They must make dear Nola happy. I must say,

Nola didn't look too happy either, poor thing. Damned torture being locked in a room with my aunts. And your mother, no offense, Carr."

Gabriel frowned. What the devil was going on? Nola was always happy. That idiot Belcraven was too drunk to make any sense.

"I wouldn't put it past them to try to hitch her to St. Fell," Belcraven said. "He is a duke."

St. Fell shook his head sadly. "I don't have a feather to fly with. Girl would have to be very hard up to want to marry me."

"Or very rich," Swann said. "Know lots of men who'd be lining up to show you their daughters, and settle a fine fortune on you for giving them dukes for grandchildren. Not me, though. I don't mind Carr here meeting my girls. He's no duke, begging your pardon, Your Grace. Don't want to rush into marrying into the aristocracy. Touchy business."

St. Fell nodded and refilled Swann's glass and his own and the two men toasted the morose Belcraven.

"Do you think I should marry Nola then?" St. Fell asked.

"Don't be absurd!" Gabriel said. "You don't even know her."

"I keep telling you I most certainly do! I have met her several times, haven't I, Belcraven? Tell him. Tall redhead. Lovely woman."

"Lovely woman," Swann echoed.

Gabriel choked. "You know her as well?" he asked the merchant.

"Everyone knows Saint Nola," Swann answered. "She helps the helpless widows."

"I suppose I could marry her, if that was the right thing to do," St. Fell said.

Gabriel rolled his eyes. "Of course it's not the right thing to do, you idiot. You have nothing in common with her."

"I am a duke, though. Step up for an earl's daughter, and there aren't a lot of us around. Not with our own teeth."

Gabriel clenched his fists. "You're also an idle wastrel who hasn't got the faintest idea about London commerce or business or war widows or anything else that interests Nola." He hopped over to the fireplace and jabbed at the grate with the poker.

"True," St. Fell said. "But we don't have to share the same interests to have a successful marriage. She could look after all of those things, and I could concern myself with boxing and horse racing. Each one's own sphere and all that rot."

"You also have no money." Gabriel glared at him in triumph.

St. Fell looked at Belcraven. "Have to rely on my brother-in-law."

Belcraven grinned. "You'll catch cold at that. I was hoping to sponge off Nola's husband."

St. Fell sighed. "It won't work then. Shame."

"They'll come up with someone else for Nola," Belcraven said.

"Your sister doesn't want to get married!" Gabriel hopped toward the door. It was far past time he visited his mother. She could get into real mischief unless he kept an eye on her.

"It'll make no difference." Belcraven drained his glass. "They'll find someone and peck at her until she gives in, and Nola's always been the most amiable girl."

"I've got a nephew," offered Swann. "He's a partner in the business."

"Oh for God's sake!" Gabriel leaned against the door and glared at them. "Are you all stupid? They are trying to get Nola to marry me."

"They are plotting to make Lady Nola marry you?" St. Fell laughed. "That's awfully self-involved of you, Gabriel."

"Don't they know Lady Nola doesn't meet the requirements of your list?" Swann asked.

Belcraven put his hands on his hips. "Nola's a perfectly acceptable girl. Don't have to force a fellow to take her."

Gabriel sighed. "It is perfectly obvious that is what is going on. That is why my mother moved her in here and your aunts have come to haunt the place."

Belcraven shook his head. "I thought she moved in here to work on her bazaar."

Swann nodded. "Everyone knows she's been helping the widows for years."

"I say, Gabriel," St. Fell said with a crooked smile, "do you mean to say Nola has been merely helping the widows as a cover to get to you? That's playing awful deep."

"Rubbish!" Belcraven barked.

Gabriel gritted his teeth. His bedchamber was full of complete idiots. "I am not saying she made up her interest in the widows," he ground out, "I am saying my mother—and possibly your aunts, Belcraven—"

"Wouldn't put anything past 'em," Belcraven said.

"Your mother is downy," St. Fell said.

"Nothing wrong with a clever woman." Swann nodded sagely.

Belcraven poured himself another drink. "But if they are up to something, I don't think it's working."

"That's because Gabriel's a clever fellow, too. Too clever to get himself in a parson's mousetrap not of his choosing, isn't that right?" St. Fell smirked most irritatingly.

"Very clever," Swann said.

Belcraven shrugged. "Well, whatever's going on, I don't think it's working. Nola's mad as hops about you, Carr. Not that she's a screamer, of course. Absolutely no temper, Nola."

"Oh, that is just about my warehouse." Gabriel leaned against the doorway. "She is overset I will not give over my warehouse for her bazaar."

"I don't know about that," Belcraven said. "She's been mad about your warehouse for weeks now. Never shy about saying exactly what she thought about your position on that. Makes a point about being plainspoken, after all." He drained his glass. "No, Nola's vexed about something else."

"Never say you did something to set her off, Gabriel?" St. Fell leaned forward with a gleeful expression.

"Certainly not! The last time I saw her—" Damnation. Gabriel hopped back across the room. The last time he had seen Nola she was running out of his bedchamber, he assumed because Nanny had caught him caressing her hand. But Belcraven said Nola was angry, not embarrassed.

Gabriel sank down in the chaise longue. Nola had not pulled her hand away when he had taken it in his. She hadn't protested. Nothing could have happened to make her angry.

Nothing except that she had found his advances repulsive.

TEN

"Lady Nola has better things to do than visit you today." Nanny rolled the clean bandages and tucked them in the chest of drawers.

Gabriel struggled to pull on his left boot without jostling his right knee. Morning had dawned, he'd dressed, shaved, groomed his hair, eaten his breakfast, finished his correspondence, groomed his hair again, and still Nola had not come to see him.

Just as he had seen no sign of her yesterday. By the time he had finally managed to get rid of St. Fell, Belcraven, and Swann, reassuring them repeatedly he had no idea what had caused Nola's anger, Nola and all the other women had left the house. They stayed out for supper. They had not returned by midnight. So Nola had not come to visit his bedchamber.

Not that he expected Nola to visit his bedchamber after midnight. Not much. Not really. Not when he was awake.

"You could help." He pulled himself upright using

the bedpost and hopped in order to wedge his heel in his boot.

The old woman shook her head. "I don't think it's safe for you to go downstairs this morning."

"One little trip outside my room is not going to leave me with a limp."

She shrugged. "There are worse things than a limp."

Sitting in his room, waiting for something to happen was worse. He had no idea what he was going to say to Nola when he saw her, after he apologized, of course. But he had to see her, even if it meant seeing the countesses and his mother as well.

When Bartlett arrived to help Gabriel negotiate the stairs, the butler's attitude was no better than Nanny's. "I do not think you ought to go downstairs this morning, sir."

Gabriel pointed at Nanny. "I thought you two always disagreed?"

Bartlett shrugged. "Some truths are universal."

Gabriel slung his arm around the butler's thin shoulders. "Now."

The descent was awkward and painful. In his haste to get downstairs, Gabriel kept forgetting to keep his right leg lifted high enough to clear the stairs and he kept having to pause so he could clench his jaw and not moan in pain. By the time he reached the hallway he was panting.

But not panting so hard he couldn't hear the buzz of female voices. Numerous female voices.

"We tried to warn you, sir. Did you not hear the carriages arriving this morning?"

Gabriel had, but had been too preoccupied with thoughts of Nola to care. "Women?" he asked.

Bartlett nodded.

"Many?"

Bartlett nodded and smirked.

"Why?"

"Women's business, I believe, sir."

Gabriel peered down the hall at the closed drawing room door. "What kind of women's business?"

The butler pursed his lips and looked up at the ceiling. "The kind of business that would make your mother write to women to invite them to your house."

Gabriel groaned. His mother must have decided to contact his tenants about prospective brides after all. He thought he had frightened her off it. He ought to have known she would never give up so easily.

"Where is Lady Nola?" he asked.

"With your mother, sir."

Why the devil would his mother make Nola sit through the winnowing of his prospective brides? Probably because Nola was the only one clever enough to figure it out. He wanted to see Nola. But he wasn't that brave.

"Take me into my study. Quickly, before someone comes into the hall and catches me."

Bartlett looked at him gravely. "I do not think you should hide in your study, sir."

"I do not need a lecture from you about running away." Gabriel hopped and held on to Bartlett's shoulders so the old man was obliged to move toward the study with him. "I shall wait in my study until they are gone."

"You would be happier in the drawing room, sir."

"Where is your loyalty to your sex, man? The study. Now."

"Nevertheless—"

Gabriel reached down and yanked open his study door. "Do you really think I want to be launched into a roomful of females all yapping at me as if—"

He stopped dead. From within his study a roomful of females gaped at him. In utter silence.

"Damnation," he whispered.

"Your language, sir," Bartlett said. "There are ladies present."

Gabriel clutched the doorway. "You are an evil traitor, Bartlett."

"Quite so, sir."

Gabriel stared into his study. There were women on the sofa, in the armchairs, in the chairs across from his desk. The dining room chairs had been brought in, as well as the drawing room armchairs. Young women, old ladies, and every age in between, all staring at him. His mother sat in the chair at his desk. The Countesses of Belcraven faced each other in the matching armchairs in front of the fireplace. The Latour sisters were side-by-side on the sofa. He recognized several of his tenants besides the Latours.

But his gaze kept coming back to Nola, standing in front of the fireplace. Glaring at him. Damnation! There was no mistaking the fury in her eyes. He had repulsed her.

"You were not invited, Gabriel," his mother said.

"Yes, I am—I am terribly sorry." He straightened his shoulders. "Although this is my study." Trust his mother to try to make him feel guilty for disrupting her attempt to interfere with his life.

"Perhaps we should remove to the drawing room and leave Mr. Carr to his study," Nola said, her tone frosty. She was wearing a new dress. Pale green. Nice.

His mother bristled. "We cannot possibly all squeeze into that cricket cage. Besides, we have had all the chairs brought into this room, and it would take far too long to shift them all around again. Only a petty man would insist on making forty women move for his sole convenience."

He wasn't petty! "You do not have to leave," he said. Nola's new dress probably made her eyes green. It was a shame he was too far from her to see.

"I suppose you can stay," Nola said. "You may have something helpful to add."

Bartlett helped him hop across the room to his desk.

"Are you here because you have changed your mind?" His mother asked as she offered him her chair.

"I beg your pardon?" he said.

"Have you decided to join us because you have had a change of heart?" she repeated.

Lord, but women were cool customers. Whoever called them the sensitive sex obviously did not spend time in a room with forty of them ready to negotiate marriage. "Since this directly concerns me I believe I am entitled to be present."

"How does it concern you if you will not agree to let the widows have your warehouse for the bazaar?" Nola demanded.

"The bazaar?" He jerked in surprise and his knee hit the side of his desk. Pain shot through his leg. "You are meeting about the bazaar?"

"Yes, of course we are meeting about the bazaar," she said. "Why do you think we are here this morning?"

He clutched his knee and bit his lip to keep from howling. "Oh, about the bazaar, of course." He glared at Bartlett, but the butler merely smirked as he fetched another chair for his mother. Gabriel looked back at Nola and tried to smooth the pain out of his face. "I look forward to hearing about the bazaar. For my warehouse." Damnation.

"Are you all right?" Nola asked.

Of course, the only thing missing in this morning's debacle—the definitive question in his relationship with Nola. "I am fine," he said through clenched teeth. "Please continue with your meeting."

Lady Hortensia thumped her cane. "I still say any bazaar which wishes to attract customers of quality must have perruquemakers."

Lady Caroline rolled her eyes. "Only the veriest drabs wear wigs anymore."

Lady Hortensia's eyes glittered dangerously as she adjusted her wig.

Nola's sensible voice cut through the impending battle. "A perruquemaker may certainly take one of the stalls, Aunt Hortensia, but we cannot force women into trades that may not be profitable. Which is not to say," she said, turning to Lady Caroline, "that a perruquemaker would not be an excellent addition to one of the stalls. It is simply we must encourage variety so all of our ladies may have a chance to sell."

The assembled women murmured their approval. Nola's aunts let their canes drop.

For the next hour, Gabriel watched Nola run her meeting. Most of the women were war widows, but Nola had gathered a representative from each type of trade she thought her widows would become, including seamstresses, milliners, glovemakers, jewelers, sellers of ribbons and trimmings, potted plants, decorated paper cards, and lacemakers and knitters. She had managed to find every possible small trade widows could engage in that did not require a large investment in inventory and could be manufactured at home. She wanted the shopkeepers to teach interested widows the fundamentals of their business practices, the keeping of records, inventory, stock, supplies, even the matter of making change and taking credit.

It was brilliant. Nola was brilliant, smoothing over conflicts, keeping the discussion on topic, persuading even the most reluctant to commit to helping turn the inexperienced widows into viable stallholders.

Midway through Nola's passionate speech about the benefits of cooperation, his mother leaned over and whispered, "Would you believe me if I said Nola was not really managing this meeting?"

He didn't bother answering. Now Nola was going around the room asking for suggestions about whether there was a better method than letters of reference of selecting who could operate a stall. Anyone could see it was all Nola's doing. He grinned with pride. She really was the cleverest woman he had ever met, with the best understanding of retail commerce. If the widows' bazaar happened it would all be due to her.

Next, she divided the room into groups so the women from each trade could compile a list of suppliers and estimate the outlay needed for a workable inventory. He was glad she had a new dress to flatter her elegant grace. Her bright shining curls made everyone else's hair look faded and dull. As for her figure, he sighed in pleasure. It was an excellent figure. He looked around at the other women and shook his head in pity. She made the other women seem blousy or boxy or—he shuddered—positively drooping.

No, Nola was obviously the most beautiful woman there. She looked up from her discussion with Aline Latour and met his gaze. He smiled warmly.

She turned on her heel and walked to the other end of the study to consult with the women at the bow window. Her skirts swayed around her hips.

She looked fine from the back, too.

If Nola was in any doubt about the importance Gabriel placed on bosoms before the meeting, watching him ogle every woman in the room every time she looked over at him was more than enough to convince her. The man was obsessed.

She knew she really shouldn't be upset. She knew he had a list of criteria and she didn't meet it before she had moved into his house. It hadn't bothered her then. Why on earth should it disappoint her now?

She sighed. Because now she no longer thought he was stubborn, selfish, and self-absorbed. He was intelligent, kind, had a sense of humor. And was stubborn, selfish, and self-absorbed. And absorbed with women's bosoms. Other women's bosoms, since hers was too small to warrant his appreciation.

She wasn't exactly sure why his judgment of her bosom upset her more than the other ways she did not meet his list of requirements, but it did. It seemed to her a bosom figured quite prominently in one's married life, although she wasn't quite sure how except when she contemplated the subject of married life, her poor bosom seemed quite interested.

Yet he was not interested in her bosom.

Mrs. Carr was right. Men were idiots.

Bartlett and Agnes and Mavis carried in the trays of refreshments. Everyone cooed over Chef's rendition of Marshal Blücher in rock cookies and spice cake. Nola met Gabriel's eyes, and he smiled and he tilted his head and lowered his eyelids in a way that made her pulse race.

Complete idiots.

He was smiling at her in the same way he had before he took her hand yesterday. He was smiling at her and thinking the whole time her bosom was too small. She narrowed her eyes. Her bosom was too small, she was too managing, too plainspoken to be soothing and didn't give a fig about running his household. Who did he think he was to judge her, just because he was so handsome?

She sighed again. It wasn't his fault he had a list. Or rather it was his fault, but it wasn't his fault she didn't meet it. Nor was it his fault his mother and her aunts and the Latours and everyone else had decided to try to throw them together. That was another thing clear yesterday after Mademoiselle Eloise's revelation, no matter how much the women had protested.

She looked around the room at the widows and shopkeepers, working hard, heads bent in discussion. Gabriel Carr's devotion to his stupid list wasn't the only thing that had not changed. The widows still needed a location for their bazaar. They needed his warehouse. He was close to giving it, she was sure. He had no tenant and he was smart enough to see the bazaar was workable. And he was kind.

She walked over to where he still sat at his desk. He smiled even more and tilted his head again. She averted her eyes from the dimples.

"Can we have your warehouse?" she asked.

"I was impressed by the way you ran your meeting. Your ideas are ingenious. You were brilliant."

Her heart leapt with pleasure at the compliment, even though it meant she was failing to meet another one of his stupid requirements. He did not want a clever wife.

"Perhaps we could discuss it later, when the crowd has thinned," he said.

Why did he have to lower his voice in that intimate way when he talked about business? It was annoying and it made her stomach turn over in a most disturbing manner. "I do not think we should be alone," she said.

He flushed. "If I upset you yesterday in my bedchamber, I hope you will accept my deepest apologies."

Her face flamed. She was trying to forget yesterday morning. "No, not because of that. Because—" She lowered her voice. "I am afraid you are going to be overset when you hear this, but I am beginning to suspect people have been scheming to make us marry."

He grinned. "No!"

"I mean to each other," she said.

His grin didn't fade. "Whatever gave you that idea?"

She certainly wasn't going to tell him about the fichu down the front of her dress. "I think your mother and my aunts and the Latours—and frankly, I must include Nanny and Bartlett in the plot—have been arranging for us to spend time together."

"Ah." He raised his eyebrows in encouragement for her to continue.

She looked around the room. Her aunts and Mrs. Carr and the Latours were busy talking. "I even suspect they have been putting bones under your bed to keep Fig there in the hopes I will be obliged to come to your bedchamber to fetch him."

"Really?" He was laughing outright now. She

supposed it must be very amusing to be so handsome as to be chased in such a manner.

"I do not think it is funny!" she said. "I am here to work for the bazaar, not force you into marrying me."

"What do you suppose we ought to do about it?" he asked.

"I certainly do not think we should spend any time alone. I have discussed the matter with your mother and my aunts and the Latours. They deny it, but I am not completely convinced they have abandoned their plans. Until they do, we will have to be very careful, or they will have us at the altar." As she uttered the words she realized it was the perfect opportunity for him to declare he actually did want to marry her. She waited. He just sat there with the grin on his face.

"I should think you would be more concerned," she said impatiently. "It is one thing to try to trick me, everyone knows I am so amiable I will agree to anything and not lose my temper. But you! To try to subvert your principles? Are you not shocked?" She had given him another perfect opportunity to renounce his list. She held her breath.

"What do you think we ought to do about it?" he repeated.

Her shoulders sagged in defeat. Why would the handsomest man in London renounce his list in favor of a flat-chested, managing earl's daughter? The idea was ludicrous. "I think my brother was right. My aunts and I should leave. Take another house in London. Now that you have agreed to give your warehouse to the bazaar, perhaps someone else—"

"But I have not agreed to give you my warehouse."

She folded her arms across her chest. Her flat chest. "I thought you said you were impressed by our meeting."

"I said I found you impressive. I am still not convinced about the bazaar. It is all very confusing. I think you must explain it to me. Perhaps you could visit my study this afternoon."

She flushed. "I have already said I do not think we should be alone together. I do not want to be forced to be married." Not to a man who did not want to marry her.

"I have an idea!" He snapped his fingers. "Why do we not pretend we are interested in marrying each other to trick them and take them off the scent."

She frowned. "How would that help matters?"

He shrugged. "I have no idea. You are so clever, I thought you might know."

"I do not see how it would serve. It seems more like the plot of a Minerva Press romance."

"But it always works in the romances, does it not?"

Poor man. He must not have read very many romances. Otherwise he would know such pretenses inevitably ended with the couple married by the end of the book.

She shook her head. "I think we should not be alone."

He leaned forward and looked into her eyes. "You are certain you were not overset yesterday morning in my bedchamber when I took your hand and—"

"Certainly not!" She pressed her hands against her somersaulting stomach, annoyed at herself for blurting out the declaration even before she saw the smug gleam in his eyes. She might be too amiable and a terrible liar, but she certainly wasn't going to admit how deeply she was affected by the touch of a man who did not find her attractive.

"How did you find it, then?" he asked, still gazing into her eyes and using that rasping tone that made her knees weak.

"It was—" She swallowed, wracking her mind for something truthful to say that wouldn't embarrass her. "It was very brief."

His jaw dropped.

"Gabriel!" Mrs. Carr trotted across the room toward them. "Lady Nola has a great deal of work to do."

"Very well," he said, turning to his mother and shaking his head as if to clear it. "Lady Nola and I can continue to discuss the merits of her bazaar after the meeting."

Mrs. Carr frowned at him. "Lady Nola cannot hang about at your convenience anymore, Gabriel. If you want her bazaar you shall have to do something to get it yourself."

His lips thinned. "I am not sure if I want her bazaar. That is why I would like to speak to her."

Mrs. Carr put her hands on her hips. "You know perfectly well you are panting for her bazaar but you are simply too stubborn to admit it."

He jut out his chin and folded his arms across his chest. "I think it is very broad-minded of me to consider her bazaar at all since it was not what I had in mind in the first place."

"Piffle! Since you were out of your mind in the first place, one would think you would leap at the chance to come to your senses. In any event, if you wish to speak to Lady Nola again, you may come to the drawing room today at three o'clock. We are having guests."

He smiled at Nola. "I would be happy to attend another meeting about the bazaar."

"It has nothing to do with the bazaar," Mrs. Carr said. "I have invited a few young women who meet the criteria of your list." Nola gasped. Mrs. Carr shot her a stern look, and Nola bit her lip, ashamed at the wave of misery that washed over her at the announcement. She clasped her trembling hands behind her back and forced herself to smile.

Gabriel began to pull himself to his feet. "You cannot seriously expect me to—"

His mother shoved him back down in his seat. "It seems to me you are making a fuss when I am merely trying to help fulfill your own wishes."

"I do not make fusses," he said grimly.

Mrs. Carr shrugged. "Suit yourself, but that is where Lady Nola will be if you wish to see her."

Nola grabbed the older woman's sleeve. "Mrs. Carr! You are not still trying to matchmake between myself and your son, are you?" She did have some pride.

"Certainly not! Why would I find young women who meet the requirements on his list if I was? I fear you are becoming cynical, my dear. Too much association with my son."

She took Nola by the arm and swept her off to a clutch of milliners still lingering over their tea. Nola looked over her shoulder at Gabriel, who sat scowling at his desk, likely brooding in worry they were still scheming to make him marry her.

ELEVEN

Gabriel spent the next two hours working at his desk. It was pleasant to return to a familiar routine in his customary surroundings, to replace the ledgers and account books on their appropriate shelves, to file his correspondence in the proper drawer, to write his letters and seal them and arrange them clockwise in the silver tray on the left hand side of his desk, just as he had done every day for the past five years.

It was soothing. Soothing in a way that thinking about marriage used to be. Now thinking about marriage made his breath ragged, set his blood aflame, and made his head ache. All because of the confounding problem of Nola.

It was a good thing Nola hadn't agreed to see him in his study. He had no idea what he would say to her if she walked through the door right now. He stared grimly at the door. She didn't walk in. Which was a good thing. Every time he saw her he said or did something more idiotic. This morning he had suggested they pretend to go along with everyone's scheme to marry them off. What kind of a responsible, sober, hardworking man with business interests said such a stupid thing? No wonder she had looked at him as if he were addled.

He was addled. The longer he spent in her company, the more addled he became. Over a plain-spoken earl's daughter who told him repeatedly she cared more for his warehouse than for him. Over a woman who when asked to describe a caress which had kept him up all night thinking about it, the only thing she could say was that it was brief. Brief! It was not so brief as all that! It would not have been so brief had he not been interrupted by Nanny! He would show Nola next time—He threw down his pen, not caring when the ink spattered the letters on the tray. There would be no next time. He couldn't very well be kissing Nola's hand or Nola's anything unless he offered for her.

And if he offered for her, everyone would know he had renounced his list of requirements and his perfectly sensible method of acquiring himself a bride. His mother would gloat. The servants would gloat. The Countesses of Belcraven would thump their walking sticks, argue, and gloat. Even St. Fell would gloat because as much as he loved winning bets, he enjoyed gloating even more. The recollection of St. Fell's bet at White's made Gabriel moan. Hadn't he shouted at White's he wouldn't marry Nola? All of London would gloat.

On the other hand, would they really gloat if it wasn't his fault he married Nola? After all, he wasn't actually admitting he was wrong to have a list of requirements if he was forced to marry Nola because everyone wanted them to marry.

Except Nola, who objected to being thrown at him and who was so plainspoken she had to tell him she objected. He clutched his head and disarranged the hair he had spent fifteen minutes on this morning. Who cared? Why the devil should he marry Nola? She laughed at him and was too managing. She met none of the criteria on his list, not that he even remembered what the devil they were anymore, except she was amiable. But she was too amiable. If she hadn't been so amiable, he wouldn't be in the mess he was in now. Only the most insanely amiable woman would agree to his mother's henwitted plan and move into his house. Only the most irrationally amiable woman would let herself get thrown at him until he had no choice but to want to marry her.

If only everyone had not found it so diverting to shove her at him. If only his mother and the Latours had minded their own business instead of scheming to pair them up. He never would have met Nola. He wouldn't be wasting precious time worrying about what to say to her. Or even more time brooding about what she thought of him. She made him miserable. It was obvious she was completely unsuitable as his wife.

He rested his forehead on his desktop. It was all so confusing. So unsettling. Not the least what he had in mind when he wanted to find himself a wife.

What he ought to do was avoid her completely. Refuse to show up like some gapeseed moonling paying a call in his own house. It would serve everyone right. Of course, the fact that Nola had agreed to be in a drawing room full of marriage candidates for his consideration might mean that she was not averse to marrying him. Or she might just be being amiable and allowing them to push her at them. Which also might not be so bad.

Or maybe it was. He couldn't think straight anymore. The very thought of Nola made him think of fusses. But he was the one in danger of making a fuss.

He rang for Bartlett and ordered his carriage. He would work this afternoon. Visit Garrard House. Just because Nola assured him everything was proceeding exactly according to plan didn't mean she was right. He should confirm the details for himself.

Two hours later he limped back through his front door. Of course Nola was right. Garrard House was in perfect shape. He was not. His knee throbbed, he kept barking himself in the shins with his new walking stick, and he had shouted at poor John Coachman when the traffic on Pall Mall made it clear they were going to be late returning home.

He did not like being late. Even for an event he had no intention of attending.

The drone of women's voices was audible as soon as he walked through the front door. He ignored Bartlett's pointed look and headed for his study, first putting his ear to the door to make sure the women were in fact in the drawing room down the hall.

His study was quiet. He opened the door. Quiet but not empty.

St. Fell lounged in the chair opposite his desk, his overpolished Hessians propped on the edge of the desk. Belcraven prodded the fire with a poker. Swann poured glasses of brandy.

"What are you doing here?" Gabriel hobbled to his desk. Somehow he doubted male companionship would ease his confusion. Not this band of sapheads, anyway.

"We could ask the same thing." St. Fell sipped his brandy. "Aren't you supposed to be in the drawing room?"

"I suppose my mother sent you to fetch me?"

Gabriel sat in his chair. Without banging his knee. He was only clumsy around Nola. He stifled the moan that rose in his throat at the thought.

St. Fell tilted the chair back on two legs. "You are missing the point, Gabriel. You are letting our side down by hiding in your office while the women lay claim to your drawing room."

"You just want me to marry before I turn thirty so you can win your bet at White's."

"You make it sound so sordid." St. Fell tipped his chair even farther back.

"I say, Carr." Belcraven looked up from the fireplace. "You haven't actually looked at the betting book at White's, have you?"

St. Fell let the chair drop with a crash. "Gabriel does not gamble! He wouldn't debase himself by snooping in the betting book."

"I have never gambled in my life," Gabriel said. "But I am more likely to read the betting book at White's than go into my drawing room this afternoon."

Belcraven frowned. "That sounds like a wager to me."

"You are right!" Swann clapped Belcraven on the back. "Clever boy!"

"One would have thought you would have learned not to make sweeping statements by now, Gabriel," St. Fell said. "Are you sure you won't have a drink? It would give you something to blame it on other than your own stupidity."

Gabriel crossed his arms and glared at him. "Why are you here?"

St. Fell's smile was innocent. "I am merely here to ask why you're not in your drawing room surveying the women who meet your every requirement. Or have you given up on the idea of finding a bride according to a list?"

Gloat? St. Fell wouldn't gloat. He'd crow. He'd be in his study drinking brandy and crowing for the next twenty years. Gabriel clenched his teeth. "I am merely tired of everyone's interference in my life," he said.

"You look tired," St. Fell said. "Everyone's interference must be keeping you up at night."

It was none of St. Fell's business what was keeping him up at night. "That still doesn't explain why you are here today."

St. Fell shrugged. "Perhaps I am thinking of acquiring a bride myself."

Gabriel snorted. "Perhaps they will begin racing pigs at Epsom."

"Do you think?" asked Belcraven.

"Have a drink, son," said Swann.

"And who would you be marrying?" Gabriel leaned forward and clutched the edge of the desk. He'd be damned if he'd listen to St. Fell ramble on about marrying Nola again, even if that dolt Belcraven was too dense to put a stop to it himself. Any idiot could see St. Fell would be the worst possible husband for Nola.

"I don't know." St. Fell shrugged. "I'm fairly new to the idea. The only decision I have reached is that it won't be a Swann—only because Swann himself has told me so."

"Don't hold with marrying dukes. Especially poor ones that game excessively." Swann nodded sagely. "Told St. Fell so from the beginning, didn't I?"

St. Fell poured himself another brandy. "Honest to a fault, is Swann. But that doesn't mean no other papa will have me. And you have twenty marriageable females traveling through your drawing room this afternoon, most of them with dowries large enough to stake me for the rest of my life."

"Twenty-three, actually," Swann said. "Have to count Mrs. Carr and the countesses."

Gabriel turned to stare at him. The man had obviously lost his senses.

Swann's face grew even redder. He squirmed in his seat and looked away. "Well, they are marriage-able," he muttered quietly.

Gabriel rubbed his temples. "What about you, Belcraven? I thought you were terrified about the prospect of marriage?"

"I'm a trained soldier," Belcraven answered. "I've been craving danger since I decided to sell my commission."

"Swann?"

The merchant's ears grew red. "I brought my daughters and my nephew. May as well wait for them to finish."

"Your nephew?" Gabriel asked.

Swann bristled. "Perfectly acceptable boy, my nephew. Sober and reliable, and damned fine fortune, I don't mind saying. Belcraven's met him and approved. He's just as eligible as any of the other young men invited."

"Why the devil would my mother invite eligible men when she is trying to find me a bride?"

"Did you not know?" St. Fell grinned. "She is also trying to find Nola a husband."

Gabriel gaped at him.

Bartlett appeared in the open doorway but before he could speak St. Fell's younger brother Toby elbowed past him.

"Not too late for the show, am I?" he asked, straightening the jacket of his Guards' uniform.

"Just in time." Belcraven drained his glass. "Say, when was the last time you saw my sister?"

*   *   *

Two hours later, Gabriel was no closer to understanding how he managed to find himself in the drawing room, trapped in the armchair in front of the fireplace, his throbbing knee on a footstool and his head aching from the strain of being polite to Miss Swann and her younger sister, the three Coulter girls whose father's bank was the largest in the City, and eight or nine or possibly fifteen other young women and their mothers from families in business, the girls all amiable, interested in household management, responsible, calm and dignified, blond, brunette, and completely irritating because they kept blocking his view of Nola.

Nola had not come to speak to him once. Not that she could, not with St. Fell and his brother and Joseph Swann's nephew and the horde of cousins and brothers of the perfect young ladies pestering her all afternoon. Of course, she was too damned amiable to do anything other than smile and laugh at their irritating jokes. Just as the men were too stupid to realize they bored her.

He glared down at his glass of orgeat. Damned if his mother had not managed to make his own drawing room more repulsive than Almack's.

"You do not look as if you are enjoying yourself."

He looked up to find Nola standing before his chair smiling down on him, her hazel eyes sparkling. She no longer looked the slightest bit angry with him. His spirits soared.

"I think I am going to have to kill my mother," he said. "I shall use my walking stick and blame it on your Aunt Hortensia."

"She is only trying to help you."

"Your Aunt Hortensia? I think not! She spent fifteen minutes telling me in her day gentlemen did not do something or other. I could not hear because she kept thumping at the crucial moment."

As he hoped, Nola laughed. "I think she likes you." She looked around the room and lowered her voice. "Although not as much as Aunt Caroline."

"I am a very likable fellow," he drawled, hoping she would agree.

"Which is why your mother wants to help you find a fine bride," Nola said.

"I do not know how even someone as amiable as you is not vexed with her." He tried to keep the disappointment from making his voice hard. He didn't want her to stop talking to him. "She is manipulating us both."

"She is no worse than anyone else," Nola said.

"Gabriel dear!" His mother loomed between them as if talking about her made her appear. "I have arranged the Coulter girls on the sofa in ascending order of age. I require you to look them over and eliminate one from your considerations. Her mama needs one for Baron Fielding. As for you, Lady Nola, that nice Swann boy needs to be thanked for the very generous donation his uncle is going to make to the widows. Just wait a moment before you go over to give me the chance to mention it." She bolted off toward Joseph Swann with a determined glint in her eyes.

"You see?" Gabriel said smugly.

St. Fell clapped his hand down on Gabriel's shoulder before Nola could answer. "I say, Gabriel," he said, "would you mind telling Arabella I was a brilliant scholar when we were at school together?"

"You were a terrible scholar," Gabriel said. He frowned. "Who is Arabella?"

"The youngest Swann daughter." Nola's eyes twinkled with glee. "His Grace wants you to deceive her. In what one might call a manipulative way."

"So what?" St. Fell said impatiently. "Unless she

is the one you want, Gabriel—is she?" He paled.
"Have you decided, then?"

"Certainly not." Why the devil did St. Fell have
to discuss such things in front of Nola? The man
was completely insensitive. Arabella Swann? Gabriel
had no idea whether she was the blonde or the
brunette Swann.

"Good man!" St. Fell rubbed his hands together.
"She is far too cynical for you anyway."

"I thought Swann had warned you off?" Gabriel
said.

St. Fell smiled. "I am a duke, dear boy. Besides,
he'll have a hard time finding someone to take that
sharp-tongued little harpy off his hands, dowry or
not." He looked over at Nola and flushed. "Not
that I am offering to do so, of course. I have not
made up my mind one way or the other." He gal-
loped across the room.

"At least he is not trying to force anyone to
marry," Gabriel said when he and Nola stopped
laughing.

She shrugged. "No one is forcing you to marry.
You want to be married."

"And you?" he asked. "When we first met, you
swore you did not want to be married. Has your
opinion changed?"

Her cheeks turned pink and she looked across
the room. "A lot of my opinions have changed."

"So do you wish to be married?" The noise of
the room faded as he watched her face.

She met his eyes briefly, then looked away again.
"It depends on whom I would marry, I suppose."

He felt ill. If she was willing to consider marriage after one afternoon of his mother's treat-
ment, then by the end of the week she would be
hitched for sure.

"I should go visit with the Mademoiselles Latour,"

Nola said. "I believe they have deciphered the meaning of Chef's seed cake." She smiled and headed off to the corner of the room where the Latours and his mother sat around the small table.

Why the devil had his mother invited the Latours anyway? The mademoiselles wanted him to marry Nola. They should not be here giving their approval to his mother's deranged attempt to shove other women at him. What the devil was wrong with everyone? They had started out trying to make him marry Nola. To change in midstream smacked of flightiness.

He watched Nola take a seat between his mother and the Latours, then she lifted her gaze and smiled straight at him. He smiled back, his heart racing. It was time he accepted the truth. He wanted to marry Nola. He sighed. But no one was going to force him to do it. He contemplated his empty glass for a minute, then took a deep breath and squared his shoulders.

He was going to have to do something drastic.

TWELVE

"I have a very good feeling that Gabriel is on the verge of breaking." Mrs. Carr popped a piece of seedcake in her mouth and smiled at the Mademoiselles Latour. "That is why I invited you—so you may share in the triumph."

Nola tore her gaze from Gabriel to look over at the older women. Mademoiselle Aline was nodding. Mademoiselle Eloise beamed at Nola with shining eyes.

"He has not taken his eyes off Nola all afternoon," Mrs. Carr continued.

Nola's heart soared. She felt the connection between herself and Gabriel as well, but it was heartening to have someone else confirm it. The small bud of hope she had been nursing all afternoon began to blossom.

Mrs. Carr waved her hand to encompass the crowded drawing room. "We have given him a selection of women who meet his every criteria, but he looks right through them as if they were not even here. Even Emily Turnbull, and that is saying a great deal."

Nola looked over to the pianoforte, where Emily Turnbull perched amongst a clump other hopefuls. She didn't see how anyone could possibly see through Emily Turnbull and her bouncing bosom but she did agree with Mrs. Carr that Gabriel had not shown the slightest interest in the girl when he was introduced to her. Even when Emily dropped her potted shrimp toast down the front of her dress. Twice.

"After all, Gabriel may be stubborn," Mrs. Carr said, "but he is not stupid."

"We can hope." Aline Latour sipped her orgeat with pursed lips.

"Mr. Carr is not stupid!" Mademoiselle Eloise peered around at the other women. "Of course, he is stubborn. Very stubborn. Extremely stubborn—possibly the most stubborn man in Lond—"

"Eloise!" Mademoiselle Aline barked.

Mademoiselle Eloise blinked. "But I am sure he will come to his senses any moment. Men are such reasonable creatures."

Aline and Mrs. Carr both reached for the plate of seedcake at the same time and shoved it at her.

"Mr. Carr is not the least bit stupid," Nola said, returning to her observation of him across the drawing room. Today he was wearing the blue superfine jacket that brought out the depth of the color of his eyes and showed his broad shoulders to advantage and one could plainly see the hint of his muscles despite the loose fit of his pantaloons. His raven curls drooped adorably over his forehead. He looked up from his glass of orgeat to smile at her and Nola could see the dimples from all the way across the room. "He is clever in business and very amusing and kind," she said.

"Yes, dear." Mrs. Carr patted her hand. "We have

all noticed your appreciation of everything about him."

"That reminds me of something I have been meaning to ask you," Nola said, her eyes still on Gabriel. "I have found of late I do not need Fig anymore to distract me when I am with your son."

"Of course not, dear," Mrs. Carr said. "A pet is only useful to keep a woman from making a fool of herself over a man's appearance. The moment you admit there is more to a man than his appearance, nothing can stop you from making a fool of yourself."

Nola nodded absently, her attention focused on Gabriel, who had taken a deep breath, jut his chin up as if he had come to a decision, and reached for his walking stick.

Since all of the girls and their mamas had been watching him either explicitly or out of the corner of their eyes, the minute he drew himself to his feet the murmur of voices in the room began to die down. He paused for a moment, then started walking slowly across the room toward Nola, his eyes never once leaving her face.

"You see!" Mrs. Carr hissed and squeezed Nola's arm.

He walked to where Nola sat, seeming to not even notice the women he dodged on his way to reach her. When he stopped in front of her chair, the entire room fell silent. Nola stood up slowly and clutched the back of her chair for support.

The expression in his eyes was so tender, so sweet and loving—everything she had ever dreamed of seeing on his face. And he looked at her. Only her. Her breath came in short gasps and her heart pounded so strongly, she was sure everyone must hear it.

He cleared his throat. "I wish to make an announcement."

"My dear boy," Mrs. Carr whispered, "isn't that something better done privately at first?"

"No." He straightened his shoulders and raised his voice so everyone in the drawing room could hear him. "I am not afraid to admit in front of everyone how wrong I have been."

Goodness! It was better than any daydream Nola had ever let herself have. She pressed her trembling lips together and prayed her knees would not give out. She kept her eyes riveted on his lips so she wouldn't miss a single word.

"Lady Nola," he said slowly, the dark honey of his voice making her stomach do somersaults, "I have been completely mistaken in my appreciation of your infinite kindness and your intelligence." He paused to draw in a deep breath. She held hers.

He cleared his throat. "Would you do me the honor of accepting my warehouse for your widows' bazaar?" he asked.

Nola stared at him.

"Nodcock," Mrs. Carr said.

Behind him, Aunt Caroline began snuffling into her handkerchief. Aunt Hortensia patted her shoulder consolingly.

The sound of Mademoiselle Aline cursing in French brought Nola back to earth. Gabriel was giving her the warehouse. Giving the widows their bazaar. It was what she had wanted all along. Exactly what she wanted. She smiled brightly. Hopefully her smile did not look like a snarl.

"On behalf of the war widows of London I accept your warehouse, Mr. Carr," she said past the lump in her throat. For a brief moment, she wondered if the war widows of London would mind if she picked up the teapot on their behalf and smashed it over their new landlord's head. She eyed the teapot. It was a Swann. She glanced up and found the eyes of Mrs. Carr, her aunts, and the Latours on her, encouraging expressions on their faces as they looked from the teapot to Gabriel's head.

Nola sighed. The widows needed the warehouse. The bazaar was more important than her own foolish disappointments.

"Wait!" Gabriel held up his hand. "I have something else to say."

One more time everyone in the room fell silent. Nola held her breath again.

Gabriel's smile deepened. "I will pay for the outfitting of the stalls and the refurbishing of the staircase myself."

"I must continue to thank you," Nola said through clenched teeth.

"Is it possible to take amiability too far?" Mademoiselle Eloise chirped.

"Perhaps we should drink a toast to the widows' bazaar," the Duke of St. Fell said, stuffing his glass of orgeat between the aspidistra's leaves. "With brandy."

Mrs. Carr fell onto the sofa. "I feel the need for brandy now."

"I would not mind a brandy," Aunt Hortensia said. Aunt Caroline thumped her approval.

"Bring the bottle," Mademoiselle Aline said.

"What about you, my lady?" Mademoiselle Eloise directed a concerned look toward Nola. "Perhaps a nice brandy would settle the nerves."

"What could possibly be wrong with Lady Nola's nerves?" Gabriel drew Nola toward the armchairs in front of the fireplace. "She just obtained the lease of my warehouse for her widows' bazaar. If she needs a drink for anything, it is to celebrate the achievement of her ambitions. Would you care for a brandy?" he asked her.

Nola shook her head. Brandy at this point might lead to teapot breakage.

"Whatever pleases you," Gabriel waited until she settled in the armchair before taking the seat next to hers. "I thought perhaps we could visit the warehouse tomorrow morning, if that is suitable?"

Nola nodded.

"I will arrange for an architect to meet us there. Mr. Oliphant did the alterations to Garrard House and I think he would be an excellent choice. Pending your approval, of course."

Nola continued to nod, still numb. Gabriel seemed to be requiring her approval a great deal.

"I want to make sure everything is according to your magnificent vision," he said. "We will have to spend a great deal of time together working out the details."

She looked at him, the shock that froze her heart beginning to thaw. He wanted to spend time with her. Giving her the warehouse was not a bad thing. It didn't mean he wasn't considering anything else between them.

"Gabriel!" Mrs. Carr tottered over to them. "Mr. Swann and the thought of brandy have reminded me how much the widows of London appreciate having your warehouse."

"Thank you." He turned back to Nola.

Mrs. Carr did not move. "We should plan a little celebration."

"Very good, Mother. In the meantime, Lady Nola and I have much to discuss."

"Tonight," Mrs. Carr said.

He clenched his jaw. "Fine."

"I will send word round to Mr. Oliphant, your

architect, to see if he can join us for dinner tonight. He is an eligible bachelor."

A vein began to throb at his temple. "I doubt he will be able to attend on such short notice, Mother."

"I expect the thought of a commission will help him decide. Besides, his widowed sister lives with him. I shall invite her as well."

"You are not going to give up, are you?" he said, glaring at her.

"Why, Gabriel? Are you going to make a fuss if I do not give up?"

"Certainly not. I will never make a fuss."

She put her hands on her hips. "And yet, you have changed your mind on the issue of the bazaar."

"I think I have shown everyone once and for all I am not so stubborn. Lady Nola has shown me the virtue of reasonable compromise." He smiled at Nola and her spirits soared.

"What about your plans to marry before your thirtieth birthday?" his mother demanded.

His jaw clenched even more tightly. "Must we discuss this now?"

"I am merely wondering how you will find a woman who meets your list of requirements if you are going to be preoccupied with the bazaar for the next few months."

He shrugged. "Perhaps I shall have to learn to compromise in that respect as well." He looked back at Nola and his expression softened.

A smug smile settled on Mrs. Carr's face and she headed off to intercept Bartlett and the tray of brandy. Goodness. Nola felt light-headed. Was he really admitting he might be interested in marrying her? She was too happy to speak.

"You know, I think I might have a brandy myself," he said.

"But you do not drink strong spirits," she said.

"You are right, as always, so I will not. But some ideas are so clever they require celebration." He smiled warmly. "I must tell you another point on which you are absolutely right. Sometimes a plan is so clever, one can recognize it as such the instant it strikes one without the need for any deliberation."

She looked at him in confusion. "Surely you do not still think the bazaar is a spur-of-the moment impulse?"

"The bazaar?" He blinked. "Oh, yes. Certainly. Of course it is not. I was referring to clever plans that strike one in general."

"I see," she said, not really seeing at all, but happy to bask in the warmth of his smile.

Sometimes a clever plan that strikes one without the need for any deliberation can be frustrated by one's mother's ninnyhammer need to celebrate. Gabriel poured himself another glass of wine and glared down the length of the dining room table.

This should have been his evening to be congratulated on his generosity of spirit and growth as a person. He should be talking to Nola about the bazaar right now. Instead he was trapped in the dining room with Nola, his mother, the Countesses of Belcraven, Swann and his daughters and nephew, St. Fell and his brother, and Belcraven. Not to mention Oliphant and his widowed sister, neither of whom had the decency to have a prior engagement.

Gabriel drained his glass and poured himself another. It was not as if his plan were so complicated. It was not. All it involved was spending the next month working with Nola on her bazaar. They would spend long hours together, perhaps even some of them alone. This would give him sufficient time to prove to her that there was more to him than a warehouse. Maybe even show her, if they had longer than a brief time alone.

Spending all this time together would likely also provoke the kind of comment which would require him to offer for her, thereby allowing him to marry Nola without embarrassing himself by publically repudiating his list. He took another sip of wine. Even if all the time with her didn't provoke comment, by the end of a month everyone's unwholesome interest in his list of requirements in a bride would likely have faded, diverted by some new scandal. It was a shame that Lamb woman's fixation on Byron seemed to have been thwarted. Perhaps she would return to London and start a new excitement. Gabriel didn't suppose she would start a new excitement if he offered her money. But one of the royal dukes might be persuaded to create a dustup for cash.

In any event, in a month or so, he could offer for Nola and marry her without any fuss.

But instead of spending the evening with Nola and impressing her with his agreeability, he was trapped at the end of the table between the Countesses of Belcraven while Nola sat at the middle of the table because his mother was more interested in idiotic precedence than in the fact that he and Nola needed to talk about the bazaar. Nola even wore a new silvery evening dress that actually showed the sweet swell of her cleavage. Gabriel drained his glass. He had always suspected his mother cared nothing for the bazaar.

At least the Countesses of Belcraven were no more concerned with polite behavior at dinner than they were anywhere else. They argued across the table about every remove and the walking sticks they jabbed at each other under the table kept smacking his knee. He didn't complain. The blinding pain was preferable to being obliged to speak to the Beasts himself. He poured himself another glass of wine and topped up the glasses of the countesses. Perhaps wine would improve their aim.

Chef marched in the room holding a silver platter aloft.

"I present the Ham Wellington," he declared with a flourish. "You will be the first to enjoy the dish on which I will make my fame."

"I still say it would have been better with beef," Cook's voice wafted in from the hallway.

Chef's mustache trembled and he dropped the platter on the table and scuttled out the door.

Gabriel looked over at Nola to share the joke, but of course his view of her was blocked by St. Fell. The idiot had been leaning over Nola all night. Probably leering down the front of her dress, the unprincipled lecher. Gabriel glared at him, but he was too far down the table to have an effect.

Not that Nola's nodcock brother would notice and put a stop to it even though he was sitting directly across from her. Belcraven was too busy horrifying the younger Swann sister Miss Whatsit with bloodcurdling tales of war. Or maybe it was the older sister. Who knew? Either way, Belcraven was obviously incapable of providing the slightest assistance to his sister. Gabriel drained his glass. Really, it was a miracle Nola had lived this long, given the utter lack of attention anyone paid to her well-being.

Gabriel tried another time to attract Belcraven's attention to the possible problem of St. Fell, but once again, the only person who noticed him at the table was Oliphant's sister, Mrs. Neville, the widow. From the overinflated size of her chest, the woman's husband must have suffocated to death.

Mrs. Neville waved at him.

Gabriel shrank back in his chair. He did not want to be noticed by Mrs. Neville. She had a gleam in her eye and was wearing the kind of dress that usually presaged a fuss. Low-cut and fancy. Apparently covered with embroidered swans, as each of the Swann girls had pointed out loudly.

He poured himself another glass of wine. Who ever heard of green swans anyway?

THIRTEEN

Immediately after the last remove the ladies left the gentlemen to their port and brandy and went upstairs to the drawing room. Aunt Caroline and Aunt Hortensia staggered over to the farthest corner of the room so they could continue their argument about the relative merits of ham versus beef in peace. The Swann sisters seated themselves at the pianoforte and began rifling through the sheet music. Mrs. Neville prowled around the edges of the room. Nola eyed her narrowly. The woman looked as if she were assessing the furnishings for auction.

"This is not nearly celebratory enough," Mrs. Carr complained. "We must go somewhere amusing when the gentlemen join us."

"It is nearly ten o'clock." Nola sat down in the armchair in front of the fireplace that Gabriel had been in this afternoon. It was very cosy. "Surely it is too late to go out?"

"Piffle! Ten o'clock is the perfect time to go out in London."

Nola stifled a yawn. Ten o'clock was the perfect

time to go out only if you stayed out all night like Mrs. Carr. "Mr. Carr and I must meet with Mr. Oliphant early in the morning at the warehouse. I think I would prefer to go to bed and be well rested."

Mrs. Carr sank down in the chair next to Nola's. "I would say you and Gabriel were perfect for each other were I not so sick of hearing it."

Nola smiled. She liked hearing how she and Gabriel were well suited.

Mrs. Neville sauntered back to the fireplace. "But it will be ages before the gentlemen are done with their brandy," she said sulkily.

"They will not linger," Mrs. Carr said. "Gabriel does not drink hard spirits."

"Really?" Mrs. Carter's thin eyebrows arched upward. "Is he a Methodist or just dull?"

Mrs. Carr bristled. "Dull, of course!"

"He is not dull!" Nola blurted out, immediately regretting it when she saw the mocking gleam in Mrs. Neville's eyes. Nola pursed her lips. She didn't like Mrs. Neville, who kept waving at Gabriel all through dinner, in her swan dress with her petite waist and her large bosom. Nola had no doubt she was the Latour customer who had her underwear embroidered with an intimate encounter in mind.

The door opened and the Duke of St. Fell was the first gentleman into the drawing room.

"It is all Gabriel's fault," he said. "Claims there's too much work to be done to linger over port like a normal fellow."

"So we brought it with us." Henry held up a bottle of port. The other gentlemen followed, carrying glasses and more bottles.

Gabriel came in last, obviously tired because he leaned heavily on his walking stick. Nola shook her head. The poor man must be exhausted. It was his first day out of the sickroom, after all. He remained standing in the center of the room, blinking and peering around as if he were having difficulty deciding where to sit. Nola wished she had sat down on the sofa so there was a chance he would sit next to her. Unfortunately, Mr. Swann took the last chair in front of the fireplace next to Mrs. Carr.

Gabriel looked at Nola and smiled. "Lady Nola and I have much to discuss about the bazaar."

Nola sighed. Dimples.

"I still think we should go out," Mrs. Carr said.

Mr. Swann puffed up his chest. "I have a theater box at Drury Lane. Of course, the play has started by now, and perhaps you have seen it."

"We do not go to see the play," Mrs. Carr said. "We go to see who else has gone to see the play."

Gabriel sat down on the sofa with a thump. "I want to stay home."

"Piffle! You always prefer to stay home, Gabriel. That is why we are not asking your opinion." Mrs. Carr turned to Mr. Swann and inquired about the precise location of his theater box.

"Perhaps I am not the only one who wants to stay home," Gabriel said loudly. "Lady Nola?" He looked around as if he could not remember where she was, even though he had smiled at her a moment ago.

"Yes," Nola said after a moment.

"Aha!" He grinned when he spotted her. "How do you feel about going to the theater?"

"Good Lord, man!" The Duke of St. Fell called out from the other side of the pianoforte. "Do you expect Lady Nola to become a drudge like you? We must go to the theater now, as a matter of principle." The Swann sisters and nephew laughed and declared their agreement.

"We could discuss the plans for the bazaar even

if we did go to the theater," Mr. Oliphant offered. "I shall just jot down a few preliminary thoughts." He extracted a notebook and pencil from the pocket of his waistcoat and sat down in the chair next to the sofa and began scribbling.

"I had not planned to go to the theater tonight." Gabriel folded his arms across his broad chest and thrust out his chin.

"We're all becoming devilishly tired of your plans, Gabriel." St. Fell banged down his glass and stamped to the sofa. "Were I not a sporting man, I would tell you what I think of them right now."

"Now, no fair beating the bushes to make the hare jump." Henry took St. Fell by the elbow and steered him back to the pianoforte.

"They are foxed," Mrs. Carr said.

"Possibly." Mr. Swann mopped his red face. "Is that not a good thing?" Mrs. Carr shrugged noncommitally and returned to her inquisition of the pedigree of his theater box.

Mrs. Neville insinuated herself onto the sofa next to Gabriel. "It seems to me this bazaar is a great deal of trouble." Her tone was still annoyingly sulky. "I have never heard of putting different sellers in the same building. It sounds like a havey-cavey idea to me."

Gabriel winked at Nola. "I think it will be a great success," he said. "And it will all be due to the efforts of Lady Nola. She is a saint, you know."

"Gabriel!" Mrs. Carr shouted.

"Not in a popish way, of course," he said.

If Nola did not know better she would swear Gabriel was foxed as well, which was of course impossible, but any thoughts she had on the matter flew out of her head the next instant when Mrs. Neville's hand touched Gabriel's thigh. Nola goggled. As she watched, the fingers of Mrs. Neville's right hand again brushed against Gabriel's thigh. Gabriel seemed oblivious.

Nola tapped Mrs. Carr on the shoulder. "What does Mrs. Neville think she is doing?" she hissed.

"She is making a fuss," Mrs. Carr whispered back.

Nola glared across the room. Mrs. Neville in her underwear designed for an intimate encounter appeared to be arranging the intimate encounter with Gabriel right now. On the drawing room sofa.

"Perhaps we should give him some assistance?" Nola whispered. Like marching across the room and giving Mrs. Neville a smart smack topside her excessively coiffed head.

Mrs. Carr shook her head. "Gabriel has dealt with fusses before."

"You may well credit Lady Nola if it is a success." Mrs. Neville casually dipped her shoulder so that her silk shawl dropped down to cover the space on the sofa between her and Gabriel. "But I wonder if you will blame her if the bazaar is a failure." Her right hand disappeared underneath the shawl.

"I am not interested," Gabriel said with a squeak, his left hand also disappearing under the shawl, "in thinking the bazaar will be a failure." His hand reemerged, gripping Mrs. Neville's wrist. He dropped her hand back over her lap and untidily folded the shawl clear of his thigh.

"The whole topic of commerce is tedious." Mrs. Neville jumped to her feet and stalked off to the pianoforte.

Mrs. Carr patted Nola's hand. "I really think it is merely a matter of time before he proposes to you, dear," she murmured.

Nola blinked at her absently. Mrs. Neville's words

were just as disturbing as her actions. Perhaps more. She quickly crossed the room to the sofa.

"I think Mrs. Neville was right," she said, sitting down next to Gabriel. "If the bazaar is a failure, you will blame me."

He beamed at her. "The bazaar will not be a failure. With your organization of the widows and the support you have garnered amongst the *ton,* and your organization of the widows—" He paused and frowned. "What were we talking about?"

"What if the bazaar is a failure?" she asked urgently.

He shook his head sadly. "You are brooding. It will not do. You will be pouting again next, and we all know where that leads."

She bit her lip. He would blame her if the bazaar was a failure. How could he not? Her heart sank, but she tried to keep her voice steady. "Do you really believe the bazaar belongs in your warehouse?"

He looked indignant. "I most certainly do! I would never agree to it otherwise."

She took a deep breath and plowed on. "But perhaps it is merely a matter of my being here, every day, wearing you down and away from what you originally wanted."

He grinned at her. "Well, of course it is. Isn't that why you moved into my house?"

She didn't return his smile. Suddenly, she felt very much like running away to the theater tonight.

It was difficult to negotiate the back stairs with a walking stick, a bottle of port, and a candle, but a good businessman did not quail in the face of difficulty. Besides, all were necessary—the candle to see, the port because he did not drink hard spirits, the walking stick so he would not develop a hideous limp that would repulse Nola even though she was the sweetest, most amiable girl in the world and would never—

Gabriel blinked at the threshold of the dark, empty kitchen. Why the devil was he here? Nola wasn't in the kitchen. She was at the theater with that idiot St. Fell and his brother, and that over-educated egghead Oliphant and Swann's overpaid nephew, all of whom would right now be yammering at her or worse, trying to take advantage of her good nature by proposing to her.

"Why are we here?" he asked Fig. The dog merely panted with its tongue hanging out. Gabriel bent down and patted its head. Stupid dog.

Gabriel took a swig of port. Of course, the plan! The new plan, since barely half an hour after everyone left for the theater he had realized that the old plan was stupid. The old plan meant he would have to wait a month to have Nola. A whole month of not having her, a whole month during which some other idiot his mother pushed in her way could propose. Which Nola might agree to because she was the most amiable woman in the world.

He tucked the bottle of port under his arm more securely so he could lift the latch on the cold pantry with the handle of his walking stick. Chef's ham lay on the middle shelf, covered with a linen cloth. Not that amiable was bad. Certainly not. It ensured that she would consent when he proposed to her. But it also meant she might consent to some other idiot's proposal.

Fortunately, a successful businessman can modify his plan when he has to. It would be a challenge. It would test his very character. But he was equal to it. He squared his shoulders. He was the

kind of man who could manage a ham platter, a
port bottle, a candle, and a walking stick without
flinching. Could St. Fell or Oliphant or those Swanns
claim the same?

Not so very many attempts later he managed to
thump the ham platter down on the kitchen table
without losing the meat, the port, or the flame on
the candle. He had to go back to the pantry to
chase Fig out with the walking stick though. Stupid
dog.

He found a cleaver on a hook on the wall. Slicing
the meat off the bone with a cleaver was a simple
matter. Or it would have been if not for the damned
ham's slippery sauce and devious pastry. Nor did
the dog's fervent fascination with the task make it
any easier. Gabriel took a long swig of port to steady
his hand and gripped the slippery end of the bone.
He swiped with the cleaver. The ham went skitter-
ing across the table and landed on the kitchen
floor.

The dog dove at it. Gabriel grabbed its back legs
and dragged it out from under the table. It took a
minute to pry the ham from its jaws, but at least
the process dislodged most of the sauce and pastry.

Gabriel put the ham back on the table and shot
Fig a dirty look. The dog was too busy licking the
ham trail on the floor to notice. Stupid dog.

Gabriel wiped his hands on the cloth and grabbed
the cleaver again. This time he kept a tight grip on
the greasy ham. This time the cleaver nicked him
in the thumb.

The dog didn't even look up as Gabriel howled
and hopped around the kitchen clutching his
thumb. Damn thing would probably just as soon
eat his thumb as Ham Wellington.

Gabriel held his thumb up to the candlelight.

Not much of a cut. Not worth wasting port on. He took another drink from the bottle, took his jacket off, unwound his cravat from his neck, and wrapped it around his thumb.

Which gave him a much better purchase on the ham bone. Soon he had a clean bone and a pile of cut meat, most of which was on the table. He swept the meat into the platter and assembled it back into ham shape over the cleaver. He couldn't find the cloth that had covered it. The dog had probably eaten it. So he took the cravat and draped it over the meat and returned the platter to the pantry. His thumb had stopped bleeding anyway.

No one would ever know he had been here. He took another swig from the bottle, and carried the bone, the bottle, and the candlestick back to his study.

Fig followed. Clever dog.

In the study, Gabriel set the candlestick and the ham bone on his desk and took a long swig of port while he assessed the situation. His chair behind the desk and the two in front of it were comfortable enough, especially if he rested his feet on the desktop. But from underneath the desk, Fig would not be visible.

The pair of armchairs that flanked the fireplace were a possibility. He could move them closer together so he could settle his head and shoulders in one and his legs across the other, but that might be uncomfortable. He took another drink of port. No reason to be uncomfortable.

The window seat in the bow window at the opposite end of the room would be very comfortable. It had the advantage of overlooking the front of the house so he could hear the carriage. But there was no space underneath for the dog.

The sofa opposite the window seat had the perfect space underneath for the dog. But it faced the wrong way.

He sighed and took another drink of port.

His mother was right, he realized mournfully. They should switch the location of the drawing room and his study. He downed another mouthful of port. The drawing room sofa was perfectly visible from the doorway and faced exactly the right way. But he would never be in the drawing room in the middle of the night. It completely lacked credibility. Damnation. He ran his hands through his hair. Damnation! Now his hair smelled of ham.

He gritted his teeth. He would just have to move the sofa. Slightly. If all went according to plan, it would be the least thing noticed. And there was no question, this time, everything would go according to plan.

The evening at the theater was wretched. Not the play. Nola always enjoyed *Richard III*. Edmund Kean was magnificent. Everyone in Drury Lane held their breath when he dropped his sword and staggered backward and writhed upon the stage after Richmond delivered the mortal blow. The rest of the time, everyone chattered without stopping.

Mr. Oliphant insisted on comparing the dimensions of this Drury Lane with all of the previous Drury Lanes. If the previous theaters had not already burned to the ground, Nola would have set fire to them herself just to make him stop talking.

Mrs. Carr kept declaring that Mr. Kean was so handsome, a girl would need two kittens to distract her. Which naturally prompted Aunt Hortensia and Aunt Caroline to argue about other notable two-cat men.

At least Mrs. Neville found friends to visit in other boxes. As for why Miss Swann needed to giggle so energetically every time Henry opened his mouth, Nola could not say. He was her brother. He was not that amusing.

But it wouldn't be fair to blame her misery on everyone else. Because throughout it all, despite the play and the other distractions, Nola could not stop thinking about Gabriel. She brooded. She tried not to, but she did. She couldn't stop thinking about the drawing room conversation. Because it forced her to face what she should have known of all along.

Before he met her, Gabriel didn't want the bazaar any more than he wanted to marry her. He had a vision of his ideal bride. He made a list of requirements. He had a list. He had a plan.

Mrs. Carr seemed to think he would eventually ask Nola to marry him. It was possible. Perhaps even likely, given his complete lack of interest in any of the other women today. He had told his mother in the afternoon that he might compromise on the requirements of his list.

Nola pressed her hands against her burning cheeks, grateful the shadows in the corner of the box hid her face as she pretended to concentrate on the actors below. Marry Gabriel. Spend the rest of her life with him. He was everything she wanted—intelligent, kind, amusing, and handsome. Extremely handsome. She took out her handkerchief and fanned herself. Ridiculously handsome.

If she married Gabriel, it would seem like heaven.

But actually it would be hell.

Because although he was the man of her dreams, she was not the woman he wanted. She was the woman he would settle for because he did not get the wife he really wanted. And wouldn't they both know it, when her plain-speaking didn't soothe him? When their house was run haphazardly because she was more interested in finding a tenant for the building on the Strand than in making sure he had his wretched beef tea?

When he reached over in the middle of the night for the wife of his dreams and found her flat bosom instead?

She could never marry Gabriel Carr.

Gabriel stood in the doorway and squinted at the sofa. All he had needed to do was turn it a few feet to the right and it was perfectly visible from the hallway. Even the color of the upholstery was in his favor. Blue always brought out the depth of his eyes. Everything could not be more perfect. He scattered a few ledger books on the carpet next to the sofa and put the candle on the table near them.

The clatter of the carriage wheels shattered the quiet of Brook Street. He drained the port and grabbed the ham bone. Fig followed. Gabriel tossed the bone under the sofa and the dog scooted after it. Clever dog.

As the night porter greeted the coachman, Gabriel closed the door to his study. He heard the carriage door scrape open, the women's shoes scuffling on the stone steps as they climbed to the front door. The sound of the door opening was muffled by the rattle of the carriage as it continued on to the stable.

Then he listened to the women's footsteps on the stairs, the steady twin thumps of the countesses' sticks, his mother's rattling on about the number of cats Byron required, Nola's gentle murmured reply lost as they passed the landing on this floor on their way to their bedchambers, the sound of their voices fading as they went around the landing.

As soon as he heard the sound of their doors close, he opened the door of the study and dashed back to the sofa. He lay down on his back and crooked his right arm behind his head and draped his left arm so that it hung down, palm up, for that added touch of vulnerability. Not as comfortable as crossing both arms behind his head, but to better effect. The exhausted businessman.

His left profile was to the door. The candlelight flickered shadows across his face. His shirt was undone to the third button. The dog's rump jutted out from underneath the sofa. The perfect romantic setting.

In a few moments, Nola would come looking for Fig. She would be drawn by the light in his study. She would have to come and get the dog, who as always, would not cooperate. Or cooperate perfectly, depending on one's point of view. Gabriel would wake up, slowly, of course, so as not to startle her, and there they would be, alone in the candlelight in the study in the middle of the night. A completely compromising position. The result was inevitable. Not that he intended to do more than hold her hand, perhaps kiss her, he was no rake after all. Just enough to ensure that she would agree they had no alternative but to marry.

The best thing about the plan was that it was absolutely foolproof. Even if they were discovered, they would still be obliged to marry. Perhaps even faster. Either way, he would marry her without humiliating himself by admitting his list was foolish.

"Fig?" Nola's whisper sounded as if it came from hall outside the study door. Then silence. She must have seen him. Gabriel dared not open his eyes, not yet. He waited, keeping himself still—or at least, keeping those parts of him still that he could, for lying in the darkness waiting for Nola to come over was so delicious an experience he was grateful the candle was positioned to illuminate only his face and leave the rest of him in shadows.

The moments stretched. Then finally, he heard the soft padding sound of footsteps into the room, slowly, quietly, irresistibly toward him. A soft swirl of air brushed against his cheek and the candle-light flickered against his closed eyelids. She must be standing over him. Lord, it was a most erotic experience, lying vulnerable, on his back, being watched by Nola. He only hoped she was enjoying it as well. If not yet, then soon, when he took her into his arms and showed her that he was not always so brief.

Finally, he couldn't stand it any longer. He languorously stretched his arms, and slowly lifted his eyelids.

To see Bartlett standing next to the sofa, holding his grimy jacket and blood-speckled cravat. The butler's gaze encompassed the tumble of ledger books, the empty port bottle, and the new position of the sofa. He pursed his lips thoughtfully.

"I thought you said you were not interested in the theater tonight, sir."

Nola locked the door of her bedchamber and leaned against it. Gabriel had been lucky she had seen Bartlett coming around the corner. If she had been caught in the study with him, he might have been obliged to offer for her.

But it was completely unfair for Gabriel to lie

around the house with his shirt unbuttoned! Did
he think she was so saintly she would not enter the
room, so saintly she would not be tempted to
brush the raven curl from his forehead, run her
hands over the muscles of his arms, his chest, perhaps even press her lips to his—she forced herself
to take a deep breath. She wasn't sure what she
wanted to do. But she wanted to do it to him. A
month ago she had no idea how a woman could
ever think of having an illicit liaison. Now she wondered how one ever thought of anything else.

   She crawled into bed and tried to concentrate
on Gabriel's warehouse instead.

FOURTEEN

"You're late!" Nanny stuck her head in his room, then popped it back out and slammed the door behind her with the kind of enthusiasm that could only mean Bartlett had regaled everyone with the details of last night's adventures.

When he was confident that the sound had not actually made the top of his head explode, Gabriel tried once again to force his trembling hands to fold the neckcloth into a durable cravat. He hadn't held any real hope that the butler would keep his mouth shut. Who could blame him? Jug-bitten like a chuckleheaded mooncalf. At his age. He winced at the reflection of his bloodshot eyes in the looking glass. On port, of all things. He deserved to be embarrassed.

Of course, being jug-bitten wasn't half as humiliating as the memory of his insane scheme to manoeuver Nola into a compromising position so that he could offer for her without having to publically repudiate his list of requirements. Of course it didn't work. Nola wasn't the kind of girl who would be tempted by his appearance. She was above such things. He sighed. But not beyond them. He remembered her reaction to the kiss on her palm. All she needed was a little encouragement to see him as more than a warehouse.

He tucked the end of the neckcloth under and patted the finished knot. It held firm. Excellent. He certainly did not want a flopping front on the day he proposed to Nola. He was done with playing games, with trying to win her with subterfuge and schemes. It was time to tell the truth. They were perfectly suited for each other. The minute they were alone, he would ask for her hand in marriage. It wasn't as if her brother would mind or even notice. All they had to do was keep it a secret for a month or so until everyone forgot about badgering him about his list of requirements. The solution was so obvious he was an idiot for not realizing it before.

When he edged his way down to the foyer, his mother and Bartlett stood waiting. Nola was not there. Odd. She was always punctual.

"Gabriel! You are late." His mother frowned. "Whatever is the matter with you this morning?"

Damnation. Why did she have to shout? He clung to the bannister for support. "I find it hard to believe Bartlett did not tell you," he said.

"Of course he told me. I thought he was exaggerating."

"Impossible, madam," Bartlett said.

"I hope we're not too late!" Cook barreled down the hallway toward them before Gabriel could ask where Nola was. Chef trailed behind her carrying a stack of boxes that reached all the way to his mustache. From the admiring looks they gave each other, they had obviously resolved the issue of beef to their mutual satisfaction.

"Too late for what?" Gabriel asked, pressing his fingers against his temples. Chef's boxes contained food. The odor was unsettling.

"No, certainly not," his mother said to Cook. "We are still waiting for Lady Nola. She has gone to fetch something." She turned to Gabriel. "Chef needs to visit his new premises and since they are right next to the warehouse, he will drop you and Lady Nola off. Cook is accompanying him."

"Because one Frenchy isn't enough to chaperone the likes of you." Cook eyed Gabriel as grimly as if he were French.

"Lady Nola and I do not need a chaperone." Gabriel rolled his eyes. It hurt like the devil.

His mother inspected him. "You are pale, your cheeks have a hectic flush, your eyes are shadowed, and you have a limp. You must either go with chaperones, or stay home and write romantic poetry."

"I am back!" Nola shouted from the landing, making Gabriel jump. She descended the stairs backward, bracing herself against the bannister as she pulled Fig down the stairs by his leather lead with both hands.

Gabriel's heart sank. She was not only wearing the pink monstrosity, she had jammed one of the bucket bonnets on her head. It would be difficult to kiss her in that bonnet without losing an eye. He would have to remember to get her to take it off before he proposed.

"Fig wants to go for the ride," she said brightly when she reached the foyer. She met Gabriel's eyes for an instant then looked away, a rosy blush flooding her cheeks. She was panting from the exertion of battling the dog. Her soft lips were parted and the gentle swell of her chest lifted with each breath.

"No chaperones," Gabriel ground out.

His mother merely snorted and shepherded Cook and Chef to the front door.

Nola followed, tugging the lead. Fig rolled over onto his back and eyed Gabriel woefully as Nola dragged him along the marble floor.

Gabriel cleared his throat. "I think perhaps he would rather stay in the house."

"You are hardly in a position to give an opinion on the dog's whereabouts, Gabriel," his mother said. She turned to Nola. "However, my dear, there is only so far one can go with a pet. You are long past that point." She held out her hand. Nola sighed and gave her the dog's lead.

Nola climbed into the carriage after Chef and Cook, wedging herself between them. Gabriel was left alone on the opposite seat with only Chef's boxes for company.

It was surely the longest it had ever taken to drive from Brook Street to Soho Square. Gabriel braced himself with his walking stick as the carriage turned from Brook onto Swallow Street. At least his hands had stopped trembling. He leaned his aching head against the side of the carriage. It would be pleasant to close his eyes for a second, what with the morning light being uncommonly blinding for October, but he still did not trust his stomach with the smell from Chef's boxes. Casting up his accounts on Nola's shoes would not be the best harbinger to his proposal.

"Of course, a nice English ice is just as good as Frenchy sorbet." Cook laced her hands over her ample waist and leaned past Nola to eye Chef.

Chef nodded, the rapture in his face as he beamed at Cook making him look like one of her beloved English beef cows. Poor idiot was not even objecting to the woman calling him French. Pathetic to see the depth of humiliation the man was willing to endure in the name of love.

"If folk want to pay twice the price for a Frenchy name, there's nothing to do except charge them for it," Cook continued. "It's a perfectly respectable English business practice. Traditional, in fact."

Nola gave Gabriel a conspiratorial smile in appreciation of Cook's comments. He smiled back, even though it hurt his teeth. She was so beautiful. With any luck, Oliphant would also be late and he and Nola would have a few minutes alone. It wouldn't take long to settle the matter. His straightforward question. Her simple answer. Perhaps even time for a kiss, if Oliphant cooperated long enough to let them settle the matter of the bonnet.

But Oliphant was not late. He bounded over the instant the carriage lurched to a stop in front of the warehouse and unlatched the door and helped Nola out before the coachman or Gabriel could, then steered her through the central doorway the minute the watchman unlocked it.

Gabriel trailed behind, cursing his knee, the walking stick, and his head for making him slow. That turnip sucker Oliphant was acting as if it were his warehouse and his idea to agree to Nola's bazaar.

Nola halted abruptly in the doorway. "It is much better than I expected!" The look of bliss on her face matched the hushed tone of her voice as she turned a full circle to gaze around the whole hall.

Oliphant flipped through his notebook. "The interior dimensions are sixty-two by thirty-six feet," he read out. "The exterior dimensions are larger, naturally, but not relevant for our purposes."

"I meant it was beautiful." Nola grinned at Gabriel behind the architect's back.

Gabriel sighed. It would have been the perfect

romantic moment to take her hand and murmur in her ear that she was more beautiful than any warehouse and then propose. He glared at Oliphant, but the insensitive clod was too busy scribbling in his notebook to leave.

"I can picture the mahogany counters running down the length of the hall!" she said, her eyes shining as if they were already built and the widows standing behind them right now.

Gabriel followed the direction of her gaze. She was right. It was a beautiful room, enormous, with high ceilings and the rows of arched windows along the north and south walls, too beautiful for a warehouse. It would be an excellent retail premise. Her organized bazaar of well-trained widows would do well.

The rest of the morning flew by as she danced up the curved staircase and inspected every floor of the building with glee. She loved every inch of his warehouse, from the vaulted arches in the cellar where Oliphant would fit the custom-made stoves large enough to heat the whole building, to the ground and first floors where the bazaar would go, and the upper floor where they decided to put the kitchen and dining room for the widows.

Throughout it all, she peppered Oliphant with intelligent questions, not afraid to ask more until she could make sense of his answers. Gabriel couldn't help laughing when she somehow managed to get the architect to agree to finish the work a month early. The widows' bazaar could open in February.

It was exhilarating to watch the woman he would marry revel in taking another step along the path of her dream. It would have been even more exhilarating if he could have shed Oliphant long enough to propose. On the other hand, over the course of the inspection, at least Gabriel's head cleared and Nola's bonnet fell victim to an ambitious cellar cobweb. She had removed the bonnet to clean it but it had slipped unnoticed from her fingers when Gabriel suggested they pace off the fifty feet for the dining room.

But she remembered of course, when they returned to the ground floor at the end of their tour. She ran her fingers through her hair and fluffed her curls up delightfully as she peered around for it, asking both men if they had seen it.

Oliphant merely looked blank and announced he needed to reconsider the placement of the stove pipes. He walked off muttering toward the east wall.

Gabriel's heart leapt. "I think your bonnet is in the cellar," he said. "I will help you go look for it." The damned bonnet was upstairs on the first floor but the dimly lit cellar was more romantic for a proposal.

He took Nola's arm and steered her toward the staircase, calling over his shoulder to Oliphant that they would be back shortly. Gabriel smiled to himself. Shortly, but not briefly.

"I do not think it is a good idea for us to be alone together," Nola said, however her steps were as hurried as his. Perhaps faster, as she did not have an aching knee and a walking stick.

"Nonsense. There is nothing to worry about being alone together." Gabriel tried not to bark his shins with the walking stick as they went down the stairs. "We will be spending many hours together working on the bazaar."

"But my part in the bazaar is mostly done," Nola said. "You could easily supervise the renovations to the warehouse without me."

He tucked her hand under his arm more tightly

and sped up. "You must participate in every aspect of the bazaar. Without your intelligence and plain-speaking and amiability and goodness and kindness there would not be a bazaar in first place." He didn't think he could justify mentioning her beauty as being a reason for the bazaar. He would just have to bring it up separately.

"Goodness! I do not think you should say such things to me." Nola sounded wonderfully breathless, but that might have been because of their rate of descent.

Gabriel stopped abruptly as soon as they reached the foot of the stairs. He tucked his walking stick under his arm and took Nola's hand in both of his. "I merely want you to know how much I admire you."

Even though the light was dim, he could still see the blush on her cheeks before she lowered her head to stare down at the floor. "But you make me out to be such a saint," she murmured. "Believe me, I am not."

He turned her hand over in his, stroked his thumb over her palm, raised her hand to his heart—and nearly had a heart seizure when the walking stick clattered to the floor because it had slipped from under his arm.

Gabriel looked down and the blood drained from his face. Nola had squealed and jumped toward him at the noise. Now her fingers clutched the lapels of his jacket. His hands spanned her waist.

She did not move away. He did not move his hands.

"Is everything all right?" Oliphant's voice sounded from the top of the staircase.

Gabriel swallowed. Nola's face was tilted up to his and her eyes had a glazed expression that

made the breath catch in his throat. Her lips curved
into a small smile and parted slightly.

"Fine," he rasped loud enough for Oliphant to
hear, never taking his eyes off Nola's.

If Oliphant came downstairs, he would kill him.

"Quite fine," Nola whispered. Her cheeks grew
pinker but she didn't lower her gaze.

If Oliphant spoke again, he would kill him.

But Oliphant didn't speak. He merely walked
away from the staircase, and the echo of his footsteps faded to silence.

For a few seconds, Gabriel didn't move. Then,
slowly, very slowly, to give her the chance to pull
away, he lowered his head toward Nola's. She didn't
pull away. Her eyes fluttered shut and she leaned
closer. He brushed his lips against hers.

Surely now she conceded he was more than a
warehouse?

He returned his lips to hers. A shiver went
through her body and she slid her arms up to his
shoulders and wound them around his neck.

Definitely more than a warehouse.

He ran his hands up the elegant line of her back
to hold her face tenderly with one hand and stroke
the nape of her neck with the other. He deepened
the kiss. She moaned and pressed herself against
him. He felt dizzy, on fire and lost in the taste of
her, and the small sounds of pleasure she made in
the back of her throat made him burn even more.

His fingers drifted back down her side, as he
reveled in the softness of her body against his,
then he gently cupped the side of her bosom. Her
perfect bosom. He feathered his thumb and she
arched and moaned into his mouth.

He shuddered in pleasure. Kissing Nola was
heaven. But it was not right. Or rather it was right,

the most right thing in the world, but it was not right yet.

She gasped when he lifted his lips from hers to rain kisses along the delicate line of her jaw.

"My dear Nola—" He took another shuddering breath, closed his eyes for a moment, then tried again. He looked into her face, smiling at her deliciously dazed expression. "My dear Nola, would you do me the honor of marrying me?"

She looked down at his hand then back into his eyes, blinking as if she didn't know what to say. He helpfully brushed the pad of his thumb against the swell of her breast and she moaned and arched into his arms once again.

"No." She tangled her fingers in his hair and pulled him closer.

He kissed the soft hollow at the base of her throat. "What do you mean, no?"

"I mean no, I will not marry you."

He nuzzled her earlobe. "Do you refuse me so you may accept when I ask again tomorrow?" He wouldn't have guessed someone so plainspoken would feel the need to be coy, but refusing the first time a proposal was offered was a well-known female prerogative.

"I will not accept no matter how many times you ask." She closed her eyes and tilted her chin up. "But I would very much like to continue kissing."

He lifted his head. "Have you promised to marry someone else?"

"No." She didn't open her eyes.

What the devil had come over her? He dropped his hands and took a step backward. "Now is not the time to be impulsive, Nola. Marriage is a very serious matter. You cannot just blurt out the first answer that springs to mind when I propose. Especially if it is no!" He reached out and braced himself against the wall. He still felt dizzy, but not just with desire.

She opened her eyes and smiled. "I am not being impulsive. I have given the matter considerable thought."

"How could you have given the matter considerable thought when I have just asked you?"

Her smile vanished. "For goodness sake, Gabriel! Everyone in London knows you are looking for a wife. They have been throwing me at you for a month. How could I not have thought about it?"

"Oh." He considered the matter then nodded as he understood. He moved toward her and wrapped his hands back around her waist. "That is the problem. You have deliberated too long. You should not brood about it so much." He smiled warmly at her. "Just follow your impulses and accept."

She smiled back and smoothed her hands against his chest. "My impulses tell me we should stop spoiling the moment by bringing up the subject of marriage."

He leaned his forehead against hers and forced himself to speak calmly through his clenched teeth. "But we have barely begun to speak of it."

"And we are already arguing." She tilted her head back. "Why will you not kiss me? Was it not enjoyable?"

"Of course it was enjoyable. It was wonderful. Which is exactly why we must now speak of marriage."

"Really?" she asked. "I did not know if I was doing it properly. Was I right to put my tongue in your mouth when your tongue—"

"Damnation, Nola! We are talking about marriage, not tongues!" He removed her distracting hands and stepped a full foot away from her. Any more talk from her about tongues and he would be battling the cobwebs in the corner so he could show her all the other things they could do with their tongues.

She frowned at him. "No, you are talking about marriage. I would rather talk about tongues."

He smothered a curse. "You are obviously still plainspoken. Why can you not still be amiable as well?"

She put her hands on her hips. "I suppose an amiable woman would agree to marry you?"

"Yes!" Considering the scorching kiss they had just shared. With tongues. Her tongue. He ran his hands through his hair. "An amiable woman would agree we are perfectly suited for each other."

She folded her arms across her chest. "What about your list?"

Relief flooded though him. He smacked his forehead in contrition. Of course! He was a brainless idiot too caught up in the kissing to think clearly. "Never mind my list!" He smiled. "All we need do is keep our betrothal a secret for a month or so until everyone is distracted by a new scandal." He reached for her.

She slapped his hand aside. "I have already said I will not marry you." Her tone was belligerent. "Now I do not want to continue kissing you either."

"You know you do not mean that." From the furious glint in her eyes and the thin line of her mouth, that was not the right thing to say either. But he was man enough to know the right thing to say. He cleared his throat. "I—" He swallowed. "I love you, Nola."

Her eyes narrowed. "How can that be when I do not meet the requirements of your list?"

He stared at her, dumbfounded. He had just made the supreme declaration. She was supposed to say she loved him back, not glare at him as if he were spinning a tale to avoid paying the rent.

Her steady gaze didn't waver. "I said, how can you love me if I do not meet the requirements of your list."

"But you know my list was merely designed so I would not be judged by my appearance and fortune," he said soothingly.

She pursed her lips. "I should think you would be eager to be judged by your appearance and fortune given the poor state of your character." She picked up his walking stick and swung it ominously back and forth. "Any man with a decent character would continue to kiss a lady when she asked."

He took a step backward. "You are being unreasonable. I would be most happy to continue kissing you. Once you agree to marry me."

"I suppose my agreeing to marry you was part of your plan?"

"Yes of course—" He stopped himself, but it was too late. Now the amber flecks in her eyes looked sharp enough to cut his throat. "It is most unlike you to be in a temper. Perhaps we should discuss the matter another time."

"I think not."

"But I do not see why you are making a fuss."

She stamped her foot. "Everyone makes a fuss except you, Gabriel!"

She snapped the walking stick across her knee, flung the pieces at his feet, and bolted up the stairs.

"I cannot call a man out for refusing to take advantage of you, Nola." Henry tugged nervously at the sleeves of his jacket. "It's just not the done thing."

Nola pinched the bridge of her nose and took a deep breath. She didn't really want Henry to shoot Gabriel. She had taken Gabriel's carriage and tracked her brother down at St. Fell's after she dropped Chef and Cook off because she couldn't face going inside and explaining to Mrs. Carr and her aunts why she was home alone.

She didn't really know what she wanted. She was too plainspoken, too managing, and too flat-chested for Gabriel Carr. The only criteria of his she had ever met was amiability and her behavior this morning had just destroyed any illusion of that. She wanted to hide. She had sunk so far from being the paragon Gabriel had admired. She had admitted to improper thoughts about him. She had shouted. She had broken an injured man's cane and stolen his carriage.

She had made a great big fuss. She swallowed the lump in her throat.

Henry patted her back consolingly. "I mean, I'd be well within my rights to shoot him for kissing you. But it hardly seems fair given he's offered to marry you."

She folded her arms across her chest. "I will not marry him."

"Now that's not like you. I thought you liked him. Loved him, even."

She stared out the window at the gray stone front of the Duke of St. Fell's mansion. She did love Gabriel. She loved him enough to make a fool of herself.

Henry sighed at her continued silence. "Well, he likes you."

Not enough to do the same for her. "Gabriel Carr likes having his own way," she said.

Henry smiled. "Yes, but he also likes you, Nola. Everyone knows it. Even if he didn't say. You should not make yourself miserable for the rest of your life just because the man cannot find the words to express his love."

"It does not make any difference if he told me he loved me! They are just words, Henry. Words do not matter."

Her brother frowned in confusion. "Then what does?"

She opened her mouth to tell him, but realized she didn't know the answer. She could tell the coachman to bring her back to the warehouse and she could agree to marry Gabriel. They could wait until everyone had stopped trying to embarrass him about his list and they could marry before his thirtieth birthday. What did it matter if she wasn't his ideal bride? There was nothing wrong with reasonable compromise.

That was the amiable thing to do. She was an amiable person. Everyone said so.

She slumped back in her seat. She didn't know what mattered.

All she knew was that she loved Gabriel Carr and she had never been more miserable in her life.

Gabriel waved his thanks to Oliphant for the ride and hopped up the stairs to White's, ignoring the salute of raised quizzing glasses when he passed the bow window. Thankfully there was no one he was obliged to speak to inside so he was left in peace in his dark corner to nurse his coffee.

He tilted the cup and stared into the dregs. His life was a disaster. Nola didn't want him. Or rather, she wanted him. But not to marry. He smiled bitterly. To think he had worried she didn't think he was handsome. She thought he was handsome.

Handsome enough to kiss in his warehouse, but not enough to marry.

He had told her he loved her! What more did she want? She was supposed to say she loved him back. He drained his cup and winced at the bitter taste. He ought to be happy she had turned him down. Now he could resurrect his list and find himself the ideal bride.

Damnation! He pressed his hands over his eyes. He didn't want anyone else. He hadn't wanted anyone else since the day he met her. He didn't even remember what was on his damned list. The last time he'd even thought of it was sitting here in White's telling St. Fell how Nola didn't meet his requirements. Lying about how he didn't want Nola when it was only because she didn't want him.

St. Fell had been so convinced by his performance that he'd gone to wager Gabriel would marry his ideal bride before his birthday. Gabriel snorted derisively. St. Fell was usually smarter than that. The hairs began to prickle on the back of Gabriel's neck. St. Fell was usually a lot smarter than that.

Gabriel pushed himself to his feet and crossed to the hall table where the betting book was kept. He'd never actually looked in it before. He opened the heavy leather cover. The wagers were listed according to date. He ran his finger down the entries for September until he recognized his friend's handwriting.

"The Duke of St. Fell offers ten to one odds that Gabriel Carr will marry Lady Nola Grenvale before this December 7th."

The words swam before his eyes. St. Fell had bet he would marry Nola? Right after Gabriel had explained why she would never meet the requirements of his list. "That bast—"

"I must agree with your mother, Gabriel." St. Fell loomed up behind him. "Your language has become abysmal. Personally, I think it is a cry for attention."

"What the hell does this mean?" Gabriel jabbed the line in the betting book.

St. Fell shrugged. "It means I thought you would marry Nola."

"Right after I told you about my list of requirements and how she did not meet them?"

His friend nodded, barely making the effort to suppress the smirk that lurked behind his pursed lips.

Gabriel crossed his arms. "And ten to one odds means—"

"Yes." St. Fell sighed. "For every guinea bet I'd pay ten if you didn't marry Nola. But we figured it was the only way to get anyone to take the bet, what with you and Nola being so perfectly suited for each other."

"We?"

St. Fell's eyes looked up at the ceiling as he thought. "Belcraven. Your mother, of course. Swann and his nephew, the Latour sisters, my brothers, my cousin Alonzo, but I told Toby to get money up front from him first, he's a bit of a rum—"

"You all thought I would marry Nola?" Gabriel ground out between clenched teeth.

"I don't know why you are in such a taking about it. I told you I was entering a bet."

"You told me you were betting I would marry the ideal woman not—" He clamped his mouth shut at St. Fell's mocking look.

"Well, you don't have to worry about it." St. Fell pointed to the betting book. "No one has taken me up on the bet."

Gabriel clenched his fists. "Which means?"

St. Fell's smirk emerged unfettered. "Everyone else in London thought you would marry her too."

Gabriel reeled against the edge of the table. Everyone in London knew he had made a list, yet they all believed he would marry Nola. Even though she did not meet the criteria of his list. Because everyone in London thought his list was stupid and so was he. He looked around the room. Every man in White's was now watching him. Just like his mother would be when he went home, and the countesses and the entire biddy brigade. As well as the Latours and every one of his tenants. Hell, probably even the blessed war widows. Every single one of them knew that if he married Nola, he would have to concede his list was a failure.

Admit he was a complete idiot for having a list, and an even bigger idiot for not admitting it.

"Bloody hell." He slammed the betting book shut.

FIFTEEN

"My lady! My lady! You must wake up."

Nola rubbed her eyes with the back of her hand and peered around her bedchamber. Agnes stood next to the bed, holding a candle. Mavis rifled through the wardrobe.

"It is still dark outside," Nola protested. The journey to Kent had been tiring and she was not in the mood for an early walk. She planned to spend the week in bed with the covers over her head. Perhaps the next month. Possibly the rest of her life.

"I can't believe we didn't pack the new clothes," Mavis wailed, shaking out the pink bombazine Nola had worn all day. "This will have to do."

"Everything will be sent down in a few days in Aunt Hortensia's carriage." Nola tried to fend off Agnes's attempt to pull her out of bed. "What time is it?" She hated country hours.

"Three o'clock in the morning," Mavis said smugly.

Nola stared at the maids. "Why must I get up?"

"You have a visitor." Agnes's grin was as broad as her sister's.

Nola's heart began to pound.

It was still pounding five minutes later when dressed in the pink bombazine with her hair barely tamed, the maids pushed her into the Dower Cottage drawing room and closed the door behind her.

She blinked in the contrast from the darkened hallway. Every lamp in the drawing room blazed. A new fire glowed in the grate. The sole occupant of the room was sitting in Aunt Hortensia's rocking chair.

Gabriel.

Nola slumped back against the door.

Gabriel had followed her to Kent.

He strode across the room and took her trembling hands in his. He was dressed in the same clothes he had worn this morning, now as disheveled as his hair. He grinned. The stubble on his chin didn't hide his dimples.

Even rumpled and travel-weary, he was beautiful. She looked into his eyes and her knees buckled at the tender expression she saw there. If he asked her to marry him again, she wouldn't refuse. What did it matter if she would never be his ideal bride, if she was a compromise? She looked down at his strong hands enfolding hers. He was the only man she wanted. If he said he loved her, she would tell him she loved him back and they would live happily ever after. He would probably never regret settling for her.

He continued to smile down at her without speaking, his eyes never leaving hers, as if he could not get over the sight of her. She swallowed. She couldn't fool herself. She did not need another declaration of love. If he kissed her she would marry him. She swallowed again. If he kept holding her hands she would marry him.

She cleared her throat. "What are you doing here?" she whispered.

His smile faltered. "Is it not obvious? I am making a fuss."

"Oh." She considered the implication of his statement and a shiver of excitement ran through her. She smiled, almost afraid to ask. "Have you come to make a fuss until I agree to marry you?"

"No," he said and grinned again.

She yanked her hands out of his grasp and staggered to the fireplace. She hefted Aunt Caroline's Chinese vase off the mantel. The minute he mentioned the bazaar or his warehouse, she would crack it over his thick skull.

He followed on her heels and drew her arm to turn her to face him. "I certainly hope you will agree to marry me," he said, his smile still steady, "but that is not why I am making a fuss." He pried the vase out of her hands and replaced it on the mantel. "First, I want to reassure you that if you do not agree to marry me, I will not be making fusses at you for the rest of your life, springing out at you when you are going about your business, trying to convince you to have me when you do not want me. However, if you do decide to marry me, I should warn you I am likely to persistently engage in fusses for the rest of our lives." He stopped abruptly and ran his hands through his hair. "I am terribly sorry. It was a long carriage ride. Too much time to think."

She nodded even though she was not certain what he was talking about. She felt even more confused than she had this afternoon. She still didn't know what she wanted. Now she didn't even know what he was offering. Perhaps matters of love should not be decided in the middle of the night.

He reached out to stroke his finger down her cheek. "I came to make a fuss because you are worth it."

She caught her breath.

He took her hands in his again. "You are worth standing on a table in White's, announcing I was going to throw myself at your mercy, worth listening to my mother crow she told me so, worth leaving London for the Kentish wilderness, worth annoying dowager countesses in the middle of the night. You are worth every fuss and many more."

Nola looked down, overcome. She suddenly recognized this was exactly what she wanted.

He ducked his head down to meet her eyes. "My vanity requires me to presume those are tears of joy?"

She nodded, too happy to speak.

"Excellent. A few more heartfelt declarations, and if you are agreeable, we shall proceed to kissing."

Two loud thumps sounded from the wall.

"What is that?" he asked.

Nola sighed. "My aunts must be in the dining room listening through the wall."

Gabriel looked at the wall and frowned. "Surely they are not going to object to a kiss? Not after I made such a spectacular fuss?"

Two more thumps sounded.

"A betrothal kiss?" he shouted.

Silence.

"Very well, then." He straightened his shoulders with a satisfied smile and turned back to Nola. "There were a number of other matters I needed to mention. Such as I love you."

"I love you as well," she said.

"I think you are the most intelligent and beautiful creature I have ever met."

"I think you are as well," she said.

"Nola!" He held her at arm's length and inspected her face. "You are amiable again!"

She shrugged. "I am beginning to suspect it might depend."

He tilted his head and smiled. "I do not mind." He lowered his voice to the tone that made her knees weak. "We cannot have you being too saintly."

Thump. Thump.

He glared at the wall. "Your aunts have very good hearing."

"I think Bartlett has been giving lessons."

Gabriel shook his head. "Thank goodness we are nearly at the kissing part." He raised his voice to carry through the wall. "My dear Lady Nola, will you do me the honor of accepting my humble hand in marriage?"

"Oh, Gabriel." She sighed. "What about your list?"

"What?" He blinked, a bewildered look in his eyes.

"Your list of requirements in a bride," she continued despite his darkening expression. "What about your list?"

"Devil take my list, Nola! I—"

Two loud thumps against the wall interrupted him.

"I think they objected to your use of the word devil," Nola explained.

The wall thumped again.

Gabriel clutched his head. "Where were we?"

"I was pointing out I do not meet the requirements on your list."

He smiled tenderly and reached for her hand and pressed it to his chest. "You meet the requirements of my heart."

Thump. Thump.

He scowled. "Why the dev—on earth did they object to that?"

"I think that was a thump of approval," she said.

"Excellent." He pulled her into his arms. "Now for the kiss."

As much as she ached to be in his arms, she took a step backward and put her hands on her hips. "What about your list?"

He threw his hands in the air. "For God's sake, Nola, to hell with my bloody list!"

A wild flurry of thumping erupted, followed by silence.

Nola bit her lip. "I think they may have fainted."

"Good." He stalked to the fireplace. "You are as obsessed with my list as you were with my warehouse."

She crossed her arms. "Because if we marry you will always be comparing me against the kind of wife you really wanted."

He stared wildly at her. "You must be joking! You are the only wife I ever wanted. I don't care a whit about the criteria on my benighted list. It was only pride that kept me from declaring myself, not whether or not you met my requirements—why you probably know them better than I do."

"You may be right." She grinned.

"I should have thrown the list out the minute I met you. Our courtship would have been so much more enjoyable."

"I don't know," she said. "I think we provided everyone else with considerable pleasure."

"Amusement, you mean." He enfolded her in his arms again and rested his cheek against hers.

She wrapped her arms around his neck. "Do you realize if you marry me some people might gloat?"

"Surely you quiz when you say some people. That implies there might actually be some who will not."

She patted his shoulder consolingly. "I am sure everyone will forget once a new scandal diverts them."

He sighed. "I do not think England can afford a scandal of that magnitude. No, I am afraid I am going to be reminded I was an idiot for a long while to come."

She pulled her head away from his so she could look into his eyes. "Do you mind?"

"Not if I have you." He cupped his hand to his ear and waited.

Thump. Thump.

He grinned. "That was just off the top of my head." He wrapped his hands around her waist and bent his head.

"Gabriel," she asked as his lips brushed gently against hers.

"Yes, my love?" he murmured.

"What about my bosom?"

His head jerked up. "Has someone been impertinent about your bosom?" He scowled. "It is that rake St. Fell, isn't it? I knew I should have knocked him on his—"

She pressed her finger to his lips. "No. I meant do you find my bosom too small?"

His eyebrows shot up in astonishment. "Good Lord, Nola! Your bosom is perfect."

"Truly?" Her heart soared. The last piece of her happiness fell into place.

He lowered his voice to a whisper. "In fact, I love your bosom."

"Oh." A wave of heat swept through her body.

"Can your aunts see us?" He continued in the silky tone that made her cling to his shoulders.

She shook her head.

He caught his lower lip in his teeth. "I could show you how much I love your bosom."

Goodness. The way his eyes roved over her body made her bosom love him. "Does it involve tongues?" she asked when she was able to speak.

He swallowed. "Possibly."

She tightened her arms around his neck. "Very well."

His fingers stroked the side of her face and he lowered his head to hers. She quivered as she waited for the touch of his lips.

"Just a moment!" He lifted his head.

She moaned in disappointment.

He looked down at her with narrowed eyes. "You never answered. Will you marry me?"

"Yes, Gabriel," she said.

He smiled. "Then it definitely involves tongues."

He lowered his head.

If her aunts thumped, she didn't notice.

AUTHOR'S NOTE

The bazaar Nola wanted to build actually did come into existence in February, 1816, when wealthy London businessman John Trotter converted his Soho Square warehouse into a bazaar so the widows and daughters of men killed in the Napoleonic Wars could sell their handiwork to the public. The Soho Bazaar was a huge success and benefitted countless women for decades.

As for Gabriel's Garrard House, it is modeled directly on Schomberg House in Pall Mall. Its groundbreaking department store opened several years before Gabriel's, so when Nola and Gabriel agree that Garrard House is completely original, I'm afraid it's a case of love being blind. For which most of us are very grateful.

More Regency Romance
From Zebra